THE BILLIONAIRE AND THE BURGLAR

GRUMPY BILLIONAIRE ROMANTIC COMEDY

TALIA HUNTER

CHAPTER 1

Scarlet

The gloomy hour before sunrise is the perfect time to get mugged in LA.

Most women feel a little vulnerable when they're walking alone in the semi-darkness on a deserted street. Like right now, for example. It's five thirty on a quiet Monday morning, and I'm striding along the sidewalk toward the gym in my workout gear, my gym bag slung over my shoulder.

But the difference between me and most women is that I don't feel vulnerable. Even though, thanks to the flickering streetlight overhead, it feels eerily like the re-enactment scene of a Netflix true crime show. The only thing missing is the creepy music.

There's only one other person in sight: a woman about my age who's just arrived at the gym's entrance. She's in front of the security access pad, rummaging in her bag for her access card. The bright security light is shining down on her, so I can see her clearly. She's short, her blonde hair is in a ponytail, and she's paired black leggings with a pink long-sleeved top.

I'm about fifty yards away from her when a dark figure sprints around the other side of the building. He's dressed all in black and even has a balaclava pulled over his face, like he picked out a mugger costume from a fancy dress store. But this guy is clearly serious, and he has the woman in his sights.

Like I said, it's a great time to get mugged in LA.

The woman jerks her face toward him as he pounds toward her, covering the ground in a rush. She lets out a little cry and stumbles away, but he's on her in seconds. He grabs her gym bag, but she doesn't let him have it. She clutches onto one strap while he yanks at the other.

Game on!

Dropping my own bag, I sprint toward them.

"Let go!" I yell at the mugger. "Let go, you creep!"

Then I perform a Taekwondo roundhouse kick.

It's a showy kick. I aim a little high so my foot connects with his torso instead of his stomach, and I'm wearing rubber-soled sneakers. But the mugger still grunts and staggers backward, letting the bag go.

"Get out of here," I snarl, dropping into a martial arts stance. "Unless you have a death wish. In which case, bring it."

My taunt is dramatic enough, and maybe I should stop there. But I can't help myself. I've been practicing Taekwondo for years, and sure, I spar in competitions, but there's nothing like getting to use my skills on the street.

And yes, okay, it's fun to show off.

Not that this should be fun. It's wrong to be enjoying myself right now, I'm aware of that.

Still, from my fighting pose, with knees bent, arms lifted, and fists loosely curled, I stretch one hand toward the mugger and point between his eyes. Then I motion with my fingers, beckoning him to come at me. The move is right out of a cheesy martial arts movie, and I've always wanted to do it. Who cares if I'm five inches shorter and at least a hundred pounds lighter than the mugger, and my hair is relentlessly curly? I'm still a bad-ass.

At least, I feel like a bad-ass. Hopefully I'm coming off that way.

The mugger stares at me. Behind the balaclava, his eyes flash. His hesitation stretches out for a long moment as if he's not sure what to do next. But then he gives a furtive sideways glance, like he's thinking about making an escape.

I don't want him to run. I want him to attack me.

"Come on," I urge, bouncing on my toes. "Come at me!"

If he lunges at me, I'll get to do a spinning jump kick. Or I could throw him. That would look cool.

His eyes are wide. He gives a tiny head shake.

Then, to my disappointment, he wheels around and sprints away.

As he vanishes around the corner, I turn to the woman and grasp her upper arms in a reassuring way. "Are you okay?"

"I think so." Her eyes are wide and her cheeks a little pale. "Thank you. You were amazing! How did you do that? That kick was straight out of an action movie!"

"He didn't hurt you, did he?"

She clutches her bag to her chest. "I'm shaken, that's all.

My heart is going crazy. If he'd gotten away with my bag, he would have had everything! My phone, my credit cards. Even the clothes I'm going to change into. You're a real-life superhero. The way you kicked him..." She's speaking quickly, clearly hyped on adrenaline. "My name's Melissa, by the way."

"I'm Scarlet. Nice to meet you. Sorry about the circumstances."

She grabs me into a hug, pulling me in against the bag she's still clutching. "Thank you, Scarlet," she mumbles into my hair. "Really."

"It was nothing." I hug her back. She's not shaking, but clearly needs the comfort. She's an inch taller than me and judging by her unexpected strength, she must be a regular at the gym. She's gripping me more tightly than she must realize. "You're safe now," I murmur breathlessly, seeing as she's starting to squeeze the air from my lungs. "He's long gone."

"But how did you do that?" she asks. "Can I learn it?"

"Taekwondo. It's part of my job." When she lets me go, I drag in a grateful breath.

She draws back, her expression hopeful. "Do you teach it?"

"I have something better." My gym bag is still lying where I dropped it, and I root around in it, then pull out a small personal alarm. "Take this." I press it into her hands. " If you ever have trouble again, press the button to activate the siren. It's so loud, it'll scare an attacker right out of his shoes. No training needed. It'll keep you safe, I promise."

"Oh no, I can't take your alarm." She looks down at it, her palm open, and I can tell she wants it.

"I don't need it," I say. "Please keep it."

"Do you sell them? I'd like to pay you for it."

"Stop. Please." Reaching out, I curl her fingers around it. "I own a security company. This alarm is the best on the market. Set it off, and everyone in a ten-block radius will come running."

"Do you always go around saving people?" she asks with a little laugh. "Is this a regular day at the office for you?" The hyped-up tension is slowly leaving her body. She's talking at normal speed now, and the color's coming back to her cheeks.

"This is one of my more interesting days." I smile back at her, happy to see she's recovered enough to laugh, however weakly. Then I take a business card from the inside pocket of my gym bag and hand it to her. "I specialize in home security. If you happen to be a billionaire and you want state-of-the-art security for your mansion, I'm the best in the business."

I say it in a joking way, but her face lights up.

"I'm not a billionaire, but I work for one," she exclaims. "Have you heard of Balthazar Anders?"

Tilting my head to the side, I tap my index finger against my cheek. "I've heard that name. Why have I...? Oh, wait. Big court case recently, right? It made the news."

She nods. "That's him."

"I saw him on TV, and he had this heavy frown, like he hated everything and everyone." Even though there's still nobody around and the street's dead quiet, I lower my voice to a confidential murmur. "How awful is he to work for?"

"Honestly, I think he's gorgeous. Just don't tell my boyfriend." She screws her nose up as though regretting sharing that secret. "In fact, don't tell anyone, seeing as he's my boss and I shouldn't even be thinking about him that way."

I hold my hand up, pinkie finger outstretched. "First rule of Getting Mugged Club. Nothing you say gets shared."

She hooks her pinkie into mine with a laugh. "Okay. Then I can tell you he can be stern, but he's so swoony that I don't mind his frown."

I wrinkle my nose. "I'm not into grumpy men, but he'd be a great client for my business. Even if he *thinks* his home is secure, I guarantee I could find ways to improve his security."

"He could use you! He's had some death threats..." She claps her hand over her mouth. "I *really* shouldn't have told you that. He's a private person, and I'm not supposed to talk about him. That has to stay confidential, okay?"

"I won't say a word," I promise. "But I'd love to do a free security audit of his house. Do you think you could suggest it to him? All I need is half an hour inside his place to identify any weak spots, and I'll provide a full report. Then he can decide if he wants to hire my company to close any of the gaps."

She grabs my hand. "Of course I'll tell him about you! It's the least I can do, and you've already proven yourself."

"Thank you. But please don't feel obligated—"

"Don't be silly! You saved my life."

"Well, I don't think I saved your actual—"

"Close enough." She turns away from the gym. "I think I'm going to skip my workout this morning. How about you? Buy you a coffee instead? There's an early-morning place on the next block." Then she frowns. "Wait. Should I call the police and tell them what happened? Maybe they can catch the guy?"

"I don't know if the police will be able to do anything," I say. "We couldn't see his face and he didn't get away with anything. He'll be long gone by now." I link my arm through hers. "How about we go for coffee, and you can tell them later?"

She looks relieved. "Okay."

"And it's my treat. Seeing as you were almost mugged, you're not allowed to pay."

"I can't let you pay!"

"Sure you can."

By the time we get to the coffee shop, we've decided to have coffee *and* pastries, and make plans to catch up later in the week so I can show her some martial arts moves. Over coffee, we have a long jokey discussion about how easy it is to make new friends in this city; all you need to do is get mugged. We even come up with a name for a dating app that helps you get mugged in order to meet people—it's called The Stickup Pickup.

Anyway, she gets over her shock, and at one point we both nearly spit coffee we're laughing so hard. It's after seven by the time I finally say goodbye to her and head to work.

My office is on a run-down street in a part of LA where most people lock their car doors as they drive through. The office is in our building's second floor, over a laundromat, and the apartment I share with my two best friends is on the fourth floor of the same building. The street always stinks of pee, and at night we often get woken by the shouts of drunks staggering out of the bar on the corner. But the rent is cheap, and despite the building's faults, I love working and living with my two best friends. We started our security business together, and even if I sometimes get bored doing home security audits all the time, I get to hang out with them every day. That's good enough for me.

I find both Jamie and Kayla already in the office. It's split into three rooms, and Kayla is at her desk in the room we've nicknamed our command center, behind an enormous computer monitor. Jamie's in our training room, where we have our workout gear set up. She's clearly been hitting the speedbag. Her uncle owns a boxing gym, and she was strapping on boxing gloves as soon as she could walk.

I met Kayla and Jamie in a juvenile detention facility when I was fifteen. We shared a horribly overcrowded room in that grim hellhole, and after making a pact to watch each other's backs, we've been inseparable ever since.

All three of us were off the rails back then, but now we're respectable citizens.

Kind of.

Mostly.

"How did it go?" asks Kayla, peering around her computer monitor. She's shy, sensitive, and the smartest person I've ever met.

I drop my gym bag and slump into my chair. "Hook, line and sinker," I say glumly. "Melissa's promised to let me do a security audit of Balthazar's mansion. On Wednesday morning, she's going to show me around."

If I don't sound happy, it's because I believe with all my heart in women supporting other women, not scaring them. But as hard as I tried, I couldn't think of another way to get a look inside Balthazar's mansion, other than tricking Melissa.

Jamie walks out of the training room and into our

command center, grinning as she tugs off her gloves. She's almost six foot tall, has long black hair, and is covered with a sheen of perspiration. "You did it!" she holds up one hand. "High five!"

I grimace at her sweaty palm without lifting my own. "I don't feel like celebrating."

Actually, I feel like pond scum. It was fun in the moment, but now my guilt is overwhelming.

"Don't be upset," says Kayla, coming out from behind her screens like a deer emerging from the shelter of the forest. "You're doing this for a very good reason. And Melissa didn't get hurt, did she?"

"She was shaken. Rob looked menacing dressed in black."

Rob's my hairdresser. He's a gentle giant who owed me a favor for helping him retrieve his personal belongings from his vindictive ex-boyfriend.

"He was gentle with her though, wasn't he?" Kayla presses, looking anxious.

"Very gentle. And afterward, I took her for coffee to settle her nerves."

Jamie gives some exaggerated blinks. "You had coffee with the mark?" She makes it sound like a ridiculous over-reaction. But Jamie is so tough, she's practically a female Chuck Norris. In fact, she has a side hustle making sexy fight-club videos. She puts on a bikini, covers herself in oil, and wrestles guys until they cry for mercy. The fights are real, and she always wins. Her online fandom is huge.

"Don't call Melissa a mark," Kayla chides her.

"Yeah, I feel guilty enough," I agree. "I've arranged to teach Melissa some self-defense moves. I don't want her to be afraid of walking around in the dark because of what I did to her."

Kayla and Jamie exchange a look. Maybe they think I'm going too far to make up for scaring Melissa, but I don't care. Good reason or not, it was still a shitty thing to do.

"You're a nice person, Scarlet," says Kayla. "Melissa's the one who works for a jerk."

"You've gone soft," Jamie mutters, rolling her eyes.

"Melissa's innocent," I say. "I wish I could have mugged her boss instead. He's the one who deserves it." I turn and glower at the picture of Balthazar Anders I've pinned to wall above my desk.

Balthazar glowers back. Even in a photo, he's menacing. His dark brown eyes have a dangerous gleam, he has a fighter's jaw, and his features are as sharp as glass. Melissa called him gorgeous, and he definitely would be if his heavy eyebrows weren't drawn together with a line pinched between them. He exudes confidence, power, and contemptuous disapproval in equal measure. As though nobody and nothing will ever be good enough for him.

My phone rings and I tug it from my pocket.

"Eeep," I say nervously. "It's Aunt Alejandra." The caller-id picture is my favorite shot of her. She looks dignified in her judge's robes and is beaming her motherly smile.

Kayla widens her eyes, looking as alarmed as I feel. "You didn't tell her I let her secret slip, did you?"

"Of course not."

Several days ago, Aunt Alejandra confided to Kayla that Balthazar had inherited some compromising photos of her from when she was a young woman. She asked Kayla if there'd be any way to take the photos off the internet if

Balthazar released them online. Apparently, that's what he's threatening to do.

Kayla explained that if Balthazar released the photos, they'd be public forever. And considering how catastrophic that would be for Aunt Alejandra's career, she was worried enough to tell Jamie and me about it.

That's when I decided to use my old burglary skills to steal the photos from Balthazar before he can make them public. Doing Balthazar's security audit will give me access to his fancy billionaire's mansion. He probably thinks the place is impregnable, but now I'll be able to look for weak spots in his security so I can break in.

"Aren't you going to answer it?" Jamie nods at my ringing phone.

Kayla grabs my arm. "Aunt Alejandra's going to kill you if she finds out what you're planning. Or if she discovers I let you in on her secret. She was embarrassed enough just telling me about the photos."

"Don't worry, she won't find out until I get her photos back. Then she'll be so relieved, she'll forgive us both."

Kayla makes a squinty, hopeful face and holds up a hand with her fingers crossed. I want to do the same. It would be awful if Aunt Alejandra didn't forgive me for plotting another robbery after I promised my bad deeds were all behind me. The thought is unimaginable. But I have to risk it. I can't let Balthazar destroy everything she's worked so hard for.

I drag in a breath, pulling myself together enough to bring the phone to my ear. "Hi tía," I say.

"Hi Scarlet, honey." Aunt Alejandra's voice is as warm as ever. "Are you with your sisters?"

"Yes, they're here. I'll put you on speaker."

Though none of us are related by blood, we're still a family, so that's what Aunt Alejandra calls us. Actually, we're closer than a family after all we've been through together.

"Are you all free on Saturday for lunch?" Aunt Alejandra asks. "I need to talk to you about something."

I exchange glances with Kayla and Jamie. "Sure. What do you want to talk about?" I ask.

I'm hoping she'll say it's something pleasant, like she's going to show us how she makes her delicious empanadas, or that she's thinking about adopting another stray cat. But suddenly—unusually—there's no smile in her voice at all.

"You'll find out on Saturday," she says.

It sounds ominous.

CHAPTER 2

Scarlet

Balthazar's house is a post-modern, brutal construction made from concrete and steel. It's huge. And from the outside, it looks intimidating.

I pause at the bottom of the steps that lead up to the imposing front door so I can record the positions of the security cameras. And seeing as I'm here to do a security audit of the property, I don't even have to hide what I'm doing. If I weren't still feeling guilty, I'd be gleeful at how easy it is.

When I'm done, I shove my phone back into my shoulder bag, climb the stairs and knock.

Melissa opens the door with a smile, looking stylish in a white dress with her blonde hair loose over her shoulders.

She looks pleased and surprised when I hand her a bunch of flowers. "What are these for?"

"To say thank you for giving me a chance to do the

security audit." They're actually guilt flowers, not that I can tell her that.

She enfolds me in a hug. "Are you kidding? You're my hero! Thanks again for saving me."

I squeeze her back. When she lets go, I ask, "How fancy is this place?" Pretending to be gazing around the entrance foyer in admiration, I scan all the visible windows. The fastenings are top-of-the-line. Unfortunately, they're ones that can't be broken or jimmied open. I'll need to sneakily unlock one while Melissa's showing me around.

"Impressive, isn't it?" she says.

"*So* impressive."

Actually, the interior is cavernous, stark, and way too monotone for my taste. The walls are white, and the floor is polished gray marble. Even the art is black and white. And instead of fresh flowers, the house is decorated with sculptural plant designs in black vases made of sticks and dried leaves.

The entire place looks like it was put together by a team of interior designers from a concept sketched with black pen. It's classy, but soulless. The type of enormous mansion I'd picture a billionaire vampire living in if he was a boring jerk with an aversion to color.

"Is this where you work every day?" I ask.

"Oh no!" She gives a little laugh as though the idea is unthinkable. "Mr. Anders has an office downtown. His staff all work there, but he usually works from home. He likes his solitude."

That's good news. The fewer people that usually come and go from this enormous house, the easier it'll be to break in.

"And I have a surprise for you," Melissa adds, grinning. "I got you an interview with him!" She lets out a little squeal, bouncing on her toes as though this is amazing news.

"Balthazar Anders is here?" My heart sinks. "But I don't want to bother him. I'll just take a quick look around and send him my report. He can read through it—"

"This will be better, Scarlet, I promise! Mr. Anders is offering a contract for some short-term work, and the pay is great. I thought of you right away. And it'd be so good for your business if you got this job!" Taking my arm, she tugs me through a giant living room, and I barely have time to look at the windows before I'm pulled into a long, wide hallway. All the doors leading off the hallway are closed, and at the far end is a huge wall of glass looking over a swimming pool that any luxury resort would be proud of.

No opening windows here, and no way to break in. And three internal alarm sensors mean there's no exit route through this area that wouldn't set off the alarm. Assuming the alarm is armed when I break in, of course. If not, I'll be able to stroll down here like I own the place.

"What work, exactly?" I ask.

She drops her voice, towing me along the hallway, flowers held out in front. "I'm supposed to let him explain it. But trust me, it's a huge opportunity."

"My specialty is security audits. I should stick to what I came here to do."

She stops in front of a closed door. "Mr. Anders' home office is through here, and he said to send you right in. I told him how you saved me, and that you know about the death threats. Just go and hear what he's offering."

"I'm sorry, Melissa, I just don't think..." I trail off. Her expression has fallen and all the guilt I feel at the way I've treated her is surging back up.

"If you don't want to do it, you don't have to." She squints, letting me off the hook with obvious reluctance. "I talked you up to him because I thought it was what you'd want, but I shouldn't have assumed you'd be into it."

I sigh. My rational brain is telling me to turn down whatever this is. But if she talked her boss into seeing me, not going through with it could make her look bad. "I'll meet him," I hear myself say. "But no promises, okay?"

She perks up right away. "Great! You won't regret it. You ready to go in?"

I'm nowhere near ready, but I drag in a breath and run a hand over my blouse. It's red, because that's my color, and it has oversized buttons for a touch of fun. This blouse has positive energy.

Whatever job I'm about to be offered, all I need to do is play along until I can figure out how to steal Aunt Alejandra's photos back from Balthazar. At least this way I'll get a look at his office. Maybe he's keeping her photos in there. For all I know, he framed them and has them hanging on his wall.

Fixing on a smile, I give a decisive nod. "Ready."

"Mr. Anders is gruff, but don't let him scare you, okay? Act confident, and you'll do great." Before I can fully absorb this advice, she knocks on the door.

A deep voice comes from the other side. "Enter." His tone is curt.

"Oh, and make sure you call him Mr. Anders," Melissa adds. "He won't want you to use his first name."

She opens the door and all but pushes me into his office

before shutting it behind me. The impression I get is of a snake keeper dropping a small rodent into a python's cage.

The room is just as cavernous as the rest of the house, and just as monochromatic. The walls are white, with no pictures to interrupt a wide expanse of blankness. There's a big white meeting table in the middle of the room. It's surrounded by white chairs, and at the far end is an enormous black desk. The only decoration is another of those sculptural plant arrangements positioned against the wall. This one reminds me of a skeleton.

My red shirt is by far the most colorful thing in the room.

Balthazar—I mean, Mr. Anders—is sitting at the desk, behind an equally enormous computer monitor. All I can see is his shoulder, clad in a gray shirt, and the top of his black hair. My first glimpse of the beast in his bleak, solitary castle.

He probably needs to swallow the remains of his last victim before greeting me.

I quickly scan the room. There's only one alarm sensor, and two windows, both behind the desk. Their locking mechanisms are covered by a blind.

I'm about to step forward when there's movement from beside the desk. A white dog lifts its head and blinks sleepily at me. It's lying on the white rug, which is why I've only just noticed it. It's the size of a Labrador, but shaggy, with a cute face. Not at all the sleek, ornamental dog I might have imagined he'd have. Apart from its color, it doesn't match the rest of his decor.

Mr. Anders finally stands up and strides around his desk, coming toward me.

In person, he's so handsome it gives me a physical shock.

His photo didn't fully prepare me for how attractive he is.
Maybe it's because energy seems to crackle from him, as
though the air around him is charged with electricity.

He's wearing black dress pants with a gray work shirt,
unbuttoned at the neck, and the way he moves makes me
stare at his body in sheer admiration. His shirt clings to him
as though he's a catwalk model, and I'd bet a million bucks
that he has killer abs. But it's when I force my gaze back to
his face that my stomach tries to screw itself up and crawl
away.

He looks even more forbidding than in his photo, and his
frown is more pronounced. He glares at me as though he
finds me offensive. The sheer force of his disapproval could
wilt flowers. Maybe that's why he has skeleton twig
arrangements instead.

But as intimidating as his frown is, the intensity of his
stare is all kinds of charismatic. Now my eyes are tangled
with his, I can't pull them away. My heart is performing an
action that's too fast to be described as beating, and every
cell in my body is on full alert. He's commanding every bit of
my attention.

It takes me a minute to convince my feet to propel me
forward, moving to meet him halfway.

Fortune favors the bold.

"Hello, Mr. Anders." I make myself sound friendly and
upbeat as I stop in front of him. "It's such a pleasure to meet
you."

If anything, my pleasant greeting makes him even more
sour. His nostrils flare. His impossibly deep frown deepens
even further. He looks as though he's waiting for me to poop
on his snowy white rug.

"Sit." He nods at the meeting table. "Let's make this quick."

I'm usually an agreeable person, but there's something about the way he's barked the order that makes me want to do the opposite of what he says. So I take my time selecting one of the chairs around the meeting table and getting settled in it. I put my shoulder bag down beside me and shift about as though trying to get comfortable. I'm the princess from that fairy tale, the one who couldn't get to sleep because she had a teensy pea in her bed.

Mr. Anders' lips tighten as he watches. His frown is severe. A frown like that must make his employees tremble. The sad thing is that it doesn't keep him from being beautiful, even if he's a monster underneath.

Whatever this mysterious job is that he's about to offer me, suddenly I want to take it, if only so I can make his frown so deep that it becomes a permanent crease between his eyebrows. I don't just want to steal back my aunt's photos, I want to punish him for having them in the first place. And as my cheerfulness seems to irritate him, I make sure to beam him my widest smile.

CHAPTER 3

Balthazar

Scarlet Jones is nothing like the woman I'd expected to be interviewing, and to say I'm not happy about it would be to severely understate my disapproval.

It's entirely due to Melissa's recommendation that Ms. Jones is here for an interview at all. Apparently, she saved Melissa's life by fighting off an attacker. I was already sure that Melissa had exaggerated the story, and one look at Ms. Jones is enough to make me doubt it happened at all.

For starters, she's wearing clothing so bright, it would be suitable for directing traffic. Her blouse buttons are outlandish, twice as big as they need to be. She's shifting in her chair as though it's upholstered with itching powder, though her smile stays ridiculously wide. In all my life, nobody has ever been that delighted to see me.

She's too *much*. Her features are too generous and her hair too curly. Her lipstick is as red as her shirt, calling even more attention to her overly-plump lips. Even her walk as she came in was unpleasant. Her steps were absurdly springy, making her chocolate-brown hair bounce wildly. I'm not a fan.

Scarlet Jones isn't the serious martial arts expert I'd expected. There's altogether too much color and movement about her.

"This is a such gorgeous office, Mr. Anders," she gushes. "I love what you've done with it."

I give a grunt to communicate the intensity of my displeasure. Not only do I hate small talk, I have pages of financial data to review today, and I want this interview over as soon as possible. I've already decided she's not getting the job. The two other candidates are an ex-marine and an ex-cop, both very experienced, with impeccable credentials. Neither of them smiled or fidgeted during their interviews. Either would be more suitable.

I take a chair on the other side of the table. Just a few questions, then I can dismiss Ms. Jones and get back to work.

Ringo, my Bearded Collie, has been fast asleep on the rug beside my desk all morning, but now he's awake, watching Ms. Jones. He was probably woken by the loudness of her clothing and is as unimpressed by her as I am.

"Did Melissa tell you about the position I'm hiring for?" I ask. One of her curls is sticking up, totally out of place, and I have to bite back my urge to buzz Melissa on the intercom and have her bring in a hairbrush.

Ms. Jones shakes her head, and I'm relieved to see the rebellious curl flop back into place among the rest. "I came here to do a security audit," she says. If you'll let me take a quick walk around your house, I'll give you a full report that will tell you—"

"I already have the best security team money can buy. I don't need a security audit."

She purses her lips. I can tell she wants to argue, but after a moment she says, "What exactly are you looking for?"

"A security specialist to attend an event and watch for threats."

"You want personal protection services?"

"Exactly."

Her eyes sharpen. They're very green. The color of money. Which is ironic, seeing as my investigator informed me her security business is housed in a decrepit, low-rent building, and is unlikely to be making big profits.

"You don't have any bodyguards already?" she asks. "You just said you have a security team. They can't handle it?"

"For this job, I need specific skills." I can't help but sound impatient because she's wasting my time with her questions. And those outlandish buttons on her blouse are distracting. If I keep glancing at them, she's going to think I'm looking at her breasts.

Why have such enormous buttons? What exactly is the point of them?

"What skills?" she asks. As she shifts in the chair, the weight of her buttons drags down the fabric of her blouse, revealing a little cleavage.

Her olive skin is sun-kissed, and judging from the small glimpse of her breasts on offer, they must be spectacular. But if she's hoping her looks will help her get the job, she's going to be disappointed. Not that she's not attractive. Objectively speaking, I suppose she's beautiful. But she couldn't be more unlike the women I usually date.

My last girlfriend was an ice-cool fashion designer who

was so successful that I could be confident she wasn't with me for my money. She had sleek blonde hair, wore elegant clothes with normal-sized buttons, and had such a busy life that we only saw each other sporadically. When we did, our relationship was based around sex. In other words, she was perfect. When I get around to dating someone else, I'll look for similar traits.

"Before I tell you about the job," I say, "tell me about your criminal record."

Surprise flickers in her eyes. She can't have realized I'd have my investigator run a background check before our interview.

"My run-ins with the law happened years ago," she says, recovering herself. "Now, I make better choices. These days I protect people instead of stealing from them."

Not a bad answer. She's keeping her cool, resisting my attempt to rattle her. Time to step it up a notch.

I lean forward, rest my elbows on the table, and steeple my hands. "How could I be expected to trust someone with a burglary conviction?"

Her chin lifts. "The CIA hires ex-hackers to protect their computer systems. Why wouldn't you hire an ex-burglar for security?"

She doesn't look like a burglar. Not that I would have expected her to walk in wearing a black catsuit, but she's the exact opposite of someone who doesn't want to be noticed. Her eyes are as large as the rest of her features. They're as oversized as her buttons, with long eyelashes to match. It's probably their size that makes her look innocent. One flutter of those eyelashes and no jury would convict her of anything.

And I can't stop glancing at those damn buttons. Only three of them. If they were smaller, there'd probably be more. They'd unbutton easily, no doubt, as their buttonholes must be just as large. Just a flick of the fingers and her blouse would open, revealing more of her golden skin.

Does her bra match her shirt, or is it an unexpected color? Is it as bright as the rest of her outfit?

"Mr. Anders?" she says, her brow creasing.

With a start, I realize I was lost in thought, silently studying her for too long.

It's not like me to lose focus. Not at all.

"You're a known criminal," I point out, my tone hard. "If I hired you, every time you shook my hand, I'd wonder if you were trying to steal my watch."

Instead of denying it, her gaze goes to my wrist, and she lets out a small whistle. "That's a Patek Philippe limited edition, isn't it? Beautiful watch. I can see why you'd worry about losing it."

I grunt, half impressed that she knows the brand, half annoyed by the distraction.

Leaning back, I pointedly drop my hands to my thighs, out of sight below the table. "What exactly are your skills? Answer succinctly. Fifty words or less."

"I have a black belt in Taekwondo, advanced-level weapons certifications, and run a successful security business with excellent online reviews. Theft isn't something I usually offer, but as it's clearly what you're most interested in, I'm willing to negotiate." Her smile reappears, this time with a touch of smugness. "And thirty-nine words was all I needed. Impressed yet?"

I grunt.

She's not afraid of me, I'll give her that.

In fact, I have a certain reluctant admiration for the way she stands up for herself. If I took her absurd buttons and wild curls out of the equation, she'd be scoring higher in this interview than I care to admit.

"I've interviewed better candidates," I say. "Why should I hire you?"

"Because my background isn't a drawback, it's an advantage. Anyone with a license can do a week's training and say they're a protection agent. But I've had experience on both sides of the law."

"You think being a criminal makes you better suited for the job?"

"*Ex*-criminal." Her tone is pointed. "And yes, because I'm sharp. I notice things. Like the make of your watch."

"You notice opportunities to commit crimes?"

"That too." Her cheeks flush, but she earns more points for not dropping her gaze or backing down. "And if you've had death threats, you need someone who—"

"The death threats I've had aren't what I'm worried about," I interrupt.

She blinks her long lashes, sitting back in her chair and pushing her full lips doubtfully to one side. "Someone's threatened to kill you... but it's not your biggest issue?"

"Those threats are insignificant compared to what I expect to face in the future."

"Well, have you considered not doing things that make people want to kill you?" She gives me a little smile.

"Was that a joke?" I deepen my frown. "This a serious job. I need a professional."

"As a professional, I'm advising you to stay off as many

hit lists as you can." Her retort teeters on the edge of insolence, and her cheeks are going pinker.

The pinker her cheeks, the greener her eyes look.

I must admit, she's extremely beautiful.

But she's not the right person for the job.

When I went to court to gain possession of my father's private papers, I had no idea what was in them, and was curious to know what he'd been hiding. But his secrets were worse than I'd ever dreamed, and now I need to deal with what I've found.

My life is about to become very dangerous. I need someone who can handle it.

With my decision made, I stand up. "Thank you for coming in, Ms. Jones, but I'm not going to hire you."

Her lips part as she exhales a surprised breath. "Why not? What did I do wrong?"

"You don't have what I'm looking for."

She stays sitting, defiantly looking up at me, as though I'll have to physically eject her before she'll leave. "What do you need, exactly? You haven't told me anything."

"I want someone who's ready to face danger. Someone with quick reflexes, combat skills, and the ability to think on their feet."

"You've just described me."

"I don't see any sign of that."

"Because you haven't given me a chance."

"Goodbye, Ms. Jones."

She hesitates a moment longer, her chest going up and down quickly as though she's breathing fast. Her eyes are sparking, as though my abrupt dismissal made her angry. She stands up in a rush.

"All right, Mr. Anders," she says. "Thank you for your time." Extending her hand, she walks around the table toward me. A farewell handshake seems unnecessary, so she's probably only offering it in the hopes I'll change my mind.

I'm putting my hand out to shake hers when she stumbles over the chair leg and falls heavily onto me.

Staggering backward, I hold her up, my hands gripping her waist, while she gets her feet back underneath her.

"Whoops!" Her face angles up to mine. She seems in no hurry to steady herself. One hand is on my chest, the other moves from my forearm to my upper arm. "I'm sorry," she says, in a tone that suggests she's not sorry at all. "So clumsy."

She smells like oranges, fresh and enticing. Is it coming from her hair? That curly hair of hers is so wild, I have a strong urge to gather it in my hands, to pull it behind her head and take a good look at her oversized features. Her overly generous smile. Her color-of-money eyes. The nose that's too big for her face.

Every part of her is too much, too bright, too full. It's overwhelming.

"I was going for a handshake," she explains with a laugh. "See?" Taking my hand in both of hers, she makes a show of moving it up and down. Because she's enclosed my hand in hers, the movement seems oddly intimate. It's more of a caress than a handshake.

Her face is lifted, and she's not making any move to step back out of my personal space. Her pillowy lips are slightly parted. Her eyes have a thin ring of tawny brown around each iris, then they're light green, with a ring of darker green circling the edge of her pupil.

She's clearly flirting with me.

Her boldness takes my breath away.

With one of hands still around mine, she puts her other hand on my chest, against my shirt. Pressing her fingers into my pectoral muscle, her eyes widen as though she likes what she feels. Her tongue darts out, touches her lower lip, then vanishes between her absurdly plump, red lips.

She's a blaze of color, vivid against the muted tones of my office. Where most people would be afraid of me, she's confident to the point of arrogance. Where most would be professional, she's entirely unexpected. She assumes she can touch me, and that I won't stop her.

I have no idea what she's going to do next, and the not knowing makes my heart beat harder.

My cock stirs.

Her breasts brush against my arm. I have a powerful urge to pop those oversized buttons, one by one. They're designed to be noticed, designed to make me want to undo them, and they've performed their task to perfection.

I lift one hand, but before I can touch them, she steps away.

"Thank you for your time, Mr. Anders," she says. "Goodbye."

She turns to leave, and I'm speechless. A small part of my brain is wondering what the hell that was, but most of my brain is focused on the sway of her hips. Suddenly the bounce in her walk isn't annoying in the least. By touching me, she's cast some sort of spell over me. I'm painfully aroused. Scarlet Jones might be outrageous, but she's also extremely sexy.

She walks toward the door, and all I can do is stand and watch her hips move.

When she reaches the door, she turns.

"Before I go," she says, "One last thing."

I clear my throat. "Yes?"

"This is for you." Suddenly, she's not smiling anymore. Her face is set with raw determination, and I glimpse a depth of character I hadn't expected.

It takes a moment for me to focus on the object she's holding out toward me, and another moment to realize what it is. When I do, I almost laugh out loud.

The woman does have skills.

What's in her hand is worth half a million dollars, and I had no idea she'd slipped it off my wrist.

She's holding out my watch.

CHAPTER 4

Scarlet

I'd almost forgotten what a thrill it is to take someone's watch off their wrist.

It's a skill that takes practice, and you need to distract the person with a few other touches first. If you run your hand over their shoulder, arm, and even their chest, they become desensitized to your touch.

Only this time, the trick didn't work exactly as I'd expected. When I touched Balthazar Anders, a shiver of awareness coursed through my body. I hadn't expected his chest to be so well muscled, or to have been so entranced by the line of his jaw.

Now my heart is racing, and his scent lingers around me, making me feel dizzy. It's probably an expensive French or Italian aftershave that makes him smell so manly and delicious. The scent has unbalanced me.

In summary, touching Balthazar affected me a lot more than it affected him.

Instead of desensitizing him, I've *sensitized* myself. To him.

Ugh.

Such a despicable man shouldn't be exhilarating to touch. He should be as ugly on the outside as he is on the inside. And knowing how horrible he is, there's no way I should be attracted to him.

He's rattled me, but I can't let him see it. So I insert a little more bounce into my step as I walk back to him.

"It's a lovely watch," I say. "You should be more careful with it." I take care not to brush his hand with mine as I drop his watch into his outstretched palm.

He curls his fingers around it but doesn't take his eyes off mine. He's reassessing me, I'm sure. And now I'm close, I can sense a tightness in his stance that makes me doubt he was totally unaffected by my little trick.

"That was a gutsy move." His tone is thoughtful. "You surprised me, Ms. Jones. You're more than who you appear to be." Then he seems to make a decision because he gives a little nod. "Congratulations. You've earned yourself an audition."

A rush of triumph courses through me. My audacity paid off.

Then I realize I have no idea what he means. Earning an audition sounds like it should be good news, but what exactly am I auditioning for?

"An audition?" I ask.

He crosses to his desk to pick up a piece of paper. "I'll need you to sign a non-disclosure agreement before I explain. If you talk about the things I'm about to tell you outside of this room, the consequences will be severe."

I scan the paper he hands me. There's a lot of legal jargon but I get the gist. If I talk, he'll ruin my life, claim my first-born, and curse my descendants. The list of punishments is exhausting. What more should I have expected from an arrogant billionaire? The mere mortals who work for him need to be kept in line somehow.

The pen he gives me to sign the paper with isn't a regular ballpoint, but a fancy metal one with thick black ink. An arrogant billionaire's pen of choice.

I give the signed form back to him, and he waves at the chair. "Sit. I'll explain what I need from you."

Instead of sitting back down as well, he leans against the table. It means he's looming over me, taller than me. This angle accentuates the width of his shoulders. It also means his groin isn't much lower than eye level, and for a moment I try to resist checking out the size of his package.

But of course, I do. I'm only human, and a mean-spirited part of me hopes he's packing light, so to speak. But the bulge in his pants is impressive, dammit.

"So, an audition?" I ask, leaning back as much as I can and planting my gaze firmly on his eyes.

"I'm going to attend a ball, where I intend to meet with someone. And after our meeting, that person may try to kill me."

It takes a beat for this sentence to filter into my brain. And when it does, I'm soooo tempted to respond with sarcastic disbelief.

I mean, come on. It's hilarious, right?

Apparently, Mr. Arrogance can inspire lethal hatred from a single conversation. Though, come to think of it, it's not hard to believe. I didn't even need to meet him before I wanted to kill him. And now we've been talking for a while, I'm not feeling any less murderous.

I want to utter some of these thoughts aloud, but remembering his reaction to my remark about death threats, I manage to stay serious. And if I may say so myself, I should win some kind of award for holding in my snark.

"You said death threats weren't the problem," I say, adopting an expression that would make any poker player proud.

"I don't care about the death threats I've already had. The man I'm worried about is the one I'm about to make angry."

"Got it." I nod like I'm cataloguing the facts. "Old death threats are fine. New death threats are bad."

He narrows sharp eyes as though he suspects I might be holding back a snigger. So much for my poker-playing skills.

"I need someone to make sure I don't have a mysterious heart attack or fall out of any windows while I'm at the ball," he says. "It'll be an audition, because I have a longer event to attend a week later. I want to make sure the person I hire does an acceptable job at the ball before committing to something more intensive."

Confused, I wrinkle my brow. "But why not hire an ordinary security detail?"

"The event is only for invited guests and their partners. I can't take a bodyguard. Not unless the bodyguard pretends to be my date."

"Wait." I blink rapidly, all trace of humor vanishing abruptly. "Did I hear that right? Did you say you want me to be my *date*?"

He lets out a surly grunt as though my reaction has

annoyed him. "To clarify, you'd be there to work. My *employee*. With no real romantic overtones whatsoever."

It's insulting he thinks he needs to make that so clear. I have a perfectly good set of eyes, and a functioning brain. However large his personality flaws are, I can see he's a thirty-six-year-old billionaire who's been unfairly blessed with gorgeous looks and a body that could star in an ad for vibrators. He doesn't need to pay a woman to get a date. Hell, I bet he doesn't even need words. That surly grunt of his would probably seal the deal. Even knowing what a monster he is, something about the masculine roughness of it has given me tingles.

He pushes away from the table, pulls out a chair, and sinks into it. Thank goodness. At least now he's not towering over me. And now I'm not tempted to sneak another look at his package to confirm my earlier impression of its size.

Not that I'm interested. Nope. Not even a little.

"Let me start from the beginning." He softens his tone and drags in a deep breath. For the first time, I catch a glimpse of a weary kind of worry. As though underneath that arrogant exterior, he's carrying some serious weight. "My father recently died. You know who he was?"

I nod. "Blythe Anders. Chairman of Anders Pharmaceutical." According to Kayla, he's the one who took naked pictures of Aunt Alejandra when she was young.

"My father's will stipulated that his private papers should be destroyed," Balthazar says. "But I contested the will in court and won. Those papers were recently released to me."

"I read about it. It was in the news."

Kayla said Aunt Alejandra contacted Balthazar to ask if her photos were among the papers he'd inherited. She wanted to know if he had them, and if she could get them back.

Apparently Mr. Arrogance replied with a threat to release them on the internet if she ever contacted him again.

Thinking about it now makes me want to grab the pen I used to sign his stupid non-disclosure agreement and stab him with it.

"My father was murdered," he says.

His flat, matter-of-fact statement snaps me out of my flare of anger, back into our conversation.

"Murdered?" I frown. "The news reports said natural causes."

"He was bludgeoned to death. I arranged for it to be kept quiet."

"That's horrible. I'm sorry."

"I'm not."

The statement is shocking. Even more so, thanks to the unemotional way Balthazar delivers it.

"His killer did the world a favor," he adds. "But I don't know why they did it and whether they're going to target me. I inherited my father's share of Anders Pharmaceuticals, and I have all his personal papers. If he was killed for one of those two things, I could also be in danger."

"What's in his personal papers?" I ask. Not that I think he'll admit to having Aunt Alejandra's photos, but I want to know what he'll say.

Balthazar looks away for a moment, at the desk where he dropped the agreement I signed, as though he's reassuring himself that I won't be able to talk about any of this later.

He has the most chiseled nose I've ever seen. It's all right-angles, long and straight, with a flat bridge. It could have been sculpted by the world's best plastic surgeon, but if it's the nose he was born with, he's a lucky man.

"My father's papers are full of secrets," he says, looking back at me. "He knew damaging things about powerful people."

"Will you let me take a look at them?"

"There's no reason for that."

Unfortunately, his voice is flat and decisive. Not that I thought it would be that easy to access those papers and find out for sure if Aunt Alejandra's pictures are with them, but it was worth a try.

"I want to find out who killed my father," he says. "Some of the people with motives will be at the ball. And I'm planning to provoke at least one of them."

"Who?"

"Someone powerful. Someone not easy to get a meeting with. Even for me."

It's clear he's being cagey about the man's identity because he doesn't trust me. Winning enough trust to convince him to show me the papers would be hard. It'll be quicker—and more fun—for me to break into his house while he's asleep and take a look for myself.

"How are you going to provoke this mysterious man?" I ask.

"Do you agree to the audition? The event is on Friday night."

"Wait, *this* Friday? In two days?"

"Is that a problem?"

"I guess not," I say, though it's presumptuous of him to assume I don't have plans. I usually hang out with Kayla and Jamie on Fridays, unless one of us has a date.

"Melissa will arrange suitable clothing for you and organize payment."

"Suitable clothing?" I repeat, straightening my back in protest at his insulting tone and the way his disapproving gaze flicked to my chest. He made it sound as though I was wearing nipple tassels instead of a nice blouse.

"Whatever your usual rate is, I'll pay triple. But before you agree, you need to understand the risks." Taking some more papers from his desk, he hands them to me. "This is a legal contract. It states that you understand this assignment, and that I've made the danger clear. Whoever killed my father may target me, and this job may put you in the line of fire."

He's fond of his legal documents, that's for sure. This one is full of more legal jargon, including some super-fun paragraphs about how he's not responsible if I get injured or killed.

This isn't at all what I wanted. I'm only here for Aunt Alejandra's photos, and I can't see how signing up to protect Balthazar from a killer would help me get them back. Although, if I spent an entire evening with him, I might be able to find an innocent way to ask whether nude photos of my aunt were included among his father's private papers. Or failing that, I might get more information about his security system and how to bypass it.

But getting a good look around his house so I can figure out how to break in would be a lot better.

"I'll do the job, on one condition," I say.

Surprise passes across his face before he creases his brow. "You're not in a position to set conditions."

That growly tone shouldn't send a pleasurable shiver

down my spine. Despicable Balthazar doesn't deserve so much as a tremor from me, let alone a shiver. My only excuse is that it's entirely involuntary.

"Still," I say brightly. "I want to conduct a security audit of your house, to make sure you're safe here."

"I told you, I don't need—"

"If I'm going to protect you effectively, I want to make sure you won't be killed in your sleep by someone who broke in through an insecure entry point."

Okay, so it sounds like a flimsy reason to take a look around. But I speak with confidence, holding his gaze. Today's daily motivational quote was *Fake it until you make it,* and I'm faking the hell out of it.

After a moment, he gives a little nod and stands up. "Fine. Sign the form, and Melissa will show you around."

Yes! Arranging my expression to hide my delight, I scrawl my signature on the dotted line.

I'm now legally employed to protect Balthazar Anders.

No matter how tempting it might be to kill him myself.

CHAPTER 5

Scarlet

When I walk into our command center after my makeover on Friday morning, Kayla does a double take. Then she rises slowly from behind her array of computer screens, her lips parted, openly gaping.

"Hi," I say with a self-conscious wave.

Instead of replying, she raises her voice. "Jamie! Get in here. You need to see this."

"See what?" Jamie emerges from the training room wearing her workout gear: black shorts and a white tank. When she spots me, she stops dead. "Oh. Wow."

"Yeah," agrees Kayla. "Wow."

I pull a silly face at them, then sink into the office chair at my desk. It's hard to resist the urge to reach up and touch my hair. My regular daytime beauty routine consists of little more than forcing a brush through my curls and adding a touch of mascara. I like to put on silver eyeshadow and red lipstick when I go out in the evening, and maybe some sparkly powder on my cheekbones to make them shine.

But I've never had my hair coiled on top of my head in a complicated design before, or had someone spend an entire hour doing my makeup in tones that are way more muted than I'd usually use. The makeup artist said she was using forest tones, which is just a fancy way of saying brown.

"It wasn't my idea," I said. "Melissa arranged the appointment. I clearly didn't look good enough for Balthazar the way I was." My computer is in sleep mode, and I peer at the blank screen but can't get a good look at my reflection. Not that it matters. I took advantage of every red traffic light on the way home to check myself out in my car's rear vision mirror. I don't look like myself at all.

"You look gorgeous," says Kayla.

"Beautiful," agrees Jamie.

"Stunning." Kayla still sounds so amazed, I'm not sure whether to be flattered or offended.

I wrinkle my nose at the dark reflection on my screen, then turn back to face them. "The appointment was at a fancy salon on the Boulevard," I tell them. "Everyone in the salon had a French name, like Jacques or Brigitte or Pierre. And take a good look while you can, because you wouldn't believe what the appointment cost."

"Balthazar paid for it though, right?" asks Jamie.

"Wouldn't have gone if he hadn't," I say. "And any minute, Melissa's going to turn up with a dress for me to wear. Her boss clearly doesn't believe I know how to clothe myself." I snort. "Arrogant jerk."

"He's giving you a dress?" Jamie asks. "What if it doesn't fit?"

I shrug. "Then I'll wear something out of my closet instead."

Kayla and Jamie exchange glances. Only, I can read their faces better than I can read my own. They're my ride-or-dies, but we have way different tastes in clothing.

"What's wrong with the clothes in my closet?" I demand.

"Nothing at all," says Kayla quickly. "There's nothing *wrong* with them. But for a fancy ball?" She looks at Jamie for help.

"You wouldn't blend in," Jamie says. I can always count on her for blunt honesty.

"That's not to say you wouldn't look beautiful," Kayla adds. "But Balthazar probably needs you to blend."

"So you shouldn't wear red Doc Martin boots." Jamie looks pointedly at my feet.

"I wasn't going to wear boots," I tell her. "I have shoes."

"You have an eclectic, colorful style that totally works for you," Kayla says soothingly.

Jamie nods at the wall above my desk. "Are you going to take Balthazar's picture down before Melissa arrives?"

"Of course." Standing up, I pull the picture off the wall. Before I met Balthazar, I thought the frown he's wearing in the photo was severe. Now I know it's actually just a mildly irritated glower, at the lower end of his impressive frown range. On a scale of one to ten, the photo frown only ranks around three. In person, I managed to provoke ones that ranked a whole lot higher. A fact that gives me considerable satisfaction.

"Your irritating face is outta here," I tell the picture, crumpling it before I lob the ball at the trash can.

"I can't believe you're doing this," says Kayla. "You're not good with authority."

Jamie nods. "Remember how bad it got when we were in the hole?"

She means juvie. The 'hole' is short for the 'hellhole'. And it's true, I was always in trouble. But the guards were so mean, I couldn't help myself. It's not like I wanted to provoke them, it was more of a compulsion.

"I can't help it," I say. "When someone tells me what to do, all I want is to do the opposite."

"You're going to get fired." Jamie plonks herself down on the edge of my desk.

"I don't care if Balthazar fires me. All I wanted was to get a good look at his security system anyway."

Kayla clicks her tongue. "Well, don't let him get killed or anything. We don't need any bad publicity. We have bills, remember." Of the three of us, she's the most sensible one.

"Got it," I say. "Keep the billionaire client alive." I hesitate. "Think it's okay if he gets wounded?"

I'm joking, but Kayla gives me a stern look. I can tell she's going to say something about integrity, but luckily the bell rings from our client waiting room, cutting her off. She ducks back behind her wall of monitors, her normal protection from visitors.

"Cinderella, your fairy godmother is here," says Jamie, pushing herself off my desk.

"Be on your best behavior for Melissa." I order them both.

When I open the door, it's not just Melissa in our waiting room, but also a very stylishly dressed woman in her fifties who wheels in an entire rack of clothes. Melissa introduces her as Lucía, Mr. Anders' personal shopper. Of course Billionaire Bob has someone who buys his clothes for him. Heaven forbid he should be forced to walk into a store.

I introduce Jamie, who's still glistening with perspiration from her workout. Jamie is tall, tough and intimidating, and she usually handles the personal protection side of our security business, while I handle home security. Jamie would be better suited for the job of protecting Balthazar, but I'm the one with burglary experience. And if I get caught stealing the photos, that's on me. I won't put Jamie or Kayla in the line of fire.

Kayla sticks her head out from behind a computer screen when I introduce her but doesn't push her hair back from her face. She's in charge of cyber security, and likes to keep real-life client encounters to a minimum.

"It's just one night," I tell Lucía, gazing at the long rack of clothes she wheeled in. "Why bring all these outfits when I only need one?"

Both Melissa and Lucía are busy looking around, taking in our office with slightly horrified expressions. The place is run down, though we've made it as nice as we possibly can. Kayla likes to joke about how the next step is putting the roaches in pretty dresses and the rats in top hats.

There are three desks in our command center, one for each of us. There's also a round meeting table, a large whiteboard, and potted plants artfully arranged in front of the wall stains. The door leading into the training room is open. In there, we have mats scattered over the ancient linoleum floor, and punching bags hanging from the low ceiling. Jamie likes to spend her spare time punching things. She says it helps her think.

"Melissa estimated your size," Lucía says, turning to me. "But we have plenty of different outfits to choose from, just in case."

"You only need one dress for now," Melissa adds. "But if it goes well, you'll need more. And it's best to be prepared because I know this is going to work out!"

She's so sweet, I want to hug her. Despite the way we met, we've become friends.

I can only hope we'll be able to stay friends once I've stolen the photos from her boss. After they're safely destroyed, I'll confess our meeting was a setup and beg for forgiveness. In the meantime, I'm going to be the nicest friend there ever was. Hopefully my good deeds will weigh in my favor on my day of reckoning.

"How about this one?" Lucía pulls a black dress from her rack.

I scrunch my nose. Balthazar might live his life in a monotone, but I like to shine. "Have you got anything that isn't black or white?" I ask. "Red is my color."

"This is red, but it's not for a ball." She pulls out a gorgeous scarlet sundress.

"I love that shade." I run an admiring hand over the fabric.

"Put it aside," Melissa suggests. "When you pass the audition, you're going to need it."

Jamie grabs my fingers before I can take my hand back. "Wait," she says. "You had your nails done?"

I nod, holding up my other hand so she and Kayla can see. My fingernails have been shaped and painted with a layer of gloss.

"Pretty!" exclaims Kayla.

"They really wanted to give me long acrylic nails," I say.

"Wouldn't that have made it hard to draw your gun?" Jamie asks.

"That's what I said."

"Imagine if they could give you titanium nails," Kayla says wistfully, emerging from her shield of computer screens. "The ultimate hidden weapon." She makes a bear claw with her hand and pretends she's swiping at an opponent.

"I'd totally get those," I exclaim.

Lucía blinks at us, her brow furrowed in puzzlement.

"Does titanium go through a metal detector?" Jamie asks. "I feel like that's something I should know."

I look at Kayla, seeing as she's the one most likely to be able to answer that question. We went through weapons training together, and she can field strip an AR-15 to the extractor in thirty-five seconds. She also has a great memory for random facts.

"Titanium has a low magnetic field," Kayla says. "Not a hundred percent certain that it would go through without setting off the machine, but we could test it."

"You three are the best," says Melissa with a laugh. "Don't forget my self-defense lessons, will you?"

"First one's tomorrow morning," I remind her. "I'll pick you up at six. You're going to love it!" I've arranged for her to have a private lesson with the instructor who trained me, and I'm going along for moral support and to make sure she has fun. If we can squeeze in coffee and cake afterward, so much the better.

Lucía turns back to the rack and pulls out a lovely satin mini-dress. "This one is fun," she says to me. "Though perhaps not formal enough."

"Whatever you wear, you'll need room for a weapon," Jamie says.

"What if I carry a bag?" I ask.

"Can you supply a matching bag that'll fit a Glock 9mm?" Kayla asks Lucía.

"Or a micro-compact pistol," I suggest.

"Even a mini single-action revolver," Jamie says. "We have one that's incredibly tiny."

Lucía's elegant eyelashes flutter again. "Nobody's ever asked for that before."

I shoot her a grin that's supposed to be apologetic, though I'm enjoying myself too much to be sorry. This is a lot more fun than my normal work doing security audits for clients worried about how burglar-proof their home might be. Recommending locks and alarms can get dull. Today is anything but.

"I'm so glad you got this job," says Melissa. "I've told all my friends about how you saved me. I wish I could do what you did."

"Tomorrow morning, you'll start learning how to fight off muggers," I promise. "You'll be lethal in no time."

"What about this one?" Lucía pulls out a long, golden dress. It drops to the floor with a split up the front, and shimmers like liquid gold.

"It's beautiful," I breathe, instantly falling in love with it.

"Put it on," says Melissa. "We won't look." She turns her back.

I move behind the rack of clothes, feeling weird to be the only one undressing as I strip to bra and panties. I've barely managed to tug off my jeans when Lucía lets out a shriek of dismay.

"No!" she exclaims. "Please tell me that isn't what you're planning to wear under the dress?"

Everyone turns to stare. I jerk my gaze down to my lucky red underwear. "Does it matter?" I ask. "The color won't show through the gold fabric, will it?"

Lucía gapes at me like I suggested we kill and eat her children. "You're going to put a thirteen-thousand-dollar Natalia Ricci gown over red cotton underwear?"

"Thirteen thousand dollars?" squeaks Kayla.

"No way!" Jamie reaches out to brush her fingers lightly over the fabric. "Is it made of actual gold?"

I look back down at my perfectly good bra and panties. They're bright, comfortable and stretchy, in case I need to do any flying back kicks. The panties are boy-legged ones that look like mini shorts, and I like them because they don't ride up my butt. I never have to fish them out of uncomfortable places.

"You don't have any high-cut, nude-colored underwear?" Lucía asks hopefully.

"Not nude," I say. "Mostly red ones."

She tuts at me. "Tell me, what's your bra size?"

When I give her my measurements, Lucía gets on her phone and makes a call. Apparently, she's best buds with a La Perla store manager, and if I were the easily offended type, I might object to her calling me a desperate case who needs urgent help. Instead, I'm bemused when she orders expensive lingerie. It also makes me wonder if she has free reign with Balthazar's credit card.

Exactly how many women does Balthazar Anders buy underwear for? Will he even notice the charge on his bill?

While Lucía's busy on the call, I step back behind the

rack of clothes to pull the gold dress on over my red bra and panties. There's no mirror in this room, but the dress feels like it fits. Though I'm well-endowed in the boob, butt, and thigh regions, the fabric is stretchy.

After zipping it up, I step out in front of them.

Kayla gasps.

"Whoa," says Jamie.

"When Balthazar sees you in that dress, he's going to die," breathes Melissa.

Lucía steps forward. "And with the new bra I've just ordered, you're going to look like this." Without so much as buying me a drink first, she reaches out and cups my breasts, lifting them up and together.

"Yes!" crows Melissa.

"Incredible," says Kayla.

"Bazinga!" exclaims Jamie.

"See?" Lucía sounds triumphant. "I knew it!"

"Stop!" I'm laughing, but also a little embarrassed. And kind of happy. My figure can best be described as *sturdy*, and I've never been the type of woman to inspire a lot of Bazingas. Earning one from Jamie is high praise.

"Mr. Anders will flip out," Melissa says. "I wish I could be there, because I'd love to see his face."

"Why do you even like him?" asks Jamie in her blunt way. "Isn't he an asshole?"

"No! He's a great boss."

Kayla tugs her lips to the side, looking doubtful. "Do you have Stockholm Syndrome? Blink twice if you need our help but can't say it out loud."

"He can be grumpy, but underneath all his bark, he's

nice. And he has a compelling presence, like a force of nature. And a strong moral code."

Jamie and Kayla exchange puzzled glances with me. How does she have him so wrong? Nobody with a strong moral code would threaten to release Aunt Alejandra's naked photos. Only someone with no code and no compassion would do that.

"It doesn't matter anyway," I say. "This is a job, not a real date. I'm only there to throw myself in front of a bullet if one comes his way."

And believe me, the irony of that is not lost on me.

CHAPTER 6

Balthazar

My driver pulls the car up to Scarlet's door. She lives above her security business in a part of town I never come to. As we stop in front of her building, I'm half expecting a gang of delinquents to rush in and start removing the hubcaps from my limo.

Gordon, my driver, opens his door to go and buzz Scarlet's apartment, but something makes me tell him to stay where he is, and I get out of the car myself. I'm planning to ask her to sit quietly while I work in the car during the drive, but it feels rude to let Gordon fetch her, even if this isn't a date.

An unpleasant smell drifts from the metal security screen that guards the entrance to the laundromat on the building's ground floor. Next to it is a small lobby I can't get into without a security code. But there's a chipped, grimy doorbell for Ms. Jones' apartment, with a small speaker but no camera or screen. I press the button, and a moment later, a woman's voice comes out of the speaker.

"Who is it?" The voice isn't Scarlet's.

"It's Balthazar Anders."

"She's on her way down." The elevator doors open, and a woman steps out, her steps springy even though she's wearing high heels. I do a double-take, the air jettisoning from my lungs in a whoosh of breath.

She's gorgeous.

Scarlet's wearing a fitted gold dress that flows over her body like paint. She looks sensational. Her unruly curls have been tamed by a fancy hairdo, glittering pins groaning under the strain of holding the chaos under control. Her hairstyle is elegant, showing off her long neck. With her hair pulled back from her face, her oversized features remind me of Julia Roberts. Technically, her features may be a little too big, but I'm forced to admit it's no bad thing. Her strong features are mesmerizing, especially her eyes framed by wickedly long lashes.

And her breasts. *My God.* They're big for her frame, but they're not oversized. Perfect-sized, more like.

If I'd known what she had hidden underneath her red blouse at her interview, would I have been able to control my urge to pop open her huge buttons?

"Hello, Ms. Jones." I find myself offering her my arm.

"This is supposed to look like a date, isn't it? You'll need to call me Scarlet." She slides her hand around my elbow, walking close to me. Her arms are toned. No, more than toned, they're muscly. Her triceps are clearly defined, and even with her arm relaxed, I can see her bicep. I've dated other women who exercised a lot, but Scarlet looks like she could power lift a hundred and fifty pounds. Maybe I shouldn't find it so sexy, but with that gold dress clinging to her body, I'm finding it hard to control my reaction.

Funnily enough, I don't mind her springy steps when she's walking next to me. At least she can keep up with my long strides. And she has an energy to her that's anything but boring.

"Nice dress," I say.

"Thanks for buying it for me." Her smile widens. "I have to admit, you don't look too shabby yourself, Balthazar."

"My employees call me Mr. Anders," I say automatically.

"But I assume the women you *date* call you Balthazar?"

I give a reluctant nod. Keeping things formal is a good way to avoid blurring any lines. I suppose Ms. Jones' familiar tone is appropriate under these circumstances. But it makes me wonder, does she *like* me?

As the thought crosses my mind, I dismiss it. It doesn't matter if she likes me or hates me. My employees are paid to do what I ask, without feelings coming into it. Employees aren't friends. I learned that lesson early.

Gordon has opened the car's back door, and is standing beside it to help Scarlet get in.

"Hi," she says to him. "I'm Scarlet."

"My name's Gordon, ma'am." He holds out a hand to assist her into the car, but she grabs it and shakes it instead.

"Pleasure to meet you, Gordon," she says. Then she slides into the car without help.

I get into the other side, while Gordon shuts her door then goes to the driver's seat.

My car has a big back seat with plenty of leg room that easily accommodates both Scarlet and me. In the large gap in front of us is a fridge filled with an assortment of drinks, and a table I can pull up so I can work.

I settle myself into the seat beside her and glance over. The split up the front of her dress reveals her bare leg up to her lower thigh. Her leg is shapely, and her calf muscle bulges. Her skin is temptingly smooth, but I don't let my gaze linger. She's looking at me expectantly.

"Are you willing to tell me what the plan is now, or is it still a secret?" she asks.

I press the button to close the privacy screen so Gordon can't hear our conversation. When it slides shut, I say, "The man I'm going to see is Governor Salamanca. He's—"

Her sharp intake of breath cuts me off. She looks shocked.

"What?" I ask. "You know the Governor?"

"No." Pressing her lips together, she shakes her head. "I've never met the man. It's just that I've heard he's corrupt."

"Word gets around," I say dryly. "Anyway, the ball is a fund-raising event, and he's the guest of honor. When I see him, I'll insist on drawing him aside for a private chat. And after I talk to him, we can leave."

"Are you going to threaten him?" she asks.

"Something like that."

"And you think he might be the one who killed your father?"

I shrug. "Unlikely, but possible. He's one of many suspects."

"I'm prepared to respond if there's violence."

She sounds completely serious, but her words are at odds with the way she looks. Her dress hugs her like a lover.

She has a tiny matching handbag on the seat next to her that isn't big enough to hold a gun.

"You have a weapon?" I ask.

"Of course."

Don't look for it on her body, I tell myself. *Stop trying to imagine where it might be. And under no circumstances ask her where it is.*

"Where is it?" I ask.

Fuck.

"Don't worry," she says. "I'll be able to draw it quickly."

It must be in a thigh holster, as there's no other possible place she could have it hidden. And she's likely wearing the holster very high on her inner thigh, so it's not visible through the split in her dress.

For a brief moment, I allow myself to picture her without the dress, wearing just high heels and a holster strapped to her thigh, her curves and muscles exposed in all their sexy glory. But with my cock starting to swell, I push the picture from my mind.

"What exactly are you planning to say to Governor Salamanca?" she asks.

"You'll find out soon enough."

I don't plan to tell her because I don't know how trustworthy she is. If I don't like how the evening's going, I'll pull the plug and hire a different woman to play the part of my secret bodyguard next week.

"Okay," she says. "Then can I ask why you're going to talk to him in public, at a ball? Couldn't you organize a private meeting with him?"

"I've been investing in businesses for a lot of years, and I sit on the boards of several different companies. If word gets out that I met privately with Governor Salamanca, it could look like I'm asking for favors. I need to avoid the appearance of impropriety."

"But you can have a private chat with the governor at a ball?"

I shrug. "That way, it doesn't seem premeditated. It's just a short discussion between two people who happen to bump into each other."

"I guess that makes sense."

"Good. Now I have work to do. The drive to Pacific Palisades will take about half an hour." I wave at the fridge. "Help yourself to a drink. Do whatever you want, so long as you don't disturb me."

"You're going to work?" She blinks as though this is surprising. "You don't want to talk more about where we're going?"

"You know everything you need to." I'm already opening my car's custom-fitted foldaway table. On it, I place the folder I had my assistants pull together. It's the data from a selection of tech firms. All of them are doing interesting things and need an injection of capital, as well as guidance on their next steps. I'm going to spend the car ride reviewing their financial information and business plans so I can decide which to invest in.

I settle back in my chair, spreading out the papers in front of me. There's a lot of data, and usually I enjoy reviewing the finer details of business activity. It's exciting when I spot opportunities, both for the businesses and for myself. I have a knack for seeing ways to maximize growth and minimize risk.

Scarlet gets a cold drink out of the fridge and sits back,

sipping it thoughtfully. She's a little fidgety, and I'm trying not to be distracted, but she keeps looking at me. I can feel her eyes on me. And I can practically hear her thinking.

I find myself reading the business data without absorbing it. Part of my brain is enjoying the scent of oranges wafting from Scarlet's hair or skin. Another part is noting her movements, registering her muscles flexing and the sound of her dress sliding across her thighs when she adjusts the position of her legs.

It's maddening that she's taking my attention from where it needs to be. Does she need to move around like that? Can't she breathe more quietly?

I concentrate harder. The animal parts of me are the ones on alert. They're the parts I need to shut down. Only the analytical parts should function.

She shifts, and the gap in her dress widens, revealing more of her thigh. Why the thought of her wearing a hidden gun holster turns me on so much, I have no idea. It probably has something to do with the short-but-intense Avengers comic-book phase I went through as a boy, and my early obsession with Black Widow.

If Scarlet wore a black leather jumpsuit, she'd be all of my teenage fantasies come true.

"Would you stop fidgeting?" I ask tightly, resolving to shift all my attention back to my work. "Enjoy the view. Just don't move."

She raises both hands and flattens her lips, widening her big eyes at me to accentuate the fact she's not talking. She clearly thinks I'm being unfair.

Maybe I've hurt her feelings, but it can't be helped. My work is more important than catering to her emotions. The financials of one of the tech firms show a year-on-year profit that's surpassed my expectations, and I need to pinpoint what percentage of their growth is due to—

Scarlet taps her fingers against her exposed leg, letting out a breath that's so loud, it's almost a sigh.

I instantly forget what I was trying to pinpoint. All parts of my brain are only paying attention to her.

Giving up, I shut the folder.

"What is it?" My tone is curt. "Whatever you want to say, let's get it out of the way."

"Don't you think we should do some planning before we get to the ball?"

"What kind of planning?" If I sound impatient it's because I can't believe there's anything we need to go over that I haven't already thought of. The way I became so successful was by being meticulous in my planning and executing those plans with precision. I don't forget things. I don't overlook things.

Not often, anyway.

"Weeell." She draws out the word. "I'm posing as your date, right?"

"That's the assignment," I agree.

She tilts her head to the side. "Who exactly are we trying to fool? The organizers of the ball? Governor Salamanca? The people who'll be attending?"

"Everyone. If my father's killer is watching, I want him to assume you're harmless. If he's unaware of your martial arts skills, we'll have the element of surprise on our side."

"So everyone needs to think we're dating. And we'll have to talk to people, right?"

"There will be people there, so yes. We will likely need to speak to them."

"How convincing do we need to be? Do you want me to act like I'm hanging on your every word?" Rounding her eyes in an exaggerated look of adoration, she leans closer. Her hand slides onto my arm. "How much should I touch you?"

Her touch is so unexpected, a jolt goes through my body. The pressure of her fingers is unexpectedly enjoyable. None of my employees would dare to touch me without permission, not even a hand on my arm. But she's not afraid of me at all. She touches me as though she knows me well, not like she just met me. As though we were friends, or we were really dating.

The touch affects me more than I want to admit. Certainly more than I'd let her see. I don't want her to think I like it, or that she has any kind of power over me.

"Don't steal my cufflinks," I order in a dry tone, removing my arm from her grip.

Instead of being offended, her lips twitch up. "I could, you know. And that's a lovely Paiget watch you're wearing. Exactly how many designer watches do you own?"

"Please refrain from taking it, or from robbing anyone at the ball."

She reacts to my curtness by widening her smile. "Only if the assignment calls for it. And how do you know it won't?"

I want to be annoyed by how flippant she is, but for some reason, I'm not. "Try to keep your hands where I can see them. Now, is that all? Will you let me get back to work?"

"No, that's not all," she says, her confident brashness taking me by surprise yet again. "What shall we tell people about how we met?"

"Why do we have to tell them anything?"

"What about how long we've been dating?"

I heave an exaggerated sigh. "It doesn't matter. This is a simple assignment. We don't need to supply background information."

"Background information is exactly what we need!" she exclaims. "Whoever we talk to will ask how we met, and what will we say then?"

"They won't ask."

"Believe me, they will. And if we don't have any answers, they'll know something's up."

"Then this is our first date," I say impatiently. "We barely know each other. Satisfied?"

She rapidly blinks her long lashes as though what I've suggested is so outrageous, it's making her dizzy. "Are you serious? You'd take a first date to a politician's fundraising ball? You want them to think you have no game at all?"

It's silly. She's silly. But I find myself growling, "I have game," as though I need to make that clear for some reason. It was clearly a ridiculous thing to say, which makes my response just as ludicrous.

"Do you though?" She tilts her head.

To end this topic of discussion, I give in. "Fine. You can make something up."

"Good." She thinks for a minute, tapping her finger against one of her oversized cheekbones. "How about this? We were out walking our dogs, and somehow their leads got tangled together."

"I don't have time to walk my dog. I pay someone to do it."

"Oh, right. It needs to be a rich person meeting." She

rolls her eyes up and to the right, as though she's coming up with an elaborate scenario. Her eyelashes are so long and thick, they make a stunning frame for her green eyes.

"Let's just say we met at a party," I say.

"Sure, okay. Because I was at a party of billionaires for some weird and unlikely reason." Screwing her nose up, she shakes her head. "Or how about this? Maybe you borrowed your friend's Lotus Esprit, but you couldn't drive it, so you picked me up and I drove it for you. Then you took me to San Francisco on your private jet. We went to the opera and saw *La Traviata*, and I loved it so much I cried."

I raise an eyebrow. "Isn't that the plot of *Pretty Woman*?"

I'm clearly not the only one who's noticed the resemblance between her and Julia Roberts. Julia is twenty years older than Scarlet, but in her *Pretty Woman* days, Scarlet could probably have doubled for her.

Scarlet gapes at me. "*You've* seen *Pretty Woman*?" Her eyes are wide. "When? Why? How?'

"I saw it years ago," I tell her, secretly enjoying her incredulity. "And on the off chance that the people you're talking to have seen it too, you should make your story more original."

Her smile widens and her eyes light up as though I've delighted her. For the first time since we met, I'm certain her smile is real.

"Fine. We were flying our personal luxury helicopters and got the whirly things on top tangled up with each other," she says. "Now tell me the truth, Billionaire Bob. Underneath that forbidding exterior, are you actually a romantic? Do you harbor a secret love of rom coms?"

Did she just call me *Billionaire Bob*? Her cheek really is

astonishing. She has no concept of the employer-employee relationship. Or of any professional relationship based on respect and deference.

I have friends I play poker with and colleagues I talk business with, and none of them would dare call me anything but my name. With the exception of my stepsister, Gaby, of course. With her, all bets are off.

The thought of Gaby gives me a familiar pang. I miss her.

But I have to wonder… Is that why I'm allowing Scarlet so much leeway, because talking to her reminds me of Gaby?

No, it seems all wrong to compare Scarlet to Gaby. Gaby and I may not be related by blood, but she's my sister nonetheless, and I've never had anything but brotherly thoughts toward her. Whereas I can't help but notice how sexy Scarlet is in that gold dress.

"I don't like rom coms," I tell her, not entirely sure why I'm volunteering personal information. "But when I was twelve years old, I gained a stepsister. Gaby and I took turns choosing the movies we watched. She sat through *Kill Bill* and all the *Matrix* movies, and in return, I suffered through a lot of Hugh Grant and Sandra Bullock movies. And she made me watch *Pretty Woman* twice."

"You've seen it *twice*," Scarlet crows triumphantly, her smile growing so wide it's in danger of overtaking her face. "But how did you gain a stepsister?"

I shake my head. She already knows more about me than I tell most people. "You don't need to know about my past." I return my gaze to my papers. That gesture would signal to any other employee that I want silence and to be left alone. But not Scarlet. Oh no. She keeps right on speaking.

"That's exactly the type of thing I should know," she says.

"It'd be weird otherwise. What if somebody asks about your stepsister and I'm clueless?"

"They won't ask about her."

She sets her mouth into a stubborn line. "It's the type of thing we'd talk about on our first date. Don't you want people to believe we're dating?"

She's relentless.

And again, I give in to her nonsense. "Fine. I gained a stepsister when my father married Gaby's mother. She was his third wife. Gaby was my age, and the four of us lived in the same house for a while."

My father didn't like kids and hadn't wanted any. After finding out Mom was pregnant with me, he'd immediately had a vasectomy so there'd be no possibility of any more accidents. But after Mom died, he'd been stuck with me. And then he'd married his third wife despite knowing she already had a daughter.

Gaby and I were both lonely kids, largely ignored by our parents. We'd formed an instant bond. The two of us had made our own family, and we'd hung out together and looked out for each other. The time spent with her had been the best part of my childhood.

"Why did you only live in the same house for a while?" Scarlet asks. "What happened?"

"Gaby's mom found out my father was cheating on her. She took Gaby with her when she left. The two of them moved away and I was sent to boarding school. Dad married his fourth wife, and I didn't see my stepsister again for several years."

"Oh. That's sad."

"People leave," I say with a shrug. "That's life."

I'd had to accept it, or spend my whole life grieving for everyone I'd lost.

"Are you and your sister still close?" she asks.

I nod. "Gaby works in Australia now, but we spend holidays together when we can. And when she left the country, she gave me my dog, Ringo."

Picking up the financial report in front of me, I stare at it without reading it. Why am I sharing such personal information with Scarlet? I'm breaking my own strict rules about not getting friendly with employees. And though she's grown on me since our first meeting, and I admire her watch-stealing skills, I'm not certain I like her. She's too familiar with me for comfort.

I shouldn't have told her so much about Gaby.

And dammit, now I can't concentrate on work. My mind is full of the past.

"Honey," Scarlet says in a musing tone.

"What?" I jerk my face to her.

"Honey," she repeats, her lips twitching up on one side. "Is that a good pet name for you?"

Did she really just ask me that? Would she *dare*?

She blinks at me, as though fluttering her long eyelashes over her beautiful green eyes will make the question any less shocking. "We need pet names to make our relationship believable."

"No." My tone is curt. "We absolutely do not."

"If you don't like *honey*, I can think of a different name. I'll call you..." She hesitates, tapping her finger against her chin, a devilish smile decorating her lips.

"Careful," I warn with a growl. "The next word out of your mouth is likely to get you fired."

"What about *snuggles*?" Her sly expression broadcasts the fact she's deliberately testing my boundaries. "Because your personality is so soft and cuddly."

Her daring takes my breath away. There isn't a person I know — not a friend, a colleague, an ex-girlfriend, nor even Gaby — who'd remark on my personality, let alone call me *snuggles* to my face.

"You'll call me Mr. Anders in private and Balthazar in public," I grind out. "Anything else and I'll have my driver drop you on the side of the road so you can walk home."

She wrinkles her nose. "I'm not sure you understand how to fool people. We'll need to do a little acting or they'll never believe we're dating."

"And you've spent your life fooling people? Your criminal activity has made you an expert?"

A shadow crosses her face. "Are you going to keep bringing that up, or can we get over it already?"

"It's who you are."

She sucks her lips in, then looks away, out of her side window.

I upset her. But finally, she's silent. Now I have peace and quiet so I can work. That was what I wanted. An end to her questions.

Looking back at the financial reports spread over my worktable, it strikes me that Scarlet is a little like the start-up companies I invest in. I like to help small disrupters that are taking on established industries, turning conventional business models on their heads. And Scarlet's a maverick too. She doesn't play by any of the usual social rules.

I've never met anyone as daring. As much as I hate to admit it, she's intriguing.

I shoot a glance at her, but her face is still turned away so I can't see her expression. Surely she must feel me looking? The scenery isn't that fascinating.

Maybe I shouldn't have been so hard on her.

Now the silence is dragging on, I even feel a little regret over hurting her feelings. *Regret*, for fuck's sake!

What the hell is happening to me?

CHAPTER 7

Balthazar

"We're here, sir," says Gordon, pulling the limo into a circular driveway.

We're at the ballroom at Pacific Palisades. Two doormen are waiting outside the grand covered entranceway. A light drizzle has started falling, and one of the doorman hurries down to open the limo's door, an umbrella held overhead.

I get out of the other side of the car, then motion the doorman away so I can offer Scarlet my hand to help her out. The way she unfolds her body as she exits the car is a picture of elegance. She moves gracefully, like an athlete. And she looks so stunning the doormen gape at her, until a glare from me makes them flush and turn away.

I escort her down the hallway and into the enormous ballroom, filled with people. She walks with her hand curled around my elbow, her strides long and graceful. Her dress swishes with each step, and I can't keep from glancing down at the split that reveals her thigh. She really has incredible legs.

"Wow. Look at this place!" She gazes around with wide, awed eyes.

The room is decorated with a vast array of colored lights, but it's all I would have expected. Scarlet is acting as though she's never seen anything like it.

When I was born, Anders Pharmaceuticals was already worth millions. I grew up with wealth, and I'm so used to it, I forget that for most of the population, displays like this one aren't regular occurrences. But now she's prompted me to take more notice, I have to admit it's beautiful.

Scarlet moves closer to me, tilting her head up to speak into my ear. I bend my neck to listen, acutely aware of her breast pressing against my arm and the scent of oranges in her hair.

"There are four guards in this part of the room," she murmurs. "All armed. And there are six security cameras."

"Where are the guards?" I murmur back.

She has her hand on my shoulder so she can get closer to my ear with her lips.

It's a strange thing. I'm not used to being touched. Every time she does it, I'm hyper-aware of it.

"Don't make it obvious when you look. But the closest two are over there." She inclines her head toward two men in black suits who are standing together at the edge of the room. I'd assumed they were guests, and I can't see any obvious weapons.

Then she gasps like something has shocked her.

"What?" I demand, my muscles tensing. Surely she

couldn't have spotted an assassin? Whoever might want to kill me couldn't possibly be so blatant.

I follow her gaze to the buffet table that's on the far side of the room. With so many people in front of it, we can only see part of it. But it looks to be laden with finger food, and on one end are some extravagant deserts.

"Is that a chocolate *fountain*?" she asks. "Do you see it?"

Breathing out, I relax my shoulders. "I take it you like chocolate." Obligingly, I walk toward it, and she walks beside me. We cross the large ballroom floor together so she can get a better look, and I scan the guests as we go. I'm looking for Governor Salamanca, and on the alert for Anders Pharmaceutical board members. This is a high-profile annual event, and the rich and famous always vie for tickets. I'm sure at least some of the board members will be here, but I haven't spotted any yet.

"It's liquid chocolate in a fountain." She shoots me a delighted grin. "Look! You can dip a cup into it." Her enthusiasm is strangely endearing, and I'm tempted to smile back at her. But she adds, "That fountain is going on my vision board. I want one!"

"Your vision board?" I stop a short distance from the buffet table.

"You don't know what a vision board is?"

"Enlighten me."

"I put pictures of the things I want on my vision board, so I can manifest them into my life."

"Manifest them?"

"Using the law of attraction," she explains as though it's something that actually exists and not a steaming pile of wishful thinking. "The universe gives me the things I want."

"The universe gives you things," I say slowly, making my disbelief clear.

"It really works. You should try it." She sounds sincere, and for a moment I just stare at her, too surprised to laugh. Her little security company seems to be barely staying afloat, and she thinks she can tell me how to get the things I want?

Using my driest tone, I say, "You think the universe might make me rich if I ask it nicely?" I smooth a hand down the lapel of my tuxedo. "Oh, wait. Never mind."

She wrinkles her nose at me. "Okay Bob, feel free to scoff. But it's worked for me so many times, there's no room for doubt."

"What exactly has the universe given you?" My investigator ran a standard background check on all three of the women I was considering for the job, but the check wasn't exhaustive. Scarlet could have secrets he didn't uncover.

"Everything!" she exclaims. "My friends, a job I love, our own office—"

I make an involuntary sound of disbelief when she says 'our own office'. She and her friends run her security company from the second floor of the almost-derelict building where I picked her up. If the termites moved out, the entire place would fall down.

"What's wrong with our office?" she asks indignantly.

"I'm sure it's top notch."

She narrows her eyes at me as though she's going to press me on it, but fortunately she's interrupted by a butler holding a tray of drinks.

"Champagne?" asks the butler, offering his tray. "I also

have freshly pulped orange juice, or if you prefer something else, I can fetch it for you."

Scarlet shoots me a triumphant look. "See, I was just thinking about getting a drink, and here it is." She picks up a glass of juice and waves it in my direction. "I need to keep a clear head, but it's SO like the universe to offer me champagne at the moment I most want it."

She's teasing me.

At least, I hope she's teasing me, and not serious. Otherwise, I hired a gullible fool to protect me from mortal danger. Either way, the experience of being spoken to like this is so unlike what I'm used to, I'm not entirely sure how to react.

"I'll take a scotch," I say to the waiter. "Single malt. Something peaty." When he leaves, I motion to the crowd. "I see my cousin and his wife over there. Let's talk to them. I'll introduce you as my date."

"Are they on the suspect list of people who might be trying to kill you?"

"They own shares in Anders Pharmaceuticals, and have voting rights, but they're the only board members my father didn't have any dirt on. If they want to kill me, it's not because I know their secrets." I offer her my free arm so I can lead her through the crowded room.

"Got it." Nodding seriously, she wraps one hand around my elbow, her glass of juice held high in the other. "That means if they attack, it's entirely due to your personality. Don't worry, my weapon is ready."

She shoots me a mischievous smile that's higher on one side than the other, which somehow manages to kill any trace of the irritation I would have felt if anyone else had joked with me that way. She has no boundaries and doesn't treat me with the respect an employee should show their employer. But it seems to be a quirk of her personality, so I can't see the point in making a big deal over it. Not right now, anyway.

"Scarlet, this is Leopold and this is Loretta." I introduce her to my cousin and his wife. Leo is about my age, but I rarely saw him growing up. My father didn't socialize with his brothers or sisters, and I've never attended any board meetings, so I've only spoken to any of them at the occasional family event I've been pressured into attending. Still, for what it's worth, I've always gotten on a little better with Leo than any of the others.

"That's a lovely dress you're wearing," Scarlet says to Loretta. "And your necklace is stunning."

My cousin's wife touches the jewel at her neck. "Thank you. Your dress is beautiful too. Whose is it?"

Scarlet hesitates. "Well, Balthazar bought it. But I guess he doesn't want it back."

"I mean, who's the *designer*?"

"Oh, it's Natalia someone?"

"Not Natalia Ricci?" Loretta turns her surprised gaze to me, and I can see the cogs whirring in her brain.

I shrug. Natalia may be my ex-girlfriend, but what's wrong with Scarlet wearing one of her designs? Natalia and I parted because we were working in different countries and she didn't want to have a long-distance relationship. I'd expected Natalia to choose her job over me so it didn't come as a surprise when it happened, and I've learned to let that kind of thing slide off me.

Besides, Natalia's a talented designer who's in hot

demand. Her gowns have been gracing red carpets for the last few years.

"That's it," says Scarlet. "Natalia Ricci."

Loretta smiles. "I love that you don't mind being dressed by her. Aren't you just the sweetest?"

"Why would I mind?" Scarlet looks puzzled.

"That's right, sweetie! Why would you not wear such a fabulous dress no matter who designed it?" Loretta turns to me. "I like her," she exclaims, as though I might care about getting her approval on who I date.

Loretta is a slim blonde, wearing a silky dress in a soft shade of pink. Leo told me she was working as a model when they met, and I've always thought she was a beautiful woman. But next to Scarlet's boldness, everyone else seems muted. Scarlet has a charisma that's plainly visible in the way she holds herself. It's a silent confidence, a swagger in her walk. It's in the way she clearly doesn't worry about what other people think of her.

The waiter arrives with my drink. "Lagavulin, sir." He hands it to me as Leo claps me on the back.

"How's the investment business?" Leo asks. "Funding anything interesting?"

"Oh no, let's not talk about boring things," Loretta says. "I want to hear how long you two have been together and how you met."

Scarlet looks triumphant. "Oh, you want to hear how we met?" she repeats, raising her eyebrows at me in a silent 'I told you so' gesture that fires up my blood as though she's issued a challenge. "Well, Balthazar's dog walker called in sick, so he—"

"Wait. Is your dog walker okay?" Loretta turns her gaze to me.

I quickly swallow a sip of whisky so I can answer before Scarlet does. "No," I say. "He died."

Loretta puts her hand to her mouth. "Oh no! That's horrible."

"How did he die?" asks Leopold, his brow creased.

Scarlet gives me a questioning look, clearly wondering what I'm doing. Thing is, I'm not sure why I'm embellishing her story. Maybe I want to see if it's possible to put any more spark into those green eyes of hers.

"Scarlet will tell you," I say, enjoying how her gaze narrows on me for a moment before she smooths out her expression for her audience.

"He got rabies," she says.

"Rabies?" Leo repeats doubtfully.

"Anyway." Her tone is firm. "Balthazar had to walk his own dog."

"Why didn't you hire someone else to walk it?" asks Leopold.

"Good question." I frown at Scarlet to disguise the fact I'm having fun.

"Because the entire point of owning a dog is to look after him and enjoy his company," Scarlet says. "Why would you even bother owning Ringo if you're going to pay someone to walk him?"

"We have a walker *and* a nanny for our shit poo," Loretta confides.

"Your *what*?" Scarlet and I ask the same question at the same time.

"Shit poo." Though Loretta repeats it, Scarlet still seems as stumped as I am.

"It's a cross between a Shih Tzu and a Poodle," Leopold says.

A small sound of amusement slips from my throat.

Fortunately, Scarlet lets out a snort at the same time and somehow manages to turn it into a cough, so nobody notices my slip. "Oh, a Shih Poo," she exclaims. "I thought you were talking about a regular dog with the runs."

"With the *what*?" Loretta looks confused.

Scarlet opens her mouth to explain, and I rush to interject. "Your dog nanny doesn't walk your dog?" I ask, though I couldn't care less. It's the only question I can think of at such short notice.

Loretta looks even more confused. "Why would Sergio walk him? He's a dog *nanny*, not a dog walker. He's a highly skilled professional."

"That's right, Bob," says Scarlet. "Dog nannies aren't walkers. Everyone knows that."

"Bob?" asks Leopold. Now he and Loretta both look perplexed.

"Anyway," I say. "Back to the story of how we met. Scarlet?"

Turning to her, I can see she's biting the side of her lip, barely holding in her laughter. Maybe asking her to keep making up a story about us is a mistake. But before I can change my mind, she picks up the ball and runs with it.

"So Balthazar was walking Ringo," Scarlet says in a tone of exaggerated horror. "And clearly, that's a shocking thing to do. But prepare to be even more shocked, because he didn't know he had to pick up Ringo's shit poo!"

Loretta's brow creases. "Balthazar has a Shih Poo?"

"I mean, his dog pooped on the sidewalk," Scarlet clarifies.

"Ew." Loretta recoils, the back of her hand going to her nose as though she's worried about gagging.

Scarlet widens her eyes dramatically. "And what kind of monster leaves their dog's poop on the sidewalk where anyone could step in it while they're innocently walking?"

"But you wouldn't expect him to touch it?" Loretta asks.

"Nobody walks in LA," Leopold says, swallowing a gulp of champagne. "It's a car city."

"That's right." I raise my eyebrows at Scarlet. "It's a car city," I repeat. "And with nobody using the sidewalks, who could have stepped in it?"

"I stepped in it!" Scarlet declares.

"NO! You didn't?" Loretta wrinkles her nose. "Whose shoes were you wearing?"

"Mine."

"Which designer, silly!"

"Oh." She looks at me.

"Louboutin," I say, though I have no idea why I'm helping with this ridiculous story.

"You stepped in dog poop in your Louboutins?" Loretta sounds as though this is the worst thing she can imagine.

"It's okay," Scarlet assures her. "Because Balthazar saw what happened and went down on one knee."

Though I can see where the story is headed, I can't believe Scarlet is actually going to take it there. I'm paying her for protection services and she's going to humiliate me?

I'm about to object, when Loretta shrieks, "Balthazar *proposed*? You're getting *married*?!"

"I didn't propose," I growl.

"No, no!" Scarlet seems horrified by the suggestion. "I didn't even know who he was. He dropped to one knee so he could clean my shoes."

"Eww," Loretta's face registers disgust and awe in equal measure. "I mean, that's sweet. But eww."

"You really cleaned her shoes?" Leopold asks, as though it's an inconceivable act.

"No," I say. "Scarlet's delusional." It takes an effort to keep the irritation out of my tone. She's gone too far. And I think she knows it. When I catch her gaze, her eyes widen a little at my expression.

"He's being humble." She tucks her hand into my elbow. "It was so romantic, you have no idea."

Loretta turns to Leopold. "Would you do that for me, darling?"

"Of course, my love."

There's no way that's the truth, but Loretta beams at him anyway. She tucks her hand into his elbow like Scarlet did to me. As though Scarlet and I are a couple to emulate when it comes to romantic gestures.

My anger abates, but I move my arm out of Scarlet's grip so I can rest my hand on the bare skin of her back, well above the dip of her dress. It's supposed to be a silent reminder that she's here to do a job, not indulge in foolishness. But I feel her shiver under my touch, and I forget everything but how silky and warm her skin feels under my hand.

God, she's gorgeous in that dress.

Her chin is lifted and she's staring straight ahead, not looking at me, but I can sense her awareness of me. Her muscles are tense. And I have an almost overwhelming urge to slide my hand further down from its innocent position on her upper back. I want to follow the curve all the way to her gorgeous ass. I want to discover if she's as well-muscled there as her arms and legs.

Tempting, but highly inappropriate. Removing my hand, I cup it around my glass of whiskey.

"The funding business is as interesting as ever," I say to Leopold, answering the question he originally asked.

"I must say, I'm surprised to see you here," he says. "You don't usually come to these kinds of things."

"I've decided to take more of an interest in the activities my father was involved in."

"Really?" He raises his eyebrows. "Does that mean you're going to the board meeting next week?"

"Not just the board meeting. The entire week away."

"You are? That's not like you."

"Why would you do that?" asks Loretta. "You've never been to a board meeting before, have you?"

I shrug. "Things have changed. I own a much larger share of the company now. I've decided to run for chairman and make some changes."

"All these years of ignoring the company, and now you want to be *chairman*?" She sounds incredulous.

"You have a problem with that?" I search her face. Part of the reason I'm planning to conduct individual meetings with all the board members is to watch how they react. They're all suspects, although I can't imagine good-natured Leo being willing to kill someone.

"Loretta suggested I should take on the chairman

position, didn't you darling?" Leo loops his arm around his wife's waist. "She's more ambitious than I am."

"You'll oppose me?"

He shrugs, looking unconcerned. "I'd rather play golf than be chairman."

"Even if I tell you that I'm planning to cut the dividend for the board members?"

Loretta gasps.

"Cut the dividend by how much?" Leo asks.

"All of it."

"What? Why would you do that?" Loretta looks horrified.

"If the others find out, you won't get enough votes to become chairman," says Leo.

"What about you? Can I still count on your vote?" I'm aware of how much pressure it puts him under to ask him so flatly after dropping my bombshell. But this is a litmus test. Leo's by far the most easygoing member of my family, and the least excitable. If he gets upset, the others will be furious.

"I don't like the thought of losing that income," he says slowly. Loretta frowns at him and then me, obviously liking the idea even less than her husband.

I spot the Governor on the other side of the room and decide to give my cousin and his wife some time to absorb the news. Seeing as they have no dirty secrets, I have nothing to pressure them with. And hopefully I won't need their vote anyway.

"If you'll excuse us." I offer my arm to Scarlet. "The Governor is over there, and I want to have a word."

"Sure," says Leo distractedly. Loretta says nothing. Her expression has turned unfriendly.

Scarlet curls her hand into my elbow, and I lead her away.

"You made up a story about me cleaning your shoes," I say in a stern tone when we're far enough away that Leo and Loretta won't hear.

She gives a laugh. "Did you see how shocked they were?"

Though I have to admit—silently—that it's a little amusing, I make my tone even sterner. "From now on, do what I say and nothing more."

Looking completely unchastised, she shoots me a sideways glance. "Did your last girlfriend always do what you said?"

"Always."

The evening would be very different if I were here with Natalia. She never did things I didn't like. I knew exactly how she'd act at all times.

There's nothing predictable about Scarlet.

"The governor is over there." I nod toward the man a few yards in front of us.

She's suddenly all business. "There's no bulge in his suit, but that doesn't mean he's not armed. Can't see any protection agents. Nobody with earpieces, other than the resort's security guards we're already aware of."

We move toward him together, as though we really are a couple. He's talking to three men I don't recognize. Judging from their plastic faces and shiny smiles, they're probably politicians.

"Governor," I say. "A word?"

Salamanca steps away from the men. "Hello, Balthazar." His tone is curious and a little wary. He knows I just inherited my father's shares in the pharmaceutical company, and that I now own Dad's private papers. He must guess I now have Dad's secrets, some of which were about him.

"This is Scarlet," I say in a polite tone. No sense in forewarning him about my real intentions.

To my surprise, Scarlet gives a wide, excited smile. "I'm a big fan of yours, Governor. And this is such a lovely suit." She strokes her hands down his lapels, then steps in to kiss his cheek, transferring her grip to his waist.

The governor's cheeks turn rosy with pleasure. He gazes rapturously down her cleavage with the same hungry look he must get when he counts his dirty money.

"Scarlet," I hear myself say. "A handshake would do."

When she steps back, I put my hand on her lower back. Salamanca's smiling far too widely for my liking. I narrow my eyes at him, but he's too busy leering at Scarlet to notice.

"Such a pleasure to meet you, Governor," Scarlet says. She's clearly decided to lay on the charm, and of course the governor's lapping it up.

"Thank you, darlin'," he says, and the endearment is like sandpaper over my eardrums. "What do you do?"

"Oh, I'm in customer service." She gives a self-deprecating laugh, blinking up at him through her long lashes, her hand going back to the side of his jacket. "It's not an important job like yours."

"But your customers must love you." He's practically drooling over the front of her dress.

If I had any second thoughts about what I was about to do to the governor, they'd be gone. The sleazebag deserves everything he's about to get.

"Governor, I need a word with you in private," I grind out. "It's important."

His smarmy smile falters just a little, but he nods. "Of course, Balthazar. Give me half an hour, then I'll meet you in the smoking room."

"Fine." It takes an effort not to snap the word.

"I hope you're going to come with him, my dear," Salamanca says to Scarlet. "I'd like to hear more about your not-so-important job."

I bet he would, if it meant getting even more handsy.

Putting my arm around Scarlet, I draw her to my side, narrowing steely eyes at the governor. He may be a big shot, and possibly the nation's next president, but if he knows what's good for him, he'll back the hell away.

"Half an hour," I growl.

The governor's gaze snaps from Scarlet's chest to my face, and he starts at my expression. His cheeks lose a little color. "Uh," he says, his voice weakening. "Yes. Of course."

I lead Scarlet away and the governor turns back to his friends. As soon as we're out of earshot, I let her go. "Did you need to touch him?"

She draws her brows together, looking puzzled. "How else could I be sure whether he was armed? I thought that's why I was here?"

Blowing out a breath, I let some of my tension go. She's right. I hadn't thought of that.

"If your meeting's about to upset him, I need to know what I'll be dealing with," she adds.

Now I feel foolish for doubting her. Her tone has become business-like. She might be willing to tease me, but she seems serious about her job.

"Is he carrying?" I ask.

"Not unless he keeps his weapon in the same place I keep mine."

The reminder of her gun instantly fills my mind with sexy images. Where could it possibly fit beneath her dress? The fabric hugs her breasts and clings to her torso. It's a work of art. One without hiding places.

"Where do you keep your gun?" I demand.

She gives me a knowing smile, one side of her mouth twitching higher than the other, as though she can tell what an obsession it's becoming for me.

"Want to dance?" she asks.

CHAPTER 8

Scarlet

Balthazar is a good dancer.

There's something about having his arms around me that makes me reckless. Maybe because being held by him electrifies my body. Both his hands are on the curve of my back, and I could describe in detail how his fingers are touching my skin, including their exact position and pressure. My hands are around his neck, and the tickle of his hair against my knuckles is sending shivers down my spine. We're moving together in perfect unison, as though I can read his mind, or he can read mine. The feeling is exhilarating.

"You still haven't told me where your gun is," he murmurs into my ear.

I don't want to tell him it's in the tiny evening bag that's looped over my shoulder. There's a devilish voice in my head that says I should let him believe it's somewhere under my dress.

"A lady never tells," I say in a suggestive tone. Then I shoot him a wink.

I'm almost certain that a wink will surprise him, but his reaction is even better than I'd hoped. His eyebrows fly up in the middle and his lips part slightly. Maybe nobody has ever winked at him before.

"Did you just *wink* at me?" He uses his growly voice. Lord help me, I like it.

"Did I? Hmm." I lift my gaze to the ceiling. "You know what? I can't be sure, but that doesn't sound like something I'd do."

He lets out a hum of displeasure, but I can tell he's goading me because he likes it when I tease him. Admittedly, his enjoyment is reluctant and difficult to spot, and it's possible he's not even consciously aware of it. But I can tell by the way he's slowly loosening up around me and becoming less cold.

And although pleasing him isn't something that should be on my list of priorities, I can't help but smile a little. Secretly, of course. I wouldn't want him to catch me doing it.

"Employees don't wink at their bosses," he states flatly, drawing me back against him.

"Do you have a no wink policy? Is it in my employment contract?" I tilt my head. "What if I get an itchy eye? Will I be allowed to scratch it, or should I wait for a prescribed break?"

"Have you never been an employee before?" he murmurs into my ear. "Because you don't seem to have any idea how it works."

"Oh, please do tell me everything I'm doing wrong. Do you mind if I take notes?"

"Respect," he says. "Deference. Courtesy. Do those words mean nothing to you?"

I like having his lips next to my ear. His voice rumbles, soft and deep. His warm breath tickles my lobe. It does wicked things to me.

"Have you ever heard the words 'fake girlfriend'?" I counter. "Are you able to pretend you're not my employer? Or maybe you treat your dates like employees, making them bow to you and call you Mr. Anders." I draw back, widening my eyes. "Wait. Red Flag! Are you a toxic boyfriend?"

"A toxic boyfriend?" he repeats, as though he's never heard those words before.

He frowns at me, but I'm coming to recognize that Balthazar has many different flavors of frown. This one is more puzzled than irritated. If his frowns were chili peppers, this one would be mild. A jalapeño frown. Weirdly, it's kind of delicious.

"A toxic boyfriend is a guy who needs to control the woman he's dating," I explain. "To order her about and tell her what to do."

"I don't *need* to do that."

"But you like it?" I press.

A small smile lifts his lips and his eyes gleam. He looks wolfish and handsome, and extremely dangerous. "I think *you* might like it."

I swallow. "No," I lie.

My entire body is vibrating, feeding off the energy that radiates from him. He's so confident of his own power, it's utterly compelling.

He lifts a hand and smooths back one of the long, loose tendrils that the hairdresser left free and sprayed into place.

The back of his finger strokes my cheek, making me shiver. "You like being told what to do, so you can do the opposite," he murmurs.

He's right.

When I'm not with him, I can remember all the reasons I need to keep our business relationship polite and distant until I can steal back the photos and move on. But when I'm this close to his arrogant energy, all that fades away and I can't help needing to tease and provoke him. Maybe bend him to my will a little. That's just my nature.

My cheeks heat and I move closer to him, turning my cheek to rest against his lapel so he can't see me blush. His cologne is delicious, and I love the roughness of his suit against my cheek. He moves his hands to the small of my back but keeps his touch light. His fingers rest softly against my dress, and we move together to the music.

He's a good dancer. Probably learned how to do it in billionaire finishing school. And if dancing with him is this pleasurable, what would sex with him be like?

Not that I imagine it as we move together.

No, not at all.

But by the time we need to meet the governor, I'm hot and flushed, and I may have salivated a little on his lapel.

The smoking room is a smallish room off the hallway, at the side of the building. It has floor-to-ceiling windows that look out over the floodlit golf course. The room is decorated in an old-fashioned style, with rich wooden panels on the walls and ornate, heavy furniture. The drapes are red velvet, and there's a huge chandelier. Everything about the resort is impressively grand.

The governor walks into the smoking room shortly after

we do. I've been trying not to think about the beef I have against Governor Salamanca in case it gets in the way of what I've come here to do. Aunt Alejandra thinks he's behind the corrupt system that sent me and my friends to juvie, and if it's true, he's an evil man. But we have no proof. So for now, I'm putting my own hatred of him aside.

We sit at the big wooden table in the center of the room. The governor is on one side of it, with Balthazar opposite him, and me beside Balthazar. Salamanca looks more rosy-cheeked than usual. Maybe he's had a few drinks.

"What's this all about?" he asks.

The governor's a famous politician, often on TV. But he looks at Balthazar as though he's awed by him. Maybe even afraid of him. It's the same way I've noticed other people treating Balthazar. Everywhere he goes he seems to collect nervous looks and deferential head nods. Maybe it's because he's so rich, but most likely it's thanks to the intimidating scowl he always wears.

Balthazar's reply to the Governor's question is to take a piece of paper from his pocket, unfold it, and place it in front of him.

"What's that?" Salamanca frowns at it a moment before he pulls a pair of glasses from the inside front pocket of his jacket and puts them on.

"It's a summary of the campaign donations my father gave you," says Balthazar. He has one elbow on the arm of the chair and his legs stretched out under the table as though he's relaxed. "He paid a lot for you to kill the inquiry into Selexitron."

I rack my brain, searching for anything I remember

about Selexitron. It's a drug, but that's about all I know. I guess it must be made by Anders Pharmaceuticals.

The governor's blotchy cheeks flush bright red. He shoves the piece of paper back toward Balthazar, the movement aggressive. "This is garbage. Your father donated nothing. Campaign donations are recorded, and if he had contributed to my—"

"Of course, the money was donated through dummy companies so as not to look as though it came from him. It would be impossible for most people to trace, but I have full details of every transaction. My father kept meticulous records, including the favors you gave him in return."

Salamanca's face goes hard. "What exactly do you want?"

"I want you to make a donation to mental health." Balthazar takes a glossy brochure out of the inside pocket of his tux and hands it to the governor.

"What the hell is this?" He peers at it. "The Salamanca Foundation?"

"It's your new charity. It's been set up to help patients who've experienced a loss of brain function from taking Selexitron. All the hard work's been done for you, and all you need to do is announce it as your own brilliant idea. You'll get the credit for it."

"I don't understand. What's the catch?"

"There is no catch. Your foundation will provide specialized housing and rehabilitation. It's a good deed. You'll be a hero."

"But why?" the governor asks, and it's a question I'm wondering myself.

"Because the people who've been hurt by Selexitron need help."

"Then help them yourself!" Salamanca flicks the brochure onto the table. It slides back in front of Balthazar.

Balthazar shakes his head. "I'm about to become the new chairman of Anders Pharmaceuticals. Being publicly connected to the foundation would open the company up to fresh lawsuits. I'm concerned that too much of the money would go to lawyers instead of the people who need help."

We both study him, and I must look as surprised as the governor. Why does Balthazar care so much about the victims of this drug? He's not even frowning for a change, just giving the governor an intimidating, steely gaze.

"Selexitron is a highly profitable drug," says the governor. "And starting a foundation would bring the wrong kind of attention. Your revenue would drop."

"That's not your problem. Just announce the foundation. And that you're kicking it off with a one hundred-million-dollar donation from your own pocket."

Salamanca rears back, his red face flushing even more. "A hundred million? Are you crazy!"

"A small price to pay," says Balthazar. "Think of the good publicity."

"This is about money? You're blackmailing me for money?" He splutters. "Forget it. I'm not doing it!"

Balthazar puts a hand on the brochure and slides it calmly back to Salamanca's side of the table. "It's not a lot of money for you, Governor. When you persuaded your friends at the FDA not to look too closely at Selexitron, my father secretly routed sixty million dollars to your campaign fund. And when you pressured the Justice Department to drop the case they were building against Anders Pharmaceutical, he gave you fifty-five million. I'm letting you off lightly."

"You asshole!" The governor's roar is so loud, the people in the ballroom might be able to hear it.

Springing from my chair, I move to the door. Sure enough it flies open, and a security guard steps in. His gaze goes from me to Balthazar without recognition, but his eyes widen when he sees the governor.

"Is everything okay, sir?" the guard addresses his question to Salamanca.

"Everything's fine," I say with a smile, stepping in front of him. "But aren't you sweet to check on us?"

Though the guard's wearing a suit that covers it well, there's a slight bulge under his left arm. He's armed, and right-handed. So I take hold of that arm, pressing myself against him, my chest thrust forward. And as I'd hoped, his gaze flicks down to my cleavage.

"You'd better watch your back," the governor snarls at Balthazar. They're behind me, and I don't want to look around. But seeing as the governor's unarmed, and Balthazar has several inches on him, I figure he'll be okay without my help.

"Is that a threat, Governor?" Balthazar's voice is cold and hard. "Tell me, are you the person I have to thank for killing my father?"

"How dare you accuse me of a crime!"

The guard's eyes widen. He tries to pull his arm free. "Miss, would you please—"

"Oh, don't worry about those two," I say with a laugh, clinging hard to his firing hand. And thanks to Jamie's drill-sergeant tendencies and her insistence on doing punishing workouts together, I'm strong enough to keep him from throwing me off.

"But if you—"

"We're playing one of those murder mystery games," I say. "And we've all been assigned different parts. Look, I put my instructions right here in my bra." With my free hand I pretend to feel around inside my new La Perla push-up bra. That thing has given me miles of quivering boob flesh, and I bend slightly to take full advantage of it.

The guard's gaze follows my hand. His body stills and he stops trying to pull his arm free.

"Thank you, Governor Salamanca for your generous donation," Balthazar says from behind me. "You really must tell everyone all about it so they can appreciate how big-hearted you are."

"Fuck you, Anders! You're going to regret this."

"I'm sure my instructions are in here somewhere." I move my hand to my other bra cup with a little laugh. "Silly me. I might need to ask someone to fish it out for me. Maybe it slid right down into my dress!"

"Out of my way." The governor pushes past us, shoving both me and the guard aside as he stomps out the door.

I let go of the guard and he hesitates, looking at Balthazar as if he's not sure what to do.

"How rude," I say with a smile. "You silly men take the game so seriously!"

Balthazar steps to my side. "Game?"

"The governor wasn't the killer?" I pout. "Does that mean we've lost already?"

The guard tugs his suit down, giving his gun a fleeting touch as though to check it's still there. He looks a little flushed, and he keeps shooting glances at my cleavage.

Balthazar puts his arm around me, drawing me to his

side. "Everything okay here?" he asks the guard. His voice goes hard, and suddenly he's frowning. Maybe he's followed the guard's gaze and noticed how interested he is in La Perla.

The guard's eyes snap to Balthazar's, and he gives an audible swallow. "Uh," he says, stepping backward.

"We should stop playing, snuggles." I put my arm around Balthazar's waist and smile up at him. "I'm bored with the game. Let's go and dance some more."

Balthazar says nothing. He's still glowering at the guard.

The flush is rapidly leaving the guard's cheeks. He backs up. "Have a good evening, sir. Ma'am." He turns and flees.

Balthazar moves his gaze to me, dropping his arm from my shoulders. "Game?" he asks again.

"Of course it's a game. Aren't you having fun?" Despite the loss of his touch, I can't help but grin. "Sounded like you were having a hundred million dollars' worth of fun. Shame I can't say the same for the governor."

If Aunt Alejandra's suspicions about Salamanca are right, the thought he'll have to pay all that money makes me deliriously happy. And maybe my delight is infectious, because as Balthazar offers me his arm to escort me out of the smoking room, his lips twitch up.

I blink at him.

"Wait," I exclaim, hooking my hand into his elbow. "Did Balthazar Anders just smile? Is the moon turning blue? Are all the souls in hell suddenly wishing they had winter coats?"

His smile widens. It's even and warm, with a flash of white teeth. Who would have guessed?

"Stop," he says, steering us out of the smoking room and into the ballroom. "One more word and I won't do it again."

I seal my lips, because it would be a shame if I didn't get to see that smile again. He's a gorgeous man when he frowns, but when he smiles, the heavens could crack.

When we reach the crowded dance floor, he puts one hand around my waist and takes my hand with the other, drawing me against him.

"The game thing was quick thinking," he murmurs into my ear. "We should celebrate."

"Celebrate adding the governor to the list of people who want to kill you?"

"Celebrate a hundred million dollars going to help some people who badly need it." He looks down at me, his face close, a hint of a smile still playing over his stern lips. "And when the governor's political opponents hear about his big donation, they'll be falling over themselves to donate even more."

Resting my cheek against his shoulder, I breathe him in. He smells so good it makes my head swim.

He guides me around the dance floor with hands that are warm and sure. His body is firm against mine. He's confident and light on his feet.

I thought I knew who Balthazar Anders was. But it's impossible to reconcile the man who would be so happy about giving away money with the other things I know about him. How could such a generous man not only keep naked photos of my aunt, but threaten to release them? They can't be the same person, can they?

Who really is Balthazar?

"Why did you do it?" I ask. "Why set up a charity?"

Balthazar doesn't reply right away. In the pause, I wonder if he's deciding how much of an answer to give me. I don't know why a pang hurts my heart at the thought that he doesn't trust me. He *shouldn't* trust me, seeing as I'm here under false pretenses.

"My father wasn't a good man," he says. "I helped him do bad things. Now I have a chance to help some of the people who were hurt."

"Bad things?" I ask.

Instead of answering, he slides the hand that's on my waist to the small of my back. It feels good there. A little too good.

"I have a problem with bad karma, too," I say to distract myself. "Mistakes to make up for. And I might be in serious danger of making some new mistakes."

"I don't believe in karma," he murmurs.

His voice rumbles close to my ear. The sound is so nice, I shiver with pleasure. Then I catch myself doing it and tell myself off. I'm not supposed to be so attracted to him, especially when I have no idea who he really is. To allow myself shivers, I need to know whether he's the devil I thought he was, or an angel in disguise.

All at once I'm happy about my plan to break into his house and take the photos back. At least then I'll get to see those papers he's hiding. Maybe they'll help me figure Balthazar out.

I'll break in around three o'clock in the morning, when he should be fast asleep. When Melissa gave me a tour, I unlocked a window in one of his back rooms and mapped out a route through the house. I should be able to search every room except his bedroom. Aunt Alejandra's photos could be in a safe, but if they're not, I'll find them.

"Tell me something," he murmurs into my ear, breaking me out of my criminal daydream. "In the limo, you reacted to the governor's name. You said you thought he was corrupt. Why?"

"Because there used to be a juvenile detention center in Lancaster that was full of teenaged girls," I tell him. "The company that ran it had a contract, so the more girls they locked up, the more money they got. They didn't care how overcrowded it was, or what the conditions were like, they only cared about the money. We think the governor might have been running the scheme." I say the last part with more confidence than ever before. If the governor accepted money from Balthazar's father, it proves he's corrupt.

"Was that the place you were sent to when you were fifteen?" asks Balthazar.

I lean back to screw up my face at him. "Do you have a file on me? What about my privacy?"

"I had an investigator run a background check. You were convicted of breaking and entering, and should have gotten probation. But you were homeless, so—"

"I wasn't homeless! That was their excuse to throw me into juvie."

His brow creases. It's one of his questioning frowns. "You got out of the detention center at seventeen, but didn't move in with either of your parents."

"I only got out thanks to an amazing lawyer who was willing to fight for me. She let me live with her." I purse my lips. "My record's supposed to be sealed. How did your investigator find out?"

"I pay for the best."

"Well, I was one of the lucky ones."

"Lucky?" He raises his eyebrows. "You think you were lucky?"

"I came out of there with a real family. Aunt Alejandra changed my life."

"How certain are you that the governor was profiting from the juvenile detention facility?" he asks.

"Not a hundred percent," I admit. "We have no proof, and the place has closed now, so we'll never know for sure."

A thoughtful expression crosses his face, as though he's mulling it over. "Hmm," he mutters. "That's a shame."

"Right? If he's guilty, he's the one who should be locked up."

"Agreed." Balthazar moves his hand from the small of my back, up to the bare part, around the middle of my back, where the dress doesn't cover. Bare skin to bare skin. I swear I break out in head-to-toe goosebumps.

It feels good that he's taking my allegation seriously. When he mentioned the governor in the car on our way here, I assumed he wouldn't believe me if I told him my suspicions. But Balthazar keeps on surprising me.

All at once, the weirdness of the evening hits me. Not the meeting with the governor. For some reason, that seems like the most normal thing that's happened tonight. What's weird is him agreeing with me, and how easy our conversation is, as though we're really on a date. What's weird is my shivers, my tingles, and the warm, excited butterflies in my stomach. The possessive feeling of his fingers on the bare skin of my back, and my urge to press myself more firmly against him. To pull his mouth down to mine.

I step back from him. "My feet are getting sore." It's not

entirely a lie. I didn't want to wear heels, but both Lucía and Melissa insisted.

"Then let's go. Can you walk to the car?"

"Sure."

"Lean on me if it helps." He takes my arm again, and we go out through the enormous double doors, down the hallway, and out the front door. It's raining, but not too heavily. We stop under the eaves of the building and a doorman rushes to stand next to us, umbrella at the ready. Presumably, he's waiting to escort us to our car so we don't get wet. But we're the only ones leaving the ball so early, and there are no cars waiting in the circular driveway.

"Where's my car?" Balthazar asks the doorman.

He looks around. "I'm sorry, sir. I'll check with our valet service."

"Wait. Is that your car? The driver just flashed the lights like he was signaling us." I point to a black limo parked a short distance along the street.

Balthazar gives an irritated frown. "What's it doing all the way over there?" The way he asks, it's like the driver parked a mile away. Admittedly, he could have stopped closer, but it won't take us more than a minute or two to walk over.

"Drivers often wait there when the driveway's busy to avoid congestion," says the doorman, though it's clearly not busy now.

"Can billionaires walk on regular sidewalks?" I ask. "Or will the concrete scuff the diamonds in your shoes?"

Balthazar narrows his eyes at me. "If sarcasm were a tradable commodity, you'd be the rich one."

"What a perfect world that would be." I give a wistful sigh.

"Please allow me to escort you," says the doorman, stepping off the curb with the umbrella held up for us.

"Not necessary." Balthazar reaches out and plucks the umbrella from the man's grip. Holding it over us with one hand, he puts his other arm around my shoulder to pull me against him, presumably to make sure I'm covered by the umbrella and not getting wet.

With his arm around my shoulders and mine around his waist, we walk down the driveway, then turn onto the street and head toward the car. Balthazar matches the length of my strides, making it easy to walk together. Thanks to the rain, the sidewalk is deserted.

With the rain falling around us, it feels like we make a cozy twosome. If anyone were watching, they'd think we really were together. They'd see a normal couple and wouldn't know what an unlikely pair we are.

"Is that what billionaires do?" I ask him as we approach the limo. "Go around stealing umbrellas from doormen?"

"The hotel can bill me for it."

"If a bill arrived for five hundred dollars, would you pay it without even thinking about it?"

He answers my question, but all at once, I'm not listening to him but to the sudden sound of footsteps pounding behind us.

I spin to confront whoever it is who's approaching so quickly. Balthazar's arm around my shoulder hinders my movement and I yank myself free, moving in front of him to shield him from possible danger. But as I step forward, my high heel catches on a crack in the sidewalk, and I stumble.

A big man in a black raincoat rams into me. I react on instinct with a hook punch, landing it hard in his side. His body is muscled rather than soft. He grunts with pain, staggering sideways, but recovers quickly. He has something black tied around the lower half of his face, and the hood of his raincoat pulled low over his eyes. The raincoat billows around his tall, solid frame. He's like a black truck plowing into us.

To take him down, I'd need to perform a sweep or a throw. But with high heels and a cracked and uneven sidewalk, I'm too unbalanced. I can't even count on a kick not sending me over. As he lunges toward Balthazar, I go for an uppercut. He brings his elbow up to block the punch, driving me backward.

My heel catches again. My foot twists out of the shoe and I land hard on one bare foot, almost falling. With the handicap of my footwear, I can't count on beating him in combat. Instead, I risk looking down so I can unlatch my bag and tug out my mini single-action revolver.

By the time I have the tiny gun out, Balthazar is dodging to the side, trying to keep the man from reaching him. The attacker's billowing raincoat blocks my view of what's happening.

"Freeze!" I bring up the gun. "Put your hands up now or I'll shoot!"

Instead of obeying, the man wheels away and takes off at a run.

I hesitate with my gun aimed squarely at him. If I fire, there's a good chance he won't survive. I've never killed anyone, and I don't want to shoot him in the back.

Cursing, I lower my weapon and kick off my other shoe. The guy is fast. He's already half a block away and about to vanish around the corner. With bare feet, I have little chance of catching him. One thing for sure, I'll never let myself be talked into wearing impractical heels on a job again.

When I turn to check on Balthazar, I'm surprised to see him on the ground.

I rush over to him, ready to help him back to his feet, but his hands are pressed to his side.

Blood leaks through his fingers, instantly watered down by the rain. His expression is tight with shock.

My heart kicks up when I realize what just happened.

Balthazar's been stabbed.

CHAPTER 9

Balthazar

I'm stripped to the waist with a bandage around my middle, alone in a room at the hospital. The wound hurts like hell, but the knife didn't pierce anything vital. Thanks to Scarlet. She scared the attacker away before he could get close enough to finish me off.

She saved my life, and I have no idea where she is. What if she's not okay?

I've been in the hospital for hours, and I haven't seen her since we arrived. They brought me in here to stitch my wound, then left me to wait for follow-up medical attention. A police officer came in to take my statement, but I haven't seen a doctor or nurse for a while.

Now I'm sitting on the side of the bed, debating whether to find my shirt and leave. I've never been treated in a public hospital before, and I'm not impressed. I suppose I should be grateful they didn't leave me in a disease-ridden ward, but the room I'm in is tiny, containing only a bed, a narrow table, and two medical machines.

I'm about to get up when a nurse hurries in.

"Where's Scarlet, the woman who brought me here?" I demand.

The nurse has a small paper cup in one hand and a larger cup of water in the other. Her gaze goes to my bare torso, then up to my eyes, and she flushes. "I'm sorry, I don't know."

"Then where's my phone?"

"I don't know that either." The nurse looks nervous. Maybe that's thanks to the intensity of my frown. I'd try to soften my features, but my side is aching and apparently being stabbed isn't good for my mood.

"The doctor asked me to give you these." She hands me the small cup she's holding which has two pills inside. Then she hands me the water.

"What's this?"

"Painkillers. You can take two every four hours for as long as you need them."

I swallow the pills, and I'm about to ask for my shirt so I can get out of here when the door opens and Scarlet comes in.

A weight slides off my chest. She's wearing a worried frown but looks unhurt, if a little bedraggled. Her hair has come out of its elaborate hairdo and is hanging in long, wet curls. Her lipstick has been washed or bitten away, and there's a smudge of black stuff around her eyes where her makeup must have run in the rain.

Somehow, she's still beautiful. Not that it really surprises me. Her full lips don't need lipstick anyway, and her eyes are mesmerizing with or without the black goo around them. Also, she's still in her gold dress and high heels. And that dress gets sexier every time I see it, even under the hospital room's stark florescent lighting.

When she sees me, Scarlet's frown eases. Her gaze lingers on my bare torso and a little color stains her cheeks. Then she tears her eyes away to look around.

"Is this the billionaire suite?" she asks. "Where are the warm, scented towels?"

I bite back a laugh, my bad mood evaporating. Who knows why her smart mouth makes me feel better, but it's like a salve on my soul.

"Someone had better offer me a hot towel soon," I say in a mock growl. "Or I won't come back to this hospital next time I get stabbed."

"Are those ordinary bandages? They didn't offer you the expensive ones? Don't they know who you are?"

The nurse is backing toward the door. She was already wary of me and judging by her expression, she thinks we're being serious.

"Where's my shirt?" I ask her.

"Um. I'm sorry, I don't know. Would you mind waiting while I get your doctor?"

"Just get my shirt." I try to stand up and pain shoots down my side. "Shit."

Scarlet stops the nurse before she can go. "Wait. He's in pain. Can't you give him something?"

"I just gave him some painkillers." The nurse flees, and Scarlet turns back to me, eyeing me suspiciously.

"She seemed in an awful hurry to leave. What did you do to her?"

"Nothing. I was charming. She must have been worried about falling too far under my spell." I shift my weight and wince.

"How badly does it hurt?" Scarlet winces with me, her expression sympathetic.

"On a scale of one to having a knife plunged into my flesh?"

She flushes. "It was my fault. I was hired to protect you and you were stabbed on my watch. I'm so sorry I let you down."

My lips part as I'm momentarily lost for words.

She has no idea how impressive she was. The man who attacked us was as big as I am, and Scarlet barely comes up to my shoulder. Yet she didn't flinch or hesitate. If her shoe hadn't come off, I don't think our attacker would have stood a chance.

"You're the reason I'm not dead," I say. "I didn't know he had a knife until too late. The blade was dark and it was covered by his raincoat."

"He shouldn't have gotten close enough to use it."

"He took a wild slash at me and got lucky."

She shakes her head, chewing her lip. "Jamie's the one who normally handles personal protection. I'm qualified, but she's the real expert. If you need a fake girlfriend for anything else, she's the better choice. And I recommend having two bodyguards with you at all times."

I don't like the idea that she's taking the blame for this, or that she wants to quit.

"We'll stick with our current arrangement." My tone is firm.

"But I clearly can't protect you."

Her nonsensical statement makes me frown. "If it makes you feel better, I'll mention it when I write my Yelp review. *Saved my life but still let me get scratched. Four stars.*"

She gives me a small smile, but it's a glum smile, and that's not good enough. Her shoulders are slumped. Even her damp hair looks dejected. Although once I imagined I'd like her curls to lose a little of their bounce, now I hate to see them hanging so limply.

"How does a billionaire know about Yelp?" she asks.

"I mentored one of the company's founders. And you're not fired. You passed the audition."

"Please don't brush this off," she says. "You're not doing yourself any favors by grading on a curve."

I make a dissatisfied sound, ready to put an end to this conversation. "How tall are you?"

"Five foot six."

"And how tall am I?"

"Um. Six two?"

I nod. "About the same height as our attacker. And I work out with my trainer most days. I can lift two hundred pounds, but I couldn't stop the man who ran into us. It happened so fast, I wasn't quick enough. At least you got a punch in. I heard it land, and he's going to have a hell of a bruise. More likely, you broke his rib."

"You're not trained to—"

"We're sticking with the current arrangement. I don't want to hear another word about it." My tone is so final, she snaps her mouth shut, pressing her lips together for a moment as she studies me.

After a moment, she toes off her shoes and wriggles her

bare feet on the floor with a sigh. Her toenails are painted bright red, a fact which doesn't surprise me one bit.

"I hardly ever wear heels," she complains. "And where's your shirt?" She looks pointedly at my torso.

With her eyes on me, I sit up straighter and put some tension in my muscles to flex them. And when she bites her lip and looks away, I smile to myself.

"If your feet hurt, sit on the bed," I say.

She eases down next to me, dropping her tiny bag onto the bed beside her. Letting out another loud sigh, she lifts both feet to wriggle her red toes. "New rule. Men should have to wear high heels, and women should only ever wear flats."

"Did you get a look at the man who attacked us?" I ask.

"His raincoat hood was up, and he had something black tied over his face. All I know is he was tall and solid. Did you see anything to identify him?"

"No, but maybe the doorman saw something."

She shakes her head. "I already spoke to him. We were too far away, and it was dark and raining. He saw nothing."

I give a disappointed grunt.

"Do you think the governor arranged for you to get stabbed?" she asks.

"Maybe. But I saw several of the pharmaceutical board members at the ball. One of them could have arranged it. It was no secret I was going to be there."

"Then our list of suspects is no shorter," she says with a grimace. Putting both hands behind her on the bed, she stretches her back. The movement pushes her breasts up, and the golden silk of her dress shimmers over her curves.

I shift on the bed. The pain in my side is lessening, but now there's some blood-flow restriction in my pants.

"Why was my car parked so far away?" I ask to take my mind off it.

She drops her head back to shake out her limp curls, and I take the opportunity to adjust my pants for expansion.

"Apparently, that wasn't your car we were walking toward," she says. "I talked to your driver. While you were getting stabbed, he was in the parking garage with a flat tire."

"You've been busy."

"I wanted to interview any potential witnesses before the ball finished and they all disappeared. That's what I've been doing while you were getting bandaged up."

"Did you find out whose car was parked on the street?"

She shrugs. "Just a black limo that looked like yours. I've given a statement to the police, and suggested they check any CCTV in the area. I also suggested they check the security cameras in the parking garage in case they can see who slashed your tire."

"It was slashed?"

"Looks that way. I guess the police have spoken to you?"

"Of course," I say. "What happened to my phone?"

"I have it here." She pulls it out of her small handbag and gives it to me. The screen is crowded with message notifications, and a quick glance tells me that Melissa knows what's happened. Scarlet must have informed her.

"Gordon's waiting outside," she says. "He'll take you home when you're ready."

As if on cue, the door opens, and a doctor comes in. He checks my chart, asks a few questions, then tells me I'm free to go, but they have a rule which says I need to be pushed out in a wheelchair. He also solves the mystery of my shirt. Apparently, the medics cut it off me, and it's now in pieces. Nobody seems to know what happened to my jacket, but I get into a wheelchair bare-chested.

"We need a second wheelchair," I tell the nurse. "Scarlet is injured too. Her feet hurt too badly to walk."

"What?" Scarlet shakes her head. "No, I'm fine." She gets off the bed but can't hide a wince.

"I'm not leaving without a second wheelchair," I insist. And it doesn't take much of a frown for the nurse to fetch one. Scarlet and I are rolled out together, which she seems to think is both embarrassing and hilarious.

My limo has new tires, and Gordon's apologetic for not being there when we came out of the ball. Brushing off his apology, I accept the shirt he offers. It's loose and warm, and I button it up before easing gingerly into the back of the car with Scarlet.

We're on our way home when Scarlet says, "Some night, huh?" Then she gives me the kind of warm, shared smile I suspect you can only partake in after you've gone through a dramatic experience with someone.

Turns out there's nothing like a stabbing to really break the ice.

"Some night," I agree.

"May I ask you something?" In what I'm starting to understand is typical Scarlet fashion, she keeps speaking without waiting for my approval. "With the information you had on him, you could have blackmailed the governor into doing anything. Why set up a foundation?"

"Like I said, there are people who need that money."

"But haven't you been part of the pharmaceutical

business all along? Why suddenly develop a conscience now?"

I'm not used to justifying my actions. There aren't many people in my life who'd ask me such frank questions, but for some reason, I'm finding it refreshing rather than annoying. And after saving my life, she deserves an answer. Besides, sharing that smile with her seems to have infected me with an unfamiliar warmth.

"I inherited shares in the company when I turned twenty-one. But I wasn't interested in pharmaceuticals and didn't want to have anything to do with my father. I didn't care what the company did." I shift on the seat, my wound aching. "Then my father died, and the instructions in his will were to destroy all his private papers. That made me curious. I wanted to know what was in them."

"That's why you contested your dad's will? You were curious?"

I nod.

"And the information in his papers was about Selexitron?"

"Among other things. He had so many secrets, I'm still going through everything."

She's silent a moment, her gaze drifting to the window as she takes this in. Her hair is slowly drying and regaining its exuberant curl. I'd like to wind a piece around my finger to help it back into shape.

Her gaze comes back to me, thoughtful and direct. "When we were dancing you said you'd helped your father do bad things. How exactly did you help him?"

"I didn't go to board meetings. The chairman isn't all-powerful, and as a shareholder, I could have voted against his decisions. Instead, I chose to stay in the dark."

"You were busy elsewhere."

"But I knew what my father was like. By not voting, I let it happen. All these years, I've been earning dividends from the company, and it's been blood money."

My own honesty surprises me. I've never even thought of saying all that out loud, let alone putting it so bluntly. I haven't even spoken to Gaby about it yet. And it's strange I don't feel the urge to make excuses for myself or dodge my own complicity.

For some reason, I want Scarlet to know who I am, good and bad. And so far, she hasn't flinched.

"What exactly is Selexitron?" she asks.

"The drug helps Alzheimer's patients. Once someone has the disease, it slows progression. But when it was released, the company also pushed to get it approved as a preventative medicine."

"And they got approval?"

I nod. "The company made a lot of money selling Selexitron to healthy people who thought it'd stop them from getting Alzheimer's. And the governor helped cover up the data that showed a thirteen percent increase in admissions to psychiatric institutions for those patients."

"Wow. That's awful."

"Criminal."

Her curls are drying out of place, messy and tangled. I want to run my hands through them, to adjust them into a more ordered kind of wildness. But I keep my hands to myself.

"Will they be prosecuted?"

I shake my head. "Questions were asked a year or so ago, but the governor used his influence to kill the process. The FDA quietly withdrew approval for doctors to prescribe Selexitron so widely, and the whole thing was swept under the rug. By then, the board had made millions."

"So they got away with it?"

"Maybe. But I can still make amends. My father left me everything I need to make the company less corrupt, and that's what I'm going to do."

Also, I like the idea of my father's secrets being used to try to repair some of the damage from his bad deeds. It feels like sending his corpse a final fuck-you. Maybe that's an indulgence, but I don't care.

"Okay." Her generous lips tug up into a smile that lights up her face. "What's our next step?"

I note the word '*our*' and resist the urge to smile back at her. It's not easy. I'm impressed she still wants to keep going after everything I've told her.

"Next I'm going to talk to all the Anders Pharmaceutical board members. I'll enjoy informing them about their upcoming financial losses. Can't wait to see their faces."

"You're going to make more people want to kill you?"

I nod. "And it's likely that one of the board members killed my father. His investigator was mainly focused on them, and his papers are full of their secrets."

"Anyone you particularly suspect?" She stretches her bare feet out to wriggle her red toes. The movement exposes a lot more of her very shapely bare leg, and I'm momentarily distracted by watching her do it.

I wouldn't mind putting her bare feet on my lap to rub

those elegant arches and cute toes for her. No, I wouldn't mind that at all.

Not that it would be appropriate.

And even less appropriate would be throwing her legs over my shoulders, but that doesn't stop the image flashing through my mind.

I clear my throat. "It could have been any of them. It doesn't matter that the board members are all my relatives. Most of them love money more than their own children."

She raises her eyebrows. "It's your family who are trying to kill you? Harsh. Are they all in LA?"

"No, they're scattered. But there's a board meeting in a week, and they'll all attend. It's at a resort in San Dante, and most usually fly in a few days early, seeing as the company pays for it all. They live it up on the company's dime."

"A junket?"

"Exactly. The meeting is on Friday, but they'll start arriving on Monday. It's the perfect opportunity to speak to them all individually, and I want you to come with me."

"On one condition," she says. "I'll wear anything you want, as long as my shoes don't have stiletto heels."

"Deal."

"And I still think you need more protection than just me. At least think about it, okay?"

The car pulls up to her building. I don't like that she lives and works in such a dangerous part of town, but once I pay for her services, she can use the money to find somewhere better.

"Can you walk?" I ask, before she can get out of the limo. "I can't carry you without tearing my stitches, but I can ask Gordon to—"

"No, seriously, I'm fine. My feet really aren't that sore."

"Then I'll walk you into your lobby." I ease my wounded body out of the car while waving away Gordon's attempt to help.

Scarlet watches my slow, deliberate movements with a furrowed brow. "You're the one who's being targeted. I should be walking you into your house and making sure you're okay."

"I'm fine," I say. "I have security guards patrolling my place." Then to Gordon, "Wait here. I'll be back in a minute."

Scarlet is checking up and down the street.

"Any threats?" I ask.

She looks serious. "All clear. But let's not invite trouble." Putting her hand under my arm, she takes plodding, slow steps toward the door of her building.

"I'm not an invalid," I tell her. "My legs are fine."

"Sorry." She stops trying to support me and walks beside me. I keep our pace at half speed, but that's more for her sore feet than for my wound.

She's put her high heels back on. Even if they hurt her feet, they make her ass look incredible. I put my hand on her back as we go into the foyer of her building. Her dress is cool under my palm. It slips over her skin in a way that's entirely distracting. Her neck is very long and very elegant.

Once inside, she turns to face me. Only a few of the lobby's lights are working, so she's half in shadow. The tiled floor is chipped and stained, and one of the elevators has an *Out Of Order* sign. In her gold dress, Scarlet makes her surroundings look even dingier in comparison. She doesn't belong here. The glamor of the ballroom suited her so much better.

"I need you to understand how dangerous things could get if you come with me to San Dante," I say.

"Exactly why you need extra protection!" she exclaims.

"I'm more concerned about you getting hurt. Working for me will put you in the firing line."

"Pfft." She waves a dismissive hand. "Worry about yourself."

"The risk to your safety is real. If you want to pull out, now's the time."

Her lips lift higher on one side. I'm coming to recognize this lopsided smile as her devilish one. It's the one she usually flashes before she says something outrageous.

"Tonight was exciting," she admits. "Not the part where you got stabbed, that was awful. But the ball, and threatening the governor. It wasn't a dull day at the office."

"Not dull at all," I agree.

She glances down at my stomach and her mischievous look intensifies. It's a look that goes straight to my cock.

"Would you like me to show you a few moves?" she offers.

I take a step closer, pretending to misunderstand her. "I could show *you* some moves."

"Do you *have* any moves?" Her tone is teasing.

"Would you like to find out?" I growl.

That mouth of hers needs taming. Her full lips are begging for punishment. Her bottom lip belongs between my teeth.

When my gaze returns to her eyes, they're dark with awareness. She's watching me devour her lips with my eyes, and her breath is coming faster. I'm certain she can tell I want to kiss her, and she's not stepping backward.

"I'll send Melissa back over with more clothes." I fight through a haze of lust for clear thoughts. "You'll need more dresses, and daywear."

"No more high heels, remember. I need to be able to run. And to fight."

"I hope you won't have to."

She gives a little shrug. "If I'm your date, they won't be expecting me to be useful, so I can be your secret weapon."

My secret weapon.

The words are intoxicating. Hell, everything about her is so sexy, I can't stand it.

My cock is throbbing, and I don't just want to kiss her anymore, I *need* to kiss her.

"Then it's important to fool everyone into thinking we're dating," I hear myself say.

Her lopsided smile becomes more impish than ever. "I'll have to call you snuggles."

I step forward, moving her backward until her back is against the wall. "You won't call me that."

"Okay. Then when you're acting like an entitled billionaire, your name's Bob," she says. "When you're being a normal person, I'll call you Zar."

Zar. I like it. In fact, I like it a lot. Not that I'll tell her that. "An entitled billionaire," I growl instead, putting my hands on the wall on either side of her. "Do you know how many people would dare speak to me that way?"

She rolls her eyes. "Clearly not enough, Bob."

"We need to kiss."

The pulse in her neck flutters. She's not as calm as she's pretending to be. "Do we?"

I lean closer. "You were the one determined to make this look authentic. And I kiss the women I date."

Her pupils are huge. She gives a visible swallow. "You mean, we need to fake kiss?" Her voice is suddenly hoarse.

"How do we fake kiss?"

"It's just like kissing for real, only..." She trails off.

"Only?" I prompt.

She shrugs one shoulder. "I guess if we do it, we'll know."

In that dress, it's easy to see that her breath is coming faster, her chest rising and falling more rapidly. Her hands come above my waist as I step into her, as though she's making sure not to put them anywhere near my wound. Her fingers curl into my shirt.

Putting a hand under her chin, I tilt her face up to mine.

Warmth radiates from her body. Her lips part, and I cover them with mine. The heat and taste of her is even better than I imagined it might be. I breathe in oranges, taste the sweetness of them. When I tease her tongue with mine, her hands slide up my back. I deepen the kiss, exploring every part of her mouth. She moans softly, and my cock jerks in response.

I fit a hand around the back of her neck, under her still-damp hair. I love the feel of her skin under my palm, the length of her neck, and the way her head tilts. The eagerness of her mouth. The sharpness of her fingernails, digging through my shirt. I can't get enough of her. Her body grinds against me, her stomach pressing hard against my erection, driving me wild.

One hand goes to her ass, encouraging those tiny gyrations she's making against me, the movements that are making my balls throb. She's incredible. Squeezing a handful of her ass, I lift her higher, so she can part her legs and—

"Fuck!"

I let her go, wincing as I clutch my side. Twisting that way wasn't a good idea.

"Crap!" she exclaims. "Are you okay?"

"Didn't tear my stitches." Hopefully it's true.

I step back from her, because along with the pain has come a sharp jolt of reason.

Scarlet is my employee.

Allowing myself to give into the urge to taste her is one thing. But I can't kid myself that messing around with an employee isn't crossing a line. It's one thing to enjoy some flirting, and the push and pull of our attraction. It's another to act on it.

"Well," I say, taking a deep breath. "Now we know how to fake kiss."

She clears her throat. "It should fool anyone who sees it." Her cheeks are flushed, and a frown creases her brow as she stabs the button to call the elevator.

The frown bothers me.

Though I'm certain she enjoyed our kiss, maybe she's having second thoughts, like I am.

The thought is disturbing. I don't want her to have second thoughts. I want her to be consumed with lust. After all, I'm only holding back because of our situation. If she wasn't my employee, I'd want to go much further.

Maybe I should fire her, then date her? I could even take her on the *Pretty Woman* date, like she suggested. To Paris, for a romantic dinner overlooking the Eiffel Tower.

"Don't get stabbed again on the way back to your car."

She looks out the glass door at where the limo is waiting. Though the street's deserted, it's a sobering thought.

"Thanks for saving my life tonight," I say.

The elevator doors open.

"Just be careful getting home, okay Zar?" She steps past me, into the elevator.

Her use of the nickname fills me with unexpected heat, even as I admire the way she walks. That bounce in her step makes a series of images rush into my head, none of which feature clothing.

"I'll remind Melissa that you need some clothes you can wear at a beach resort," I say as she turns to face me. "The board meeting is in San Dante."

"When will we leave?" She stands at the back of the elevator, her hands clasped in front of her, waiting for the doors to close. That dress really is incredible on her. The elevator is mirrored, so I can see her back as well as her front. And I remember all too well the way her bare back felt under my hand.

"Next Monday. We'll stay until the board meeting on Friday, and..." I hesitate for only a split second. "We'll need to share a hotel suite to make our ruse believable. I trust you have no objections?"

"Share... *what*?"

The elevator doors slide shut, and I smile to myself. That's only the second time I've seen her look so surprised. I like the 'o' of her lips and the curving lift of her brows.

And I can't help but wonder if that's how she looks when she orgasms.

CHAPTER 10

Scarlet

Aunt Alejandra lives in a cute bungalow on a quiet, leafy Pasadena street. It's where I stayed when I got out of juvie, and I love everything about it, from the porch swing out front that always has a cat sleeping on it, to the enormous, gnarled old lemon tree that takes up most of the backyard. It'll always feel like home.

Jamie, Kayla and I head over there for lunch on Saturday, after my Taekwondo lesson with Melissa, curious about what Aunt Alejandra wants to talk to us about. When we arrive, the house smells like freshy baked bread, and we're delighted to find that she's set out a delicious lunch that includes cornbread just out of the oven. We sit around her little dining table and joke around, talking about everything and nothing while we enjoy the food.

But the whole time we're eating, I can't help but feel like I've betrayed the person I have to thank for most of the best things in my life. Aunt Alejandra has good reason to hate

Balthazar, and the memory of kissing him is still fresh, probably because I spent most of last night replaying it at least a million times in my mind.

I haven't told anyone about the kiss. Not Melissa, nor Kayla, nor Jamie. When I described the evening to them, I ended with Zar dropping me off at my door. Kissing a client is totally unprofessional, but that's not the only reason I haven't said anything. I mean, who would have thought I'd even *want* to kiss him?

But I hate keeping secrets.

For years now, I've been living a blameless life with my bad-girl days firmly behind me. But since finding out about Aunt Alejandra's photos and deciding I had to get them back, my list of things to feel guilty about seems to be getting longer and longer.

After Kayla and Jamie have finished bickering good-naturedly over the last piece of cornbread, we clear the dirty plates off the table and sit back down. Under the table, one of my aunt's rescue cats rubs against my shins, purring.

Aunt Alejandra clears her throat, growing serious. "I have something I need to tell you." She divides her gaze between Jamie and me. "I already told Kayla, and it's time I let you two in on it as well."

Jamie and I exchange a quick, guilty glance. She's clearly about to tell us about the photos, and we'll have to pretend we don't already know.

She folds her hands on the table in front of her. The whitening of her fingers is the only sign of how difficult this must be for her. "When I was twenty-four years old, I had a brief affair with Blythe Anders."

I assume a surprised expression while I do a quick

calculation. She was sixty on her last birthday, so it was thirty-six years ago. It's horribly unfair that something she did so long ago could affect her career. But if her photos went public, she could be forced out. And she'd definitely say goodbye to a Supreme Court nomination.

"I was a law intern, working with his legal team," she goes on. "He was in his fifties, a rich and powerful man, and I didn't know how to say no to him." Her cheeks have flushed, but her tone is steady and matter-of-fact, and her chin is high. "Unfortunately, I allowed him to take some photos of a sexual nature."

"You were young, tía." Kayla's voice is gentle.

"It's your body, and nobody should get to make you feel bad for however you choose to show it." Jamie sits back in her chair, arms folded, her expression set. "I can't believe your profession is so misogynistic. Bunch of dinosaurs!"

"Nevertheless." Aunt Alejandra unclasps her hands to brush imaginary crumbs off the tablecloth, and I get the impression it's an excuse to drop her gaze. But she's used to hearing shocking things in her courtroom and not letting her emotions show on her face. Her pragmatic unflappability is only one of a million reasons why she's my hero. I've always felt like I could tell her anything.

"I'd more-or-less forgotten about the photos." She frowns at a crumb that isn't there. "Until nine years ago, a case came in front of me that involved Anders Pharmaceuticals. And Blythe threatened me, saying he still had the photos and he'd release them if I didn't find in his favor."

"What did you do?" asks Jamie.

"I recused myself from the case and asked a colleague to

take over." Her face creases into a look of regret. "I should have done more. I should have reported the threat."

"I understand why you didn't," Jamie says, and I nod my agreement. Aunt Alejandra has almost reached the top of a profession that doesn't traditionally favor minorities. She's worked incredibly hard to get to where she is.

"Several months ago, Blythe Anders died," she says. "When I heard he'd passed, I hoped the photos would be destroyed. Then I saw a news report that said his son had gone to court to gain access to all his private papers. I was worried that might include the photos, so I contacted Balthazar Anders to ask for them."

"What did he say?" I ask.

"I got an email which essentially informed me that he could do what he liked with the pictures, including releasing them to the public."

"What an asshole," Jamie mutters.

"You don't really think he'll release them, do you?" I ask. Now I'm getting to know Balthazar, it's a lot more difficult to believe he'd do something like that. Could a man who's setting up a charity for Selexitron survivors really be so callous?

My vague theory that there's two different Balthazars is looking more likely. Maybe he's like Dr. Jekyll and Mr. Hyde. Or he has an evil twin.

Aunt Alejandra spreads her hands in a helpless gesture. "There's no way to know. The reason I'm telling you is that I didn't want you to be blindsided if it happens. There's likely to be a lot of publicity, but I'll handle it."

Jamie and Kayla both look at me with tight expressions. Jamie's right that people shouldn't criticize her. But they will.

Aunt Alejandra couldn't have a more high-profile job, and the scandal would start a media feeding frenzy. It would be unspeakably savage.

"What would you do?" asks Kayla. "Would you have to retire early?"

Aunt Alejandra frowns. "I don't know. Probably. But you shouldn't worry. And I don't want you doing anything reckless." Her pointed gaze moves to me, and I flush.

Okay, so I'm the one most likely to be impulsive. But I'm also the one who owes her the most. She didn't just get me out of juvie, she gave me a home. We were practically strangers then, but she cared for me a lot better than my own parents ever had. And I quickly grew to love her.

Aunt Alejandra has photos of me on her wall, including the day I graduated, something that never would have happened without her help. If she hadn't taken me in, I'd likely be dead by now, or in jail. And I don't have a single photo of myself before I came to live with her. My parents never thought to take any, but tía has dozens of them, proudly displayed. That says a lot.

"What if we could figure out a way to get your photos back from Balthazar?" I ask, just to see what she says.

"What do you mean, Scarlet?"

I wince a little, knowing she'll hate the idea. "I mean, if we could somehow just take them back from—"

"You're not thinking about trying something foolish?"

"Of course not." I try my best to look angelic while my face is burning. She'd be horrified if she knew I'm planning to break into Balthazar's house tonight.

She narrows her eyes suspiciously. The lines around her eyes have gotten deeper lately, and she's let her hair go white, but she's not getting any less astute. My aunt is smart and hard to fool. She was a lawyer for most of her life before becoming a judge.

I've never lied to her before. It's an awful feeling, and if my cheeks get any hotter, someone's going to need to call the fire department.

"I'm sorry to change the subject." Kayla shoots me a sympathetic look as she comes to my rescue. But I have something to tell you all as well."

She pauses, and when Aunt Alejandra's sharp gaze moves off me, I breathe a huge sigh of relief.

"I have a lead on finding someone from the hole," Kayla announces.

"You have?" Jamie demands. "Who!"

"Dani."

"*Dani*? No way! Really?"

Dani was one of the girls we'd shared an overcrowded room with in juvie. Though Aunt Alejandra was able to get me, Kayla, and Jamie out, plenty of others weren't so lucky. Kayla's started looking for the others, but most are either dead or incarcerated. A few have dropped off the radar. There's nothing Kayla can't do online, but a lot have dark pasts and good reasons to disappear. Take Dani for example. Back then, she was mixed up in something sinister.

"You really think you can track her down?" asks Aunt Alejandra. She looks hopeful, and I know it weighs on her that she couldn't save more of the girls who were locked up with us.

Kayla shrugs. "If anyone can, it's me." She's not being boastful, just stating a fact. She was sent to juvie for hacking websites, and even now, she does some stuff online she says it's better the rest of us don't know about.

"We should do the dishes and get back to the office." Jamie gets up. "We need to work out this afternoon, remember?"

"I'm too full to work out," groans Kayla.

Jamie puts her hands on her hips. "We can't get lazy. Our clients expect better."

I pull a face, but drag myself to my feet. "Come on, Kayla. She'll only hound us until she gets her way."

When it comes to our workouts, Jamie's bossy and unrelenting. Even though Kayla spends most of her time behind a computer screen, and I rarely do personal protection work, Jamie still insists we all work out regularly and visit the shooting range every few weeks.

We start by warming up on the punching bags in our training room, then do some weights and cardio. Jamie works us hard, and by the time we've finished we're all bathed in sweat.

After our final cool down, we head up to our apartment and take turns to shower and change. Then we flop onto our couches with some delicious drinks.

Jamie gets to make us work out, but Kayla and I always insist on having cocktails afterward. Our post-workout cocktails have become a tradition, and today Kayla has mixed up some ice-cold Margaritas. She's even given the glasses a salt rim and added a circle of lime for decoration. There may be ancient burn marks on our kitchen countertops and a mysterious funky smell in one corner of our living room, but you'd better believe we have proper Margarita glasses. We have our priorities right.

We clink our glasses together before we sip, appreciating the relief that comes with having finished another of Jamie's killer workouts. The tang of salt and lime is delicious.

"Are you still planning to break into Balthazar Anders' house?" asks Jamie, smacking her lips with pleasure.

I nod. "I'm doing it tonight at midnight."

Kayla frowns. "Are you sure you want to risk it? Doesn't he have an alarm?"

"Check this out." I pull up a diagram on my phone and hand it to her. Jamie is sharing her couch, and she puts her Margarita on the coffee table and leans over to take a look.

"Wait." Jamie peers at the screen. "Are these Balthazar's house plans?"

"Yep. And according to Melissa, when he's home, only the perimeter is alarmed. These sensors will be active." I point them out. "But get this. I asked for the remote access code and password, and *she gave them to me*. Kayla, it couldn't be easier for you to hack in and turn all those sensors off for me, leaving the house without any alarms." I shoot her a hopeful look.

"She gave you the code and password?" Kayla pushes her long hair back from her face with a slow, stunned-looking blink.

I nod. "For my security audit. She also detailed the hours his housekeepers and gardeners work, and the full schedule for his security guards. I know where everyone will be, and the way to get in to avoid the cameras. I even unlocked the window." I grin at them. "And you want to know the best part? Melissa said Balthazar usually goes out until late on Saturday night. He has a regular poker game. That's why I'm doing it tonight. He won't even be there!"

Jamie picks her cocktail back up, shaking her head. "I can't believe you had Balthazar's assistant send you all the information you need to rob him. That's diabolical."

"You call it diabolical," Kayla mutters darkly. "The lawyer prosecuting your case would call it *premeditated*."

I wince. "Once the photos are destroyed, I'll never do a bad thing again," I vow. "I'll be a law-abiding, trustworthy paragon of virtue."

"Just make sure you don't get caught," says Jamie. "Balthazar has all the money in the world. If he catches you breaking into his house, he could go after you with expensive lawyers. You might never see daylight again."

My stomach churns at the idea, but I can't let fear win. I wrinkle my nose at her. "Dramatic much?"

"No, she's right," says Kayla. "He has all the money and all the power. You're a nobody with a dodgy past."

"Hey, thanks for the pep talk," I joke. "Love the encouragement."

Kayla levels a stern look at me. "You know we've got your back. But that means giving you the hard truth when we need to."

"All we want is to keep you safe," adds Jamie.

I hate it when the two of them gang up on me, spouting their annoying common sense.

"I won't get caught," I promise. "I've stacked the odds in my favor."

"If you find the photos, will you still go away with him to San Dante next week?" asks Kayla.

"Sure. I mean, I'm committed."

Jamie's nostrils flare with distaste. "A whole week with him though? We wouldn't blame you for pulling out."

He's not so bad." I sip my Margarita.

"Not bad? Why would you say that?" Kayla's gaze sharpens on my face.

"No reason. Um. By the way, the shopper's coming back with more clothes tomorrow."

"More clothes!" exclaims Jamie. "What will you get this time?"

"Boring stuff, probably. That seems to be what Zar likes."

"Zar?"

I drain my glass in several quick swallows and stand up. "Anyone feel like another?"

CHAPTER 11

Scarlet

Just like I told Jamie and Kayla it would be, breaking into Zar's house is easy. After all, I have the security team's patrolling schedule, the alarms turned off, and a window unlocked. I'm wearing all black, including gloves and a balaclava that covers my face. I've buckled a belt bag around my waist that holds a flashlight, a set of lockpicks for opening any locked drawers or cupboards I might encounter, and a whole lot of dog treats. The treats are to distract Ringo in case I run into him.

The window I unlocked is just above Zar's large household garbage and recycling cans so I can climb on them to reach it. When I get inside, I turn on my flashlight, then walk quickly through Zar's kitchen and down the long hallway. The house has lots of rooms, including a home cinema with a full-sized movie screen, a library, and wine cellar, but I can bypass most of those rooms. They're not places he's likely to keep the photos, and I already took a good look around them when Melissa showed me through.

I'm most interested in his office. Maybe the photos are in a desk drawer. The second most likely place is in his bedroom. Melissa wouldn't let me look in his bedroom, and it's possible I'll find Aunt Alejandra's photos in there.

The door that leads to his bedroom is about halfway down the hall, and I have to go past it to get to his office. Sure enough, the room is dark, which is a good sign. Zar is at his poker game. Still, I creep silently toward it, listening hard for the sound of breathing.

I hear nothing.

But it's not until I get inside that I can be certain the large room is empty. No Balthazar, and no Ringo. Hopefully he took his dog with him.

Tugging my flashlight out of my waist bag, I aim it around. His bedroom is cavernous and spotless. If it wasn't for the rumpled bedclothes on the king-sized bed, I'd wonder if anyone actually lives here. It must have been furnished by the same interior designer who did the rest of the house, because there's hardly any color. The only furniture pieces are the nightstands beside the bed and a giant bookcase. There's also an enormous walk-in closet. That's about it.

I start in the closet, shining my light across the racks of beautiful suits. Balthazar's extensive watch collection has a shelf of its own. Thousands—no, millions of dollars' worth of precious timepieces. There are plenty of treasures in the closet, but no naked photos of my aunt, so I head over to the bookcase.

As well as lots of books on the bookcase's shelves, there

are a few framed photos. The largest is a photo of Zar as a boy. At least, I assume it must be Balthazar. But his assortment of different frowns must have been something he acquired later in life, because in the photo he's wearing a smile that's wider than I would have guessed was possible.

He looks about ten or so, and he's grinning at a woman who's too young to be his mother, perhaps in her early twenties. She's a short, pretty redhead, only a little taller than the boy. She has her arm around him, smiling back at him, and I instantly like her face. She seems like a happy person, and there's clearly real affection between the two of them.

At first I wonder if the woman might be the stepsister Zar mentioned. Then I spot some more photos of Zar as a teenager hanging out with a brown-haired girl who's his own age. Beside it is a photo taken more recently of the two of them with the distinctive ancient ruins of Machu Picchu in the background. The brown-haired girl must be his stepsister, Gaby. Which means the redhead's identity remains a mystery.

And speaking of mysteries, on another shelf is a photo of Zar wearing a black tux, his arm around an elegant blonde. She's stunning. And judging by the way they're standing together, she has to be an ex-girlfriend.

I don't like judging other women; I'd much rather be supportive. But for some reason, I find myself examining the blonde, hoping to spot some kind of flaw. Only I can't see any. Her dress is as gorgeous as her face, and her hair is sleek and perfect.

Ugh.

I'm turning away when I spot another photo of the

elegant blonde. This picture is on the front of a magazine, on top of a neat pile of them. It's *Vogue* magazine. In stunned disbelief, I pick it up.

It's definitely the same woman.

His ex-girlfriend is a cover model?

The byline says her name is Natalia Ricci, and she's a fashion designer. Wait. Isn't she the one who designed the dress I wore to the ball? Now I get why Loretta was so surprised when I told her the designer's name. I was wearing a dress designed by Zar's ex-girlfriend.

I balance the flashlight on the shelf so it illuminates the magazine's pages, and leaf through until I find the article about Natalia and more photos of her. She has such light blonde hair, it's almost white. And there's a double-page spread that shows her reclining in a tight black gown with her long hair pulled over one shoulder.

It's a dramatic shot. She looks stunning. And she's unlike me in every way.

Not that it matters.

It's not like I'm dating Zar for real, after all. But still, why aren't people more surprised when he introduces me as his girlfriend? I'm the opposite of her.

"Focus, Scarlet," I mutter out loud, putting the magazine back. "Who cares who Zar used to date. I'm here for Aunt Alejandra's photos and nothing more."

Then I hear a soft padding noise. Ringo wanders in.

"Good boy," I murmur, pulling dog treats out of my fanny pack. "Be quiet now, boy. That's a good dog."

Ringo lets out a soft, happy woof and chows down on the treats. I quickly check inside Zar's nightstands, but don't find his father's private papers. They must be in his office.

By the time I creep to the door, Ringo has wolfed down all the treats. He follows me hopefully, tail wagging, his attention focused on my waist bag.

"Be quiet now, okay?" I whisper. "I have a few treats left. If you stay nice and quiet, I'll give them to you in a minute."

He lets out a bark, and I tsk at him before sneaking down the hallway.

As I round the corner, I see light coming from the office's partially open door. Then I hear a distinctive male voice, deep and sexy.

Shit!

Zar is at home. I don't know what happened to his poker game, but he's clearly not at it. And he's not only awake at midnight, he's talking to someone.

Does he have someone in there with him?

I creep closer so I can peek through the crack in the door.

Zar's on the phone. He's wearing gray sweatpants and nothing else. He's bare-chested, and just like at the hospital, the sight of his naked torso makes my mouth dry. Though he's half turned away from me, the dim light of his desk lamp is playing over his muscles, creating beautiful shadows. The white bandage he has over his knife wound stands out, but his ridges of muscle are what draw my gaze. He's an exquisite specimen of manhood.

"Call me back when you're free," he says into the phone, clearly leaving a message.

Hanging up, he moves to his desk. Then he bends over some papers, mostly turned away from me. His sweatpants are low on his hips and the muscles in his back are as defined as the ones on his front.

Though I should really cut my losses and leave, I want to

know what he's looking at, so I risk moving a little further into the doorway. Squinting, I'm able to make out typed pages. Not that I seriously thought he'd be looking at Aunt Alejandra's naked photos, but I'm glad to know he's not.

Zar turns his face so I can see his profile. He's wearing a thoughtful, intense look. Not a frown, but a look of someone with incredible focus and determination. Like he's planning how to rule the world.

There's something about that look that's incredibly hot. Maybe even hotter than his naked torso, though that's almost impossible to beat.

Ringo shoves his nose into my crotch.

Suppressing a squeak of surprise, I try to shove him away, but he's determined to get more treats. He pushes his face into my waist bag, tearing at it with his teeth.

Zar turns to face the door, and I duck back just in time.

"Is someone there?" he calls.

I try for silence, but Ringo's insistent nose is jammed so far into my crotch, it's probably illegal. And as hard as I shove him, he just won't quit. Then there's a sharp ripping sound, and the bag releases from my waist. Ringo backs up with it in his teeth. He shakes it from side to side, making my lockpicks clank against each other. The racket is like Central Park fireworks on New Year's Eve.

"Who's there?" growls Zar. "Show yourself!"

CHAPTER 12

Balthazar

The assassin is in my house.

I can hear Ringo wrestling with him outside my office door. That asshole had better not hurt my dog or I'll tear him limb from limb.

Though I want to race out and help Ringo, it would be a good way to get myself shot. So I flatten myself against the wall and listen to the clanking sounds, trying to work out what's happening. Ringo gives a little bark. Good thing it's not a whine, or I'd have no choice but to charge out and protect him.

The intruder must be the one who stabbed me and killed my father. He must have known my poker game had been called off tonight. He intended to kill me while I slept and steal my father's papers. Good thing my wound was aching so I decided to work late to take my mind off it.

I'm awake when the assassin can't have expected it. Too bad for him.

My heart's pounding. I look around for a weapon and see little I can use. My laptop and the heavy books in my bookcase are possibilities, but a letter opener would be more useful. Pity the assassin didn't break in sometime last century when people still sent snail mail.

I'm barefoot and shirtless, which makes me feel even more vulnerable. It's not logical, seeing as a bullet would cut through a t-shirt as though it wasn't there anyway, but there you go. I wasn't expecting an assassin to break into my home, or I would have put a shirt on.

The whole situation pisses me off.

"My dog's a killer, and I'm armed to the teeth!" I shout. "You have three seconds to get out of here, or I'm coming out shooting. Get ready to die!"

The floor creaks again and I hear the muted thump of soft-soled shoes. Incredibly, my shouting might have spooked the assassin because it sounds like he's running away. Did my bluff really scare him off, or is it a trap?

Then there's the telltale scrape of someone dragging a window open. It's either a ploy to get me to come out of my office, or the assassin really is escaping.

Crossing quickly to my office door, I risk sticking my head out for a quick look down the hallway. Ringo is snuffling at something black on the floor—some kind of bag. He's pawing and biting it. The moon is shining through the skylight, and shadows play across the walls as clouds skitter across it. The hallway's empty, but I can see through to the living room where a window is open.

I switch all the lights on, flooding the hallway with bright light. Then I grab the bag from Ringo and discover it's one that fastens around the waist. It's open. Several metal lockpicks and a flashlight have fallen out of it.

"You okay, boy?" I ask, petting down his sides. He's wagging his tail and doesn't seem hurt, thank God.

Grabbing my phone, I call Alan, my head of security.

He picks up on the second ring. "Yes, sir?"

"Someone broke into the house," I say. "They've just escaped out the window."

He barely needs a second to take this in. "They hurt you?" he asks crisply.

"I'm fine. Just catch him."

"We're on it, sir. We'll find him."

"Careful, he's likely to be armed."

"Roger that." Alan's tone can only be described as excited, and I hang up with a sense of grim satisfaction. When they capture the assassin, I'll discover his identity.

Dropping the phone on my desk, I head to the window to close it. And if I take a look through it, I might even be able to spot the intruder myself.

CHAPTER 13

Scarlet

I'm dangling from the edge of Zar's window frame, and my leggings are sagging. Maybe because the elastic stretched when Ringo ripped my waist bag off, or it could just be gravity. All I know is I'm using both hands to hang on, so I don't have a spare one to hike up my leggings. They're creeping down my butt, and my lucky red panties are flashing in the bright light that's spilling from the window.

This isn't the window I used to break into Zar's house, so there are no handy trash cans below it to help me climb down. Worse, I can hear Zar coming down the hallway toward the window I'm hanging from. Once he reaches it, he's sure to see me, red panties and all.

My current position isn't something I have any desire to explain. So I desperately swing my legs from side to side, ignoring the way the movement makes my leggings creep down even further. It's not easy to grip the sill, and the muscles in my hands are already screaming. But with a couple of swings, I build enough momentum to grab onto the next window frame with one hand and drag my body across. Then I keep going, clawing my way to the next window, which—thank goodness—is still dark.

Balthazar sticks his head out of the lit-up window, and I flatten myself against the wall.

He's staring out at the grounds, looking the other way. I'm hanging several feet away, my heart pounding as heavily as a hippo mating.

If he turns his head to look across the wall and down, he'll see me.

I turn my face away so if the worst happens, he'll only see the side of my balaclava and not my eyes or mouth. Then, because any movement could catch Zar's eye, I force my ragged breaths into silence and command my aching arms to stop shaking. Clenching my thighs together, I try to stop my leggings from falling down any further by sheer force of will. At least my panties are a dark shade of red. As long as the light's not hitting them, they'll look dull, almost as good as black.

Dammit, I haven't broken into anyone's house since I was fourteen, and my lack of recent experience shows. So much for all the skills my father taught me. Mind you, he never had me break into a billionaire's house, and we always avoided places with dogs.

A man shouts from somewhere on the lawn, and another man answers. It's Zar's security team calling to each other. There are two guards on duty at night: one patrols the grounds while the other watches the security cameras. Now both are hunting for me. It sounds like they're just around the corner of the house, at the place where I broke in.

They're closing in fast.

Should I drop to the ground and try to make a run for it? There's nothing around here except neatly cut lawn stretching all the way to the fence line. There's no cover. Nothing to hide behind.

But my fingers are in serious pain and my gloves are starting to slip off the window frame. I can't hang on much longer.

The muffled ring of a phone comes from inside the house. Zar puts his head back inside. Then his footsteps move away from the window.

Thank the sweet, sweet Lord.

My relief is strong, but short-lived.

The security team start making banging noises. It sounds like trash can lids thumping open. They must be checking to make sure I'm not hiding inside the trash. One complains about the smell, then there are more thudding sounds as they put the lids back on.

Their flashlight beams get brighter. They're coming around the corner of the house toward me.

Pulling up my legs, I scrunch into as tight a ball as I can manage, positioning my body in the darkest shadow under the window frame. My fingers are trembling, and with my legs up, my ab muscles are straining. Thank heaven for Jamie's drill-sergeant tendencies and her killer workouts. She's the only reason I can hold this pose at all.

If I fall, the security team will probably catch me in seconds. And it'll be even harder to outrun them if I have to hitch my leggings up first.

The only good part of where I'm dangling is that the security camera coverage on this side of the house is patchy.

Seeing as there's no ground cover here for burglars to take advantage of, the cameras are mainly concentrated on the front of the house and swimming pool areas. And for now, the guards are pointing their flashlight beams away from me, toward the fence line rather than at the house.

The two guards stop a short distance from me. "He can't have come in through the front gate," says one. "Or the cameras would have picked him up."

"Must have come in over the side fence," says the other. "That bit where it's a little lower. He cut through the neighbor's property."

The first says, "Then he must have gone back out that way, too. There's nowhere to hide. He must have sprinted off."

"Let's go."

Both of them move in that direction. The great news is that they're striding quickly away from me. The terrible news is that they're right about how I got onto the property. That tiny section where the fence is a little lower is the only way to get off the grounds without being picked up by the security cameras. By heading that way, they're cutting off my only escape route.

My grip is slipping, and both Zar and his security guards could be back any minute.

Seizing my chance, I release my aching hands and let myself fall. As I hit the ground, I roll to soften the landing and make less noise. Then I tug my leggings back up into place before skirting silently around the house, sticking to the deepest shadows while I desperately figure out how to get myself out of this mess.

CHAPTER 14

Balthazar

My sister is on the phone, wanting to have a video call. I left her a voicemail before hearing the assassin, and now she's calling back.

I stare at the screen for a moment, about to reject her call. Then I think better of it. The intruder must be out of sight by now, and my security team will deal with him. So I may as well talk to Gaby and take my mind off the disturbing fact that a killer somehow made it all the way into my house.

"Hi Gaby," I say when her image appears on my screen. "How's everything?"

"Hey Bee." She retorts with her nickname for me. "Can't complain. But it must be the middle of the night for you? Are you okay?"

She's in her apartment in Australia. It's around five in the evening there, and she's on her couch, her phone held up in front of her. Her brown hair is tied back in a ponytail.

"I'm fine." Telling her about the intruder would only make her worry, and what would be the point of that? Still, I walk back out into the hallway. May as well check that window again while I'm talking to her.

"Are you naked?" She jokingly covers her eyes with one hand.

I keep the camera angled up at my face, not wanting her to see the bandage covering my wound. No point in worrying her about that, either.

"Of course I'm not naked! I'm wearing sweatpants. It's a warm night."

"Can't sleep, huh? That's a sign of a guilty conscience. What have you been up to?"

"Dad's estate was finally settled," I say. "I'm going to transfer half the money to you."

Dad should have left her an inheritance, but because he isn't her biological father, I guess he didn't feel he had to. As far as I'm concerned, Gaby's my sister so she's entitled to half his money. She's the only real family I've ever had. The fact Dad didn't agree means nothing.

Gaby screws up her nose. "No thanks. I don't want anything that belonged to him."

I peer back out the window. It's quite a jump from the sill to the ground. The lawn is an empty, dark expanse of grass. Near the fence line, I spot flashlights. My security team are chasing down the assassin.

"It's several million dollars, Gaby." I slide the window shut and lock it. "You can't turn that down."

She shrugs. "I don't care how much it is. I don't want a single thing from him."

Because she's not Dad's daughter, she didn't have the same complicated relationship with him that I did. There was no love lost between them; she's always flat-out hated him. It's made her life simpler than mine. But I still wish she'd take the money.

"Pretend the money's from me, and he had nothing to do with it," I suggest, padding back to my office with Ringo by my side. "Use it for something worthy. Donate it to a charity he'd hate. One that campaigns for human rights."

"Ooo, that's actually tempting." She widens her eyes at me for a moment, then shakes her head. "But even then, it wouldn't feel right taking his dirty money."

"A charity for women's equality. Picture his face."

She lets out a delighted laugh. "That's brilliant!"

"If you don't want to handle his money, I could make the donation in your name."

"Yes, please." She blows me a kiss. "Thank you, Bee. You're the best, you know that?"

I ease gently into my office chair, being careful not to bump my wound. Then I set my phone onto its stand on my desk and make myself comfortable. Ringo puts his head in my lap so I can scratch behind his ears. He must have scared off the assassin by attacking him. Once I've finished this call, I'll feed him a whole lot of dog treats. He deserves them.

"I got a big box of Dad's private papers," I tell Gaby. "It's this size." I demonstrate with my hands. "Stuffed full of financial records and notes about his illegal activity. There's also hundreds of reports his investigator compiled that are full of secrets about everyone he knew."

Like I figured it would, that makes her lean closer to the screen. "Information for blackmailing people?"

I nod. "But the worst thing was at the bottom of the box. He had a pile of photos of naked women. Explicit shots."

Her eyebrows shoot up. "All the women he slept with?"

"Seems that way."

"Like trophies, huh?" Her nostrils flare with disgust. "Knowing your dad, that doesn't surprise me. How many are there?"

"A lot. But I only glanced at the top ones, and they were bad enough."

"What will you do with them?"

"Burn them. But unfortunately, I'll need to look through them first." I grimace at the thought. "The photos could have been a motive for his murder."

"You really think so?"

"I don't know. But a Circuit Court Judge already contacted me to ask about them. Apparently she could be in one of the photos."

Gaby blinks at me. "Really? What did you tell her?"

"I had my legal team send a reply to stall her. I won't be rushed into doing anything until I get a chance to review everything in the box, and the photos are last on my list."

"Lots of dirty secrets," she says.

I smile. I'm pretty sure Gaby will appreciate what I'm planning to do with them. She's always had a moral compass that points true north. If it wasn't for her, maybe I would've become more like my father. But she was the good influence I needed, right when I needed it.

"I'm going to use those dirty secrets to clean up the pharmaceutical company," I say. "Right some of my father's wrongs. Make it less evil."

She grins back at me. "Sounds great. But how?"

"I'll blackmail the board."

"What?!"

"Dad was blackmailing them to get what he wanted. Why shouldn't I do the same thing?"

She purses her lips. "Risky tactic, Bee. He was bludgeoned to death, remember?"

"I have good security." At least, I thought I did. The fact there was just an intruder in my house could suggest otherwise.

"Just be careful, okay? And let me know if there's anything I can do to help."

I grunt.

Wasn't Scarlet supposed to be doing a security audit of my house? My security team clearly need help keeping intruders out. I'll have to check whether she's completed it yet.

The thought of Scarlet makes me picture kissing her.

"By the way," I say to Gaby. "I've met someone interesting. You'd like her."

"Someone interesting?" She leans in, her eyes lighting up. "Someone you're dating?"

"Not exactly. She's an employee."

"Oh." Gaby's expression falls as she shifts back on her couch.

"What's wrong?"

"Nothing. It's just... well, your father used to target the women who worked for him."

"I'm aware," I say dryly.

"Not that I'm suggesting you're anything like your father. You're nothing like him. All I'm saying is to be careful."

"I'm conscious of all the problems. The power

imbalance. The fact that I'm paying her. You know how careful I am with my employees. I always keep them at a distance."

She nods. My old nanny, Helena, left before Gaby came to live with us, but I told Gaby all about her. Helena was by far my favorite, but there were other nannies before her. They were all young and attractive, and they all left after a year or two. All I understood at the time was how much it had hurt when each of them left. It was only when I was older that I wondered if their leaving had anything to do with my father's predatory ways.

"As things stand, I won't take it any further," I add. "If I still feel attracted to her after her contract's over... then we'll see."

She puffs out her breath. "Okay. Good. Very sensible."

"When are you coming to LA for a visit?"

Her smile returns. "Soon. And don't forget you can come and see me whenever you like. Don't wait for an invitation. You always have one."

"Hey Gaby," I say impulsively. "Do you ever ask the universe for things?"

"What kind of things?"

"Anything. Apparently, some people believe that when you want something, you can just ask the universe to give it to you. Like a Cosmic Santa who grants wishes."

I don't know why I'm asking Gaby about it, other than I find it intriguing that Scarlet could believe life could really be so easy.

Gaby's eyes crinkle with amusement. "I think it's more about attracting what you want by believing you can have it."

"So you believe in Cosmic Santa?" I ask.

"I believe in positive thinking and the power of the mind. Don't you?"

"I believe in science."

"Positive thinking *is* science."

"Positive thinking is just wishing things were different. It doesn't work."

I know this for a fact.

Helena left me with barely a goodbye, shortly before my mother died. Then, after Gaby and I grew close, she was sent away, and I was dumped in a boarding school so Dad wouldn't have to deal with me. Later, Natalia decided she'd rather design clothes in France than continue our relationship. Even Gaby had decided to move to the other side of the world.

Not one person I'd cared about had ever stuck with me. And all the wishing in the world hadn't helped one bit.

"Cosmic Santa is a fraud," I say.

Gaby shakes her head. "I'd argue the point, but I'm starving. I need some dinner. And I can't sleep tonight, because I need to get back on the reef to watch the coral spawning. Clouds of eggs and sperm get released into the water. It's fascinating."

"Underwater loving?"

"You know how much I like a good romance." She laughs. "See ya, Bee."

After hanging up, I call Alan back. "What's happening?" I demand.

"We found where the intruder got in," he says, panting a little. He sounds like he's moving quickly. "We're searching for him, but nothing so far."

I let out a curse. "He's gotten away?"

"Possibly, sir."

"Keep looking," I tell him. "He's got to be there somewhere."

CHAPTER 15

Scarlet

I hide inside Zar's stinky trash until the guards finally give up looking for me.

They already searched the trash cans before they went running off to the fence, so I'd figure they won't search them a second time. But it's a foul, disgusting experience crouching in there on top of food scraps and other things I don't want to look closely at.

And after I finally escape and make it home, I have to wash my hair three times to get the stench out.

Then I collapse into bed and sleep all day.

I'm beyond disappointed that I didn't find what I was looking for. But the next week goes past quickly, so I don't have too long to dwell on it. I'm busy getting all our clients' jobs tidied up so I can go away for a week. I have some more Taekwondo training sessions with Melissa. And on Wednesday, Melissa and Lucía turn up to our office with a massive selection of new clothes.

On Friday, I do some research on Anders Pharmaceuticals, and learn the company was started by Zar's grandfather. By the time his five kids were born, including Blythe Anders, Zar's father, it was already worth millions. The company is still owned by Blythe's siblings and all their kids, who grew up with all that money. Most of them seem to do nothing but spend it. Zar has a successful venture capital business and a lot of investments. He's turned his millions into billions. Good for him, except it means he has so much security around his house, I can't risk trying to break in again.

Still, by the time Monday rolls around, I've recovered my optimism, and I'm ready to face an entire week protecting Balthazar in the small coastal town of San Dante while I come up with a new plan.

Especially when I find out we're going there by helicopter.

I sit in the helicopter's front passenger seat, next to the pilot, gazing through the enormous glass window in front of me. It's usually Zar's seat, but he insists I have it, and I'm not about to turn it down.

When we take off, the helicopter's noise is muffled by my headphones. We soar through the air, defying gravity. It's magical. Exhilarating. And the view is breathtaking. Ahead of us, the golden sand beach of San Dante glistens under the bright sun. The vast expanse of blue sky envelops us, and I feel as though I'm in a dream.

I turn to look behind me at Zar. He looks amused, and I realize I have an excited grin on my face. One I couldn't tone down if I tried.

"Having fun?" he asks, his voice coming through my headphones.

I nod enthusiastically.

"I like flying," he admits with a slight smile, as though it's a secret confession. And for a moment we share a wordless connection that leaves me feeling even more giddy.

"I'm going to add this to my vision board," I say into the microphone attached to my headphones. "I want more helicopter rides!"

He quirks an eyebrow. "If you're asking the universe for a helicopter, don't forget to request gift wrapping."

"How exactly would you gift wrap a helicopter?"

"Isn't that the universe's problem?"

I grin. "Look at you, understanding the concept. Now you're starting to get how it works!"

"But do you actually think the universe is your personal cosmic delivery service?" He gives me a cynical, scrunched-eye look.

"Look at all this." I sweep my hand at the incredible view. "How lucky are we? There are millions of people down there, and how many of them get to experience this? Take a good look and tell me the universe doesn't have our back!"

He does what I ask and gazes out the window. Though he doesn't reply, he has a thoughtful expression. Maybe my argument made an impression, and maybe it didn't. Either way, he's staring out at the spectacular scenery.

The resort we're staying at has its own helipad, which says a lot about how fancy it is. Flying in, it looks like a sprawling low-rise complex set on a beachfront acreage with several swimming pools and tennis courts set around the buildings.

"It's stunning!" I'm breathless with how luxurious it looks from the air.

"The resort's brand new," Zar informs me. "Completed last month."

"You were joking about us sharing a room, weren't you?"

"We're sharing a *suite*." When I blink at him, he adds, "It has two bedrooms. You'll get your own room."

I blow out a semi-relieved breath. After kissing him, I can't trust myself to stay in the same room with him. I don't know if it's his looks, his charisma, or the way he frowns at me, but I find him irresistibly sexy. My repressed bad-girl side is struggling with inappropriate desires. Even being in the same suite with him will be hard enough.

When we land, a couple of staff members are waiting with refreshing cold towels and a selection of drinks on trays, including some delicious-looking cocktails. Seeing as I'm here to work, I resist the urge to grab a piña colada, and accept something fruity and non-alcoholic instead.

I'm wearing a gorgeous blue dress printed with sunflowers that Zar's personal shopper gave me. Lucía was nice enough to supply colorful outfits to suit my taste. And she gave me some lovely flat sandals that won't throw me off balance if I need to deal with an attacker.

Zar is in a gray shirt that's unbuttoned at the neck, dark slacks, and one of his expensive watches. He looks effortlessly gorgeous. I'm glad I haven't caught him wincing, so his wound must be healing well.

A blonde, older woman introduces herself as the hotel manager and personally escorts us to the top floor of one of the buildings. She tells us about the restaurants and other amenities at the resort, including a health spa, gym, and choice of swimming pools with private cabanas. Then she opens the door to our suite, and everything else is wiped out of my mind as I walk into a beautifully decorated living room and see the enormous windows that look over the ocean.

"Holy crap," I breathe. The beach is below us and the sky and ocean stretch out in front. The sun's reflection makes the waves shimmer. I've never seen anything so blue.

When I manage to wrench my gaze from the stunning view, I see there's a kitchenette on the far side of the living room, which is small but equipped with a coffee machine. Walking past it, I find a giant bedroom. Inside it is a super-king-sized bed. And there's an attached bathroom that's just as impressive.

"Take a look at the size of the bath!" I gaze into the bathroom with my jaw loose. "It's way too big for just one person. You'd need to throw a party in there to have a chance of filling it up."

Zar moves beside me to see it. But it's not until he gives me an amused sideways glance that I realize how suggestive that might have sounded. I shoot him a look back, trying to make my expression say, *'Don't get any ideas'*. Problem is, now I'm the one with the vision in my head of the two of us having our own private party in the enormous bath.

I walk back into the living room to where the manager is standing. "Where's the other bedroom?"

"Other bedroom?" She looks puzzled. "This is the honeymoon suite. It only has one bedroom."

I jerk my face to Zar. "We're in the *honeymoon suite*?"

"Is that a problem?" The manager suddenly sounds nervous.

"We're supposed to have a two-bedroom suite." Zar's

frown is one of his stern ones, and the manager shrinks under the force of it.

"I'm sorry, sir. There must have been a mix up."

"There's only one bed?" I gulp. It might be a giant-sized bed, but will I seriously be forced to share it with Zar? In the *honeymoon suite*. I bet it has silk sheets.

"That's not what you wanted?" The manager twists her hands together, clearly flustered. "I'd offer you a second room, but I'm afraid we're full."

"We'll discuss it." Zar motions to the door. "You can wait outside." His tone is curt, and I don't love the way he speaks to her, without so much as a please or thank you.

"Mr. Anders, please accept my sincere apology for any misunderstanding with the room." She backs rapidly out. "I'll wait just out here until you're ready."

Once the door has closed behind her, he turns to me. "I'll have a second bed brought in. We'll put it in the living room. You can take the one in the bedroom."

I scrunch my nose doubtfully. "Will they have another bed available if all the rooms are booked?"

"I'll buy one."

"Buy one?"

"Melissa can have it delivered within the hour."

I let out a laugh, walking back to the bedroom and looking in. "You can't buy a bed for a short stay."

"I can." He walks up beside me, putting subtle emphasis on the word 'I'.

"You might have an entire swimming pool full of money, Bob, but buying a bed would be wasteful, unless the hotel can use it afterward. Otherwise, what's going to happen to it?"

"I'll have it donated to charity."

"Oh." I hadn't thought of that. "Still, this bed's the size of an entire country." I sit down on it and bounce a little. "I've shared a bed with both Jamie and Kayla a few times when we were traveling and couldn't afford our own rooms."

And in juvie, I shared a room that was smaller than this with eight girls. The hotel room is palatial in comparison.

But when I look up at Zar, it's immediately clear why this isn't even remotely the same thing as sharing with Jamie. The bed could be as big as Alaska, and I'd still be acutely conscious of sharing it with Zar.

What will happen if we kiss again?

How will I be able to stop myself from having sex with him if we're sharing a bed? I mean, other than knowing it would be all kinds of wrong to go that far with Zar while I'm working for him and secretly plotting to steal from him. But will knowing that be enough to help me keep control? He seems able to disengage my brain to communicate directly with my inner bad girl.

Dammit, life was so much simpler when I hated him.

He stares down at me a moment as I'm bouncing on the bed, his eyes dark and his expression unreadable. I'm wearing one of the killer push-up bras Lucía got me, and I suddenly realize my breasts are probably wobbling in my low-cut dress. I stop bouncing.

Zar gives his head a slight shake and stalks over to the floor-to-ceiling windows. Stopping in front of them, he stares out at the ocean.

"There was an incident on Saturday night at my house." His voice is tight. "Someone broke in. They were able to wander around before they escaped."

"Oh no, really?" I try to sound surprised and innocent.

"My security team let me down."

"I'm sure it wasn't their fault."

He turns to face me. Silhouetted against the windows, the width of his shoulders is obvious, but his face is shadowed.

"My team let an assassin get inside," he growls. "Then they let him escape."

Shit. I was supposed to get in and out without anyone knowing I'd been there. Now I've made his team look bad. Something else to feel guilty about. My karma is taking a hammering.

"Did any of them come with us?" I ask. "You should have extra security here to look out for threats."

"It's just you. So it's better if you stick close to me."

I swallow. "Okay."

"You're willing to make do with one bed?" His tone is curt.

"Um." I've already implied I don't mind. I can't walk that back without him wondering why. "I guess it's fine. But don't blame your security team for the intruder, okay?"

"They didn't do their jobs."

"Aren't you being too hard on them, though?"

"I don't believe I am." He walks back out of the room, and I hear him open the front door to speak to the manager. "We don't need a second room."

She babbles something grateful, mixed in with another apology. "The valet will bring up your luggage and unpack for you," she adds. "And please don't hesitate to call if you need anything else. Anything at all."

"Fine."

I wince at how impatient he sounds. No wonder she seems afraid of him. It seems contradictory that Zar is determined to put his father's evil deeds right, yet he's so tough with the people who work for him.

Getting up, I go out to see him closing the door. "What did she say about our luggage?"

"The valet's going to put our things away while we go and have lunch."

"Not mine." I shake my head. "I don't want anyone unpacking my bag."

"Why not?"

"Because I value my privacy, and I want to put my own things away."

His eyes narrow, but I hold his gaze, standing my ground, noting the nuances of his current frown. This one is puzzled and slightly irritated. It ranks low on the frown scale I'm formulating. Maybe he's hard to read sometimes, but his frowns are expressive. They're the clearest way he shows what he's feeling.

"All right," he says after a moment. "We'll let the manager know. Now, you must be hungry. Let's have lunch."

I nod, trying to suppress the doubts that are crowding in on me. What am I doing? Tonight, I'll have to share a bed with him.

And I have to admit, I might be in a little over my head.

CHAPTER 16

Balthazar

I asked Melissa to book a two-bedroom suite, not the honeymoon suite, or a room with only one bed. Still, that doesn't mean I'm unhappy with our current situation.

On the contrary.

As we take our seats at a table on the restaurant's balcony, I'm relishing the knowledge that tonight, Scarlet and I will be sleeping in the same bed.

I haven't been able to get our kiss out of my head, and I have an insatiable urge to know more about her.

"This place is so beautiful." She's staring out at the view over the water. The restaurant is on a lower floor than our room, and we're seated outside, near the edge of the balcony, under the shade of the awning. From here, we have a good view of the surfers riding the curling waves. The beach is full of people and their towels, umbrellas, and beach chairs.

"You've already mentioned that," I tell her. "Twice before we ordered."

"Well, look!" She waves her hand toward the water. "Doesn't it make you grateful to be here?"

Her wild brown curls tumble around her shoulders in the breeze. They blow across her cheeks and catch in her long eyelashes when she blinks. She's wearing a dress that's printed with yellow sunflowers on a blue background. Cheerful colors that suit her personality. The dress hugs her figure nicely, with a bodice that cradles her breasts. If my shopper chose it, she outdid herself. I've barely been able to look at anything else.

"Even the people on the beach are beautiful," Scarlet says, turning her face into the salt-tinged breeze.

I run my gaze across the line of sunbathers. She's right, there are some attractive women in tiny bikinis who are lying just below where we're sitting. I hadn't noticed them until she pointed them out, and I have no interest in sending more than a passing glance their way. I'd far rather look at Scarlet.

"Don't be hard on your security team," she says abruptly. "The break-in wasn't their fault."

I frown, surprised she's bringing it up again. "Then whose fault was it?"

When she leans in, her dress displays more of her cleavage. She has an incredible figure. If her eyes weren't so striking, it would be a struggle to keep my gaze from dropping.

"I used to be a burglar," she says. "So I know what I'm talking about when I say that if someone really wants to get into your house, it's all but impossible to keep them out."

"You think you could break into my house?"

"Of course I could. If I wanted to." Her cheeks flush as

she pushes some stray curls out of her eyes. "Which I don't, of course. I mean, why would I?"

"How would you do it?"

"In and out through the side windows. Easy."

I lift my brows, impressed. "That's how the intruder got in."

"It's not the fault of your security team. You're not going to fire them or anything, are you?" Her voice holds a plaintive note, and her expression is imploring.

I don't know why she cares so much about their jobs. If my team decided to quit working for me, they'd walk away without a second thought as so many of my employees have done. I never heard from Helena after she left, nor any of my other nannies, and who was supposed to care about me more than them?

"I'm not firing them, if that's what you're worried about," I say.

She lets out a breath. "Okay. Good." She sounds so relieved, I raise my eyebrows.

"Well," she says, "you need them to guard your father's papers while you're away."

"I didn't leave those papers behind. They're here, in the hotel's safe."

She blinks her long lashes at me. "The safe in our suite?"

I shake my head. "That safe isn't big enough. The hotel has a bigger one. When I need the papers, a security guard will bring them up to me."

"Okay!" She brightens. "That's good." Suddenly she's all smiles again as she brushes her errant curls back from her face.

Our waiter appears at our table with a large plate of

freshly shucked oysters. Scarlet has never tried them, so I ordered a dozen as a starter. They come with a selection of sauces, but first I get her to try one with just a squeeze of lemon. I watch her closely, enjoying her surprise as she chews.

"Good?" I ask.

"Weird." She licks her lips in a very distracting manner. "A little slimy. But strangely tasty."

"Try one with the horseradish sauce next."

I encourage her to go through all the sauces, to discover which she prefers. She's adventurous, eager to try them all. I like that.

When we've had enough and the waiter has taken the plate away, Scarlet asks, "What's your plan for today?"

"I'm looking for the board members I want to meet with. If they're at the resort already, I'll ambush them when they walk into the restaurant. I need to talk to them all before the board meeting."

"You're going to surprise them all?"

"That's the idea. I'll threaten them one by one."

"A fun day."

"Not for them."

"Well, they've been doing bad things, haven't they? So this is karma finally catching up with them." She sounds cheerful.

"I've never believed in karma." I tilt my head, reconsidering. "But seeing as my father died horribly, maybe there's something to it."

She lifts her eyebrows. "Do you really mean that? I mean, he was your father. Wasn't there anything good about him?"

"Nothing."

Her expression softens as though my answer triggers her sympathy. But maybe she senses I don't want to talk about him, as she steers the conversation in a different direction.

"I'm all about the karma," she says. "Mainly trying to clear my own after all the bad things I did when I was younger. Now I'm working on putting enough positive energy into the world to make up for it. And I *really* don't want to add to my bad karma." She scrunches her face. "Even though sometimes it feels like I don't have much of a choice."

I give a disbelieving grunt. "You don't actually believe there's a Cosmic Karma Mathematician sitting on a cloud, tallying up all the bad things you've done?"

"Sure, in a way. The universe balances things out."

"So if you did something bad enough, would a swarm of locusts descend to punish you?"

She gives me a smile, unbothered by my cynicism. "It might."

"Do Cosmic Santa and the Cosmic Karma Mathematician ever have after-work drinks?"

"Maybe they meet up to discuss your misdeeds." She raises an eyebrow. "You should carry a big can of bug spray in case of locust swarms."

I can't help but laugh, and her grin is wide and beautiful, lighting up her face as our young waiter arrives with our entrees. When she lifts her smile to him, he stumbles a little, blushing.

"Um, ravioli for you, miss," he says shyly, putting the plate in front of her. "And wild-caught shrimp for you, sir." He's still looking at Scarlet while he puts my food down, and although it's not very professional of him to be staring at her,

I can't blame him. With that sparkle in her eyes and her mischievous smile, she's difficult to look away from.

The waiter fusses with her cutlery and checks she doesn't want another drink before managing to tear himself away from Scarlet and leave us in peace.

Scarlet tastes her ravioli, closing her eyes for a moment and making a low moan of pleasure that seems to hum all the way through my body to my cock. She chews slowly. When she swallows and licks her lips, I get harder.

"This is amazing." She points her fork at it. "You have to try it! Here, give me your fork." It's still lying beside my plate, and she snatches it up and heaps on some ravioli, then passes it over.

I find myself with a forkful of ravioli and her expectant eyes on me, waiting for me to eat it. It's a new experience. Nobody has ever insisted I share their food before. And she's watching me with such intensity, it's as though my enjoyment might heighten hers.

Obediently, I eat the ravioli. "Delicious," I say, and though it really is tasty, I would have said the same thing even if it weren't.

Her delight feels like a reward.

She scoops more into her own mouth, and I eat some shrimp, marveling at my own response to her. What is it about her that makes me want to please her?

Watching her savor another mouthful of her food, I try to figure it out. Is it her beauty? Her sassy mouth? Her fearlessness? The way she treats me like a friend instead of an employer?

Reaching out, I pull away a curl that's trying to wind its

way onto her fork as she lifts it to her mouth. "Your curls are getting in your food," I tell her.

"The perils of eating in a breeze. It's annoying."

I tuck the curl carefully behind her ear, taking my time about it. "Do you have a barrette?"

"Afraid not."

When I lift a finger, our young waiter is with us in a moment. "Please call the gift shop in the lobby and have them send up their nicest barrette. There's a large tip in it for you if they get it here in the next three minutes."

"Yessir." He strides away.

"You can't ask him to do that!" exclaims Scarlet.

"I believe I already did."

She wags her fork at me. "Do you always get everything you want, Bob?"

"Always. Except for one thing."

"What thing?"

I level a stern frown at her. "Apparently, I can't get you to stop calling me Bob."

She shakes her head dismissively, ignoring my frown. "I already let you give me a lot of new clothes to wear at this fancy resort. And okay, I want to pin back my hair, because it's getting in the way of me enjoying this amazing food. But I can buy my own barrette."

"I'm not negotiating with you. It's already done."

She gives me a frown of her own. "Just because you have a lot of money doesn't mean I'll do everything you say."

"Shocker," I say dryly. "The way things are going, I'd be grateful for one instruction in ten."

Her frown dissolves, and she looks amused. She takes

another bite of ravioli, but she's barely finished it before our waiter is back.

"Here's your barrette, sir." He puts a box on the table.

"That was so fast!" exclaims Scarlet.

"Please let me know if it's not to your liking, or if I can do anything else for you, sir." He gives a small bow and backs away.

"Sir," Scarlet repeats, scrunching her nose as she picks up the box.

"What?" I ask.

"It's just weird, the way everyone bows and scrapes. Don't you get tired of it?"

"That's what respect looks like. You should take notes."

But she's too busy opening the box to retort. "Oh, it's beautiful!" she exclaims. "A butterfly."

"Let me." Taking the little jeweled barrette from her, I pin it into her hair, pulling her curls back from her cheek and tucking them into it. I'm careful to get them all, then spend some time adjusting the clip, enjoying the silkiness of her hair in my fingers. The barrette shimmers in the brightness of the day, adding another touch of sparkle, not that she needs it. Still, she looks more beautiful now that her hair isn't drifting over her face.

"Thank you," she says, when I finally pull my hand back. "But I still want to pay for it."

"It's not up for discussion."

"You should talk to my therapist about your need to boss people around. She might be able to help you."

"Are you really in therapy?" I ignore the part of her statement that's not worthy of comment.

She nods, lifting a forkful of ravioli. "I love my therapist.

We work on gratitude and manifestation. What about you? Do you see a therapist?"

"Of course. But I don't go to Madame Woo's circus tent for my therapy. I speak to a trained psychologist. Someone highly reputable."

"My therapist is better." Scarlet grins. "She's so good, she could help you manifest two beds."

Her joke gives me a twinge of guilt. I could easily solve the bed issue, and the fact I haven't done so is because I don't want to.

Asking an employee to share my bed is the type of thing my father would have done. I refuse to be anything like him. But in my defense, it's not like I'm going to mess around with Scarlet.

It's just that most people in my life are deferential. They want something from me, usually money, advice, employment, or validation. Scarlet seems to think I have things to learn from her, and that's part of what makes her so fascinating.

I enjoy talking to her. And though I don't believe the universe will magically provide the things she wants, I envy her cheerful optimism.

I also have a burning desire to uncover why she smells like oranges. It could be her shampoo, she might eat a pile of oranges every night, or maybe there's a citrus perfume I don't know about.

Tonight, I intend to find out.

CHAPTER 17

Scarlet

This is, without a doubt, the nicest restaurant I've ever been to.

Sitting at a lovely table on the balcony, we're shaded and cool despite the hot sun, and we have an incredible view across the beach and over the ocean. The food was delicious, but I have no idea how expensive our lunch was, seeing as there aren't any prices on the menu. That must be a rich-person thing.

I reach up to touch the barrette Zar put in my hair. It's beautiful, decorated with little diamonds that look real, and he bought it on a whim. As though it was really that important for me to eat without my hair wafting across my face.

Must be nice to have so much money. It blows my mind even trying to imagine it.

"Dessert?" offers Zar.

"I couldn't." I pat my full stomach.

"Coffee, then?"

"Yes, please."

If only the wretched, desperate girl I'd once been could see me now. This resort seems millions of miles—and millions of dollars—away from the detention center's grim walls. Back then, I couldn't even have imagined that a place like this existed.

"You've always been rich, haven't you?" I ask Zar once our coffees have been delivered.

He nods. "My father became chairman of Anders Pharmaceuticals when I was young. And he bribed or threatened enough board members to keep the position for the rest of his life."

"How many board members are there?"

"Fourteen. They're all spoiled and selfish. And I'm related to all of them."

"Do they look like you?"

"Judge for yourself. That's one of my uncles over there, the man in the ugly shirt." He motions past me. "I haven't seen the woman he's with before, but she's probably his newest wife."

I crane my neck to look and spot a big man in a Hawaiian shirt being shown to a one of the tables on the other side of the restaurant's balcony. He's with a blonde woman who looks about twenty-five and is seriously petite. She can't be much over four feet tall. He's got at least thirty years on her and is several times her size. They're so mis-matched, it's a little disturbing.

"He looks nothing like you." I squint at the man. He has dark hair, but that's as far as the resemblance goes. Even if he had the same body shape as Zar, he wouldn't have much of a chin. Plus, he's wearing a garish, short-sleeved shirt that I'm certain Zar wouldn't be seen dead in.

"Uncle Orson." Zar says his name with a touch of contempt. "One of my father's brothers."

When his uncle looks our way, Zar raises his hand in greeting. The uncle gets up, abandoning his wife, and swaggers to our table.

"Balthazar," he says. "Long time." He doesn't say it in a friendly way, or like he thinks the time should have been any shorter. His gaze is sharply assessing, and he seems wary of what Zar might want.

"Hello, Orson." Zar's tone holds even less warmth. "I didn't see you at my father's funeral."

"I was in Bermuda, on my honeymoon." Orson's gaze goes to me.

"Congratulations," I say. Hoping a smile might help the tense atmosphere, I beam one at him. But an aversion to smiles must run in the family because Orson ignores it.

"This is Scarlet," says Zar. "Sit down, Orson. We need to talk."

His uncle hesitates a moment, glancing back at his wife. She's focused on her phone, clearly not missing him, so he lowers himself onto a chair. He's wearing a lot of jewelry. Gold chains glint from under the open neck of his shirt, thick gold rings are crammed onto his fingers, and a fat gold Rolex watch dominates his wrist. He's wearing white pants and sits with his legs aggressively spread, taking up twice as much space as he needs to.

"I've never seen you at a board meeting before," Orson says to Zar. "You haven't been interested in the business."

"I am now. In fact, I've decided to become chairman of the board."

Orson leans back in the chair, his lip curling, shifting his legs even further apart. "That's not funny."

"I'm not joking."

"Listen, Balthazar, becoming chairman isn't something you can just decide. It goes to a vote. All the board members vote and choose someone." His tone is condescending, like he really thinks Zar doesn't know the process.

"I'll get the votes I need." Zar speaks with such conviction, it's impossible not to believe him. "And when I'm chairman, I'll lower the prices of essential drugs so patients pay less."

Orson scoffs. "That's ridiculous. Why would you want to do that?"

"The price we're charging for some drugs is over five hundred times what it costs us to make them."

Scowling, Orson leans in to jab at Zar with one meaty finger. "That's because we have to pay for research and development."

"It's because we've been paying such high dividends to board members. The company has been prioritizing profits over patients for too long." Zar sounds remarkably calm. Too calm. If I were Orson, I'd be afraid of what his ice-cold tone might mean.

"If you're the chairman, you'll get paid more than anyone," Orson points out.

"I won't be paid anything. None of us will. The company will stop paying dividends for the next five years, at least."

"What the *fuck*?" Orson looks wildly around as though searching for someone to share his incredulity. "You can't do that! And you sure as hell won't be chairman. Over my dead body!"

"I have something you need to see." Zar opens the leather satchel he stashed next to his chair, riffles unhurriedly through a bunch of papers, and eventually pulls out a single page, which he hands to Orson. "This is the data from the Selexitron clinical trial."

"So?" Orson peers at it.

"At the top of the page is a summary of the actual data. Underneath is the data that was sent to the FDA. The two aren't the same. Fake results were submitted."

"Then there must have been a mistake." Orson's cheeks flush red. "One of the researchers—"

"The falsified data came from you. You're the one who sent it to the FDA."

Orson blusters a little more, but now I'm distracted. The papers in Zar's satchel are clearly his father's, and he said he brought them all with him. Does that mean he could have Aunt Alejandra's photos here? Will I get a second chance to get them back for her?

"So here's what's going to happen." Zar's sharp tone brings me back to the conversation as he skewers Orson with one of his best frowns yet. "At the board meeting, I'll become chairman because you're going to vote for me. And I expect you to support all the changes I make. If you don't, I won't send this to the people who've already been paid to look the other way, but straight to the press. I have one of the country's top reporters on speed dial."

"You shit-head," snarls Orson. "I'm going to kill you!"

His face has gone from red to purple. I tense, ready to

throw myself between them if he springs at Zar. Not that he looks like the springing type, but you never know.

"That's interesting," I interject, trying to pull some of Orson's anger from Zar to me. "Was it you who already tried to kill Balthazar?"

"Fuck you, bitch!" Orson scrapes his chair back and surges to his feet.

Anticipating the movement, I leap up at the same instant and go straight into my fighting stance, hands raised, ready to strike.

Zar gets up as well. His ice-cool demeanor is gone. His fists are clenched and something dark gleams in his eyes. "You don't get to talk to her that way," he snarls.

"You'll regret this. Both of you!" Orson still looks angry, but there's a wariness in his expression as it flicks between Zar and me. He's afraid of us.

"Just go," I tell him.

Sure enough, he spins on his heel and hurries back to his wife. Zar takes a step after him, but I grab his arm to stop him.

"Don't."

Zar's expression is thunderous. "He has to apologize to you."

"Don't worry, it's okay. Negative actions have karmic consequences, remember?"

His gaze jerks to mine. "I don't believe in karma."

"Trust me, everything will balance out eventually." I offer him a little smile. "You don't need to do anything. It'll happen anyway."

Orson barks a sharp order at his wife before storming

out of the restaurant. She casts a confused look at us, then follows.

Zar's stance slowly relaxes, and I risk letting go of his arm.

"I don't think you're his favorite nephew," I say to lighten his mood.

"What gave it away?"

"Have you ever thought about collecting stamps or coins? Or anything other than death threats?"

"I warned you I wasn't here to make friends."

"And you weren't kidding." I sit back down, and after a moment, he does too. Unlike his uncle, he doesn't do the obnoxious leg-spreading thing, but the way he sits makes him look commanding. I'm not sure what it is. Maybe a mix of his confident posture, the small frown that's his default expression, and that his angular features are so arresting.

"Are you really going to do all those things you said?" I ask.

He nods, rubbing a hand across his square jaw. "The company needs to change. The board members have all made millions at the expense of patients."

"There's something I don't get. If your father was head of the corruption squad, why would any of them want to kill him?"

"Because of the secrets he collected."

"He was blackmailing them?"

"Most of them. I'm still going through his financial records, but some of them were paying him part of their earnings, while others did favors for him."

I tap my cheek thoughtfully. "Are you making a list of who did what? It might help us narrow down the suspects."

"I am, but there's a lot of data. I had copies of his bank statements sent to a financial analyst to compile a summary of payments and deposits. I'll have Melissa check on progress." He gets up. "Let's go back to the room." Moving to the back of my chair, he pulls it out for me as I stand. Whatever billionaire finishing school he went to, I approve.

While we wait for the elevator he asks, "Did you see Orson's watch?"

I nod. "A vintage Rolex." Noticing watches is an old habit from when I was a girl.

"Not just any vintage Rolex. It was owned by Max Oberon. He wore it in the first Ryder Savage movie, and it has his name engraved on the back."

I whistle. Ryder Savage is one of the biggest movie franchises in the world, and Max Oberon is the star.

"How did your uncle get it?" I ask.

"Oberon auctioned it for charity, and Uncle Orson paid sixteen million dollars for it."

"No way. Sixteen million bucks? For a watch!"

"It's a collector's item. Orson got it for the bragging rights. I'm pretty sure he loves it more than anything else in his life. Even his new wife."

"I wish I'd taken a closer look," I say as the elevator doors open. "I've never seen a watch that's worth that much before."

"You like watches?" he asks when we get in.

"Actually, my dad was the one who loved watches. He taught me to steal them, and he used to get proud of me when I snagged a good one." I wrinkle my nose. "Looking back, I can see it was a weird way of showing affection."

"Not a parenting technique from the handbook." He says it in that dry tone I'm coming to love.

"If I'd met you when I was fifteen, your wrist would have been bare in seconds." I raise my eyebrows at the Patek Philippe he's wearing. It's not the same one I took during my interview, but that's hardly surprising. I saw his collection when I broke into his house. He could wear a different watch every day of the month and not run out.

"You should steal Orson's Rolex," he says. "The man deserves it."

I shake my head. "My watch stealing days are over. I'm a reformed citizen. No more crime for me!" It's a miracle I don't flush bright red as I say it, considering how recently I broke into Zar's house.

"You took my watch."

"Only to prove I could, and I gave it right back. The only reason I'd ever risk stealing something now would be if someone I loved desperately needed me to." I'm trying not to wince, but the conversation's getting too close to reality for comfort.

"Why would they need it?"

"I don't know. It's hypothetical. Like if Kayla or Jamie had a deadly illness and inside the watch was a magical cure."

This whole conversation is a bad idea, and I'm glad when the elevator opens on our floor. Zar waits for me to get out first. All his small, old-fashioned gallantries seem automatic, as though they're things he does without thinking.

"Did you like stealing watches?" he asks as we walk down the hall to our suite.

"Stealing is wrong."

"That doesn't answer my question."

I consider for a moment. "It wasn't that I liked it, but it was exciting," I admit. "Scary but thrilling. A little addictive, even though it was a bad thing to do." I stop in front of our suite.

He studies me with the key in his hand, seemingly in no hurry to open the door. "You're an adrenaline junky."

"Maybe I used to be. Not anymore."

"You got hooked on danger when you were young, and you still crave it. That's why you loved the helicopter ride so much."

"I mean, who wouldn't love a helicopter ride?"

"But your life is less exciting than it used to be."

I give a non-committal shrug, because I run a business and have responsibilities so of course life is less exciting. It's inevitable.

When we get inside the suite, there are signs someone has put Zar's luggage away. A thriller novel is positioned on one of the nightstands, and there's a big stack of papers arranged on the desk for him. A quick glance tells me they're probably not his father's secret papers. They look like company reports and brochures.

My luggage is standing on the far side of the bed. I'm pleased to see it hasn't been opened and is still full of my things. But Zar glowers at it, as though it offends him that it hasn't been done.

"The valet would have unpacked it for you."

"I have a rule. Nobody but me touches my stuff." Bending down, I unzip my bag. "You might not mind strangers pawing through your personals, but that's one service I'll never use."

"Do you have something secret in there?"

"If I do, you'll never know."

"I don't like secrets." He hesitates. "You must understand why."

"Sure. But I value my privacy, and you need to respect that."

He frowns at me.

The ranking system I'm putting together for Zar's frowns is almost complete. The most common ones are his thoughtful frown, his puzzled frown, his exasperated frown, his irritated frown, and his angry frown. I've labeled those frowns numbers one through five. But my favorite is his stern frown. Frown number six. It's a dangerous expression that demands to be obeyed, and therefore tempts me to disobey.

And the fact he's aiming frown number six at me in the honeymoon suite where we'll be spending the night alone together sends a secret, delicious shiver down my spine.

It's the opposite effect to the one he intends, and I'm painfully aware I shouldn't like it so much. I'm not here for sexy fun times. No matter how sexy or how much fun I imagine they could be.

Turning away, I busy myself with unpacking my luggage, hanging the beautiful dresses Lucía gave me in the room's enormous walk-in closet.

I'm planning to leave my more personal stuff in my suitcase so Zar doesn't see it, but when I pull out a pair of capri pants, one of my crystals gets caught in its folds. It drops to the floor and rolls.

"What's that?" Zar frowns at it. "You travel with rocks?"

Oh well. I guess we're having this conversation now after all.

And now he's about to see this side of me, I get a tingle of anticipation. I'm pretty sure I know how he'll react, and I find I'm actually looking forward to it.

Picking up my quartz, I quirk an eyebrow at him before setting it on my nightstand, silently challenging him to give me his best shot.

"I travel with crystals." Pulling more from my suitcase, I hold them up one by one. "Amethyst for inner peace. Jade for luck. Moonstone for vitality."

"You think your rocks have magical powers." His tone is flat, disappointing me not at all. "Did you buy them from someone who told you they'd grow into a beanstalk?"

"Hmm. If only I'd thought to bring some smokey quartz to clear negative energy." I tug my aromatherapy candle out of my suitcase, setting it on my nightstand next to my crystals. Smiling to myself, I light it. Poking the bear is fun. I like the way he growls.

He wrinkles his nose. "That candle smells."

"I'll just burn it for a minute, to lightly scent the room. It's frankincense. Helps with mental clarity."

"Mental clarity? If you think your rocks are magic, it's not working."

"Better stand closer to the flame," I tell him. "You need it more than I do."

He holds my gaze for a moment, attempting another of his stern looks. Only the hint of amusement in his eyes softens the expression.

So far, the only people I've seen him interact with seem to be afraid of him. And I'm pretty sure he enjoys it when I don't yes-sir and no-sir him, like everyone else seems to.

Giving his head a little shake, he sits at the desk. "If you can continue quietly with your nonsense for the next hour or so, I need to catch up on a little work."

I nod at the big stack of papers laid out for him on the desk. "What is all that?"

"Financial reports and data from companies that are looking for investment."

"You really bought a whole lot of work to a beach resort?" I sit on the edge of the bed with my half-unpacked bag at my feet. "You didn't think you'd be busy enough while you're threatening people and trying not to get murdered?"

He's opening his mouth to answer when there's a knock on the door. "Mr. Anders?" calls a woman's voice. "It's the hotel manager with a gift."

"We don't want it," Zar calls back.

"Wait!" I scramble to my feet. "We're not turning down free stuff!" I fling open the door. The manager is holding out a gift basket, an apologetic smile fixed to her lips.

"I've reviewed Mr. Anders' assistant's conversations with our booking staff." Her gaze tries to focus on me but keeps flicking over my shoulder, searching for him. "His assistant requested a two-bedroom suite, and the mistake was made on our end. Our staff member has been reprimanded, and I'm here to extend my sincere apologies for the hotel's mistake. Please accept this small gift as a token of our regret."

"Thank you." I take the gift basket from her, eyeing up the yummy treats inside. Chocolate, cheeses, and a bottle of wine. Awesome!

"We're busy," Zar calls from his desk, his tone grumpy.

Her smile vanishes. "Yes sir," she calls back. "I'm so sorry to have disturbed you."

"Don't mind him. He's full of negative energy." I speak loudly enough for Zar to hear. "The gift basket looks lovely."

She gives me a final quick nod as though afraid to say anything else, and hurries away.

"Did you need to be rude?" I ask Zar as I carry the gift basket in.

"Apparently so," he mutters, focused on a sheath of papers covered with graphs and charts.

"She must think you're still angry about the room mix-up."

He turns a page. "I didn't ask for a gift basket."

"Someone made a mistake. She's clearly trying to make up for it."

Sighing, he tears his gaze from his graphs to look at me. "All I ask is that she does her job. Nothing more, nothing less."

"You could be more polite."

"I thank people who do their jobs correctly. More importantly, I pay them, and I tip well."

"As usual, my quote of the day was perfect for today," I mutter.

"Your quote of the day?"

"Every morning, I pick a card from my pack of motivational quotes. Today I pulled a card that said, *Kindness costs nothing but means everything.*"

I lift my eyebrows, daring him to respond.

In return, he gives me his number two frown of pure puzzlement. "Why?"

"Why do I choose a motivational quote? So I can think about it during the day."

"Again, I ask why."

"For self-improvement."

"I also have a quote of the day," he says. "You want to hear it?"

Scrunching my face, I squint at him. "I'm going to regret saying yes, aren't I?"

"Reading quotes for self-improvement is the same kind of logic as putting a treadmill in your closet and expecting to stay fit."

"Then what do you do to improve yourself?"

His lips twitch up as he returns his gaze to his papers. "Who says there's room for improvement?"

CHAPTER 18

Balthazar

That night, Scarlet and I dine together in the restaurant before we go back to our room to turn in. As Scarlet walks through the living room and into our bedroom, she lets out a squeal of delight. "Hey! We have chocolates."

When I follow, I see someone has turned down our bed and left chocolates on our pillows. Scarlet pounces on them, eating hers with relish, then devouring mine when I tell her I don't want it.

"Free chocolates taste the best." She licks her fingers.

Come to think of it, I'm pretty sure she's already eaten all the chocolates that were in the gift basket.

"What's this?" I lift an envelope from the bed that has my name on it and open it to find gift vouchers for the resort's health spa. "Another gift from the hotel manager." I hand the vouchers to Scarlet. "Hopefully the last one."

"Try being nicer and telling her you're okay with the room mix-up."

"Reward her incompetence?"

"If you keep being rude, she'll keep sending gifts." I make a sound of disbelief, and she says, "Mark my words," in a tone so dire, it makes me smile.

Scarlet grabs some personal items, then heads into the bathroom. "I'm going to shower and change into my pajamas," she says as she shuts the door.

Pajamas? Do I have any of those?

If not, I'm going to need some.

I message Melissa, then sit at the small table in the bedroom where I stacked my financial reports. But a moment later, I hear the shower start up, and suddenly I'm picturing Scarlet getting undressed and into the shower. She's probably standing under the water with her face lifted to the jet, bare limbs wet and slippery.

Now I have a boner.

Kicking off my shoes, I get on the bed and tug the bedcovers loosely over my lower half to hide it. I stuff some pillows behind me to lean back on. Then I lie in a heightened state of awareness, listening to the water run and indulging in images of Scarlet's wet, naked body. Soap bubbles sliding down her stomach and clinging to her legs. Her long curls damp on her back. Water gliding over her breasts and between her thighs.

I want to jerk off. But I put both hands behind my head, forcing them to behave. I'll wait until it's my turn in the bathroom before I indulge.

The shower cuts off, and a few minutes later, Scarlet emerges wearing bright pajamas. They're red and silk. They make a swishing sound as she walks, gliding around her limbs. They're baggy, and maybe they aren't supposed to be sexy, but I harden even more.

She stops, raising her eyebrows. "What's wrong? Why are you staring at me?"

I force some moisture into my dry throat. "I'm trying to make out the design printed on your pajamas. It looks like an animal."

"They're dragons. They have wings, see?" She holds out an arm to give me a better look at the creatures printed on the fabric, making it swish again.

My cock jerks in response, like Pavlov's dog.

"Is that what you always wear to bed?" I ask.

She makes an indignant sound. "What's wrong with these pajamas? Your personal shopper didn't buy them, if that's what you're asking. But you can't complain, seeing as I didn't expect to be wearing them in front of you."

"Dragons." I give my head a shake as though dragon pajamas are ridiculous. But what's actually ridiculous is how sexy they are, especially considering the silky fabric covers so much of her body.

It's absurd. Who gets turned on by dragon pajamas?

"Get into bed," I order.

"Sheesh! So bossy." She slides in between the sheets, mercifully pulling them up to cover her pajamas. Still, I know she's wearing them. And my cock knows she's wearing them. I keep the blanket strategically positioned to hide my boner.

"Who doesn't like dragon pajamas?" she mutters with a grimace.

I roll over a little to face her. "Where did you find a pair of adult-sized pajamas that are clearly meant for children?"

She folds her arms over the sheets, pretending to pout. Her hair is loose, her curls wild. I like them that way, splayed over the white pillow. They're as unruly as she is.

"Don't worry, I'll try not to get any color on your side of the bed. I mean, you must be allergic to color, right? That's why you and your house are so black and white. Will you swell up if you touch something bright? Do my red pajamas make you itchy?"

Surprised, I frown at her. "My house isn't black and white." I try to picture it like a stranger would see it. Okay, maybe it has white walls and black furniture. But there's some color in there, isn't there?

"Are you kidding? When Melissa was showing me around, I thought it was exactly what watching TV must have been like in the olden days. And what's the deal with the dead tree branches you keep in vases instead of flowers?"

"My interior designer did those arrangements."

"Does she hate you?"

"I like them," I say, even though I've never given them a thought. They're just objects the designer installed that I've always ignored.

"Where are your pajamas?" she asks. "Are they black? Are they made from the tears of widows?"

I press my lips in a stern line. Mostly so I don't smile.

"I don't have pajamas," I retort.

Her eyes widen. "You don't have pajamas? What do you usually wear to bed?"

"I sleep naked."

Her cheeks flush red. "Oh," she says, in a tone that's far less certain than the one she was just using to tease me.

I like the idea I might have flustered her. Her gaze darts

over my reclined form, and I'm sure the pretty flush on her cheeks is because she's imagining me naked.

"I've never seen the point of wearing clothes in bed," I add with relish, tucking both hands behind my head again. Under the blanket, I have a rod of iron. Any harder and it'd rip right through the bedsheets.

She swallows, but quickly recovers her composure. By which I mean, she goes back into teasing mode.

"So you can't afford pajamas," she muses. "And you can't afford a second bed. Do you need a loan, Billionaire Bob? Or is this your not-so-subtle seduction technique?"

The sass is back in her tone, but the red from her cheeks is spreading to her ears. And her pupils are dilated as though she's as turned on by the sexually suggestive conversation as I am.

Dammit, we're straying into dangerous territory.

It's so enjoyable, I don't want to change the subject, and my cock sure as hell doesn't want me to. But I'm her employer. I have responsibilities.

"Actually, I've asked Melissa to have a pair of pajamas sent up." I force my gaze away from the delicious green of her eyes. Turning my focus to her nightstand, I nod at all her woo-woo paraphernalia. "Tell me, why did you bring so much stuff with you?"

"I like having my things here." She wrinkles her nose at me. "It might seem silly to you, but I never had much of anything growing up."

"Is that why you stole things?"

She gives a little shrug. "I was just brought up that way. But I had nothing at all in juvie, and not even a little bit of space that was my own. That was one of the things I hated most. Everything in there was public property. So now you know why I value my privacy." A defiant edge creeps into her voice. "And why I didn't want anyone going through my stuff."

Maybe she expects me to make fun of her confession about juvie. But the fact she was willing to share it with me is strangely touching and I'm not about to mock her for it.

"My childhood was the opposite. I had all the possessions I could ask for and a lot of privacy." I stop myself before I can admit everything I'm thinking, which is that I had far too much privacy seeing as my parents had mostly ignored me.

She rolls right over to face me, tucking her hand under her cheek. Now we're only a couple of feet from each other. I'm propped up on pillows, and she's lying flat, so I'm gazing down on her. But talking while we're both in bed feels strangely intimate.

"We're so different," I say softly. I wonder if that's why she fascinates me so much.

"But we're the same in a lot of ways," she says.

"How are we the same?"

"Neither of us had the best family, and instead of messing us up, it made us stronger."

My investigator gave me a summary of her history. Her father is a long-time criminal, in and out of prison. Her mother is a drifter, with a long list of addresses.

"Tell me more about your family," I ask, wanting to hear about it from her perspective. "What was your mother like?"

"She went from boyfriend to boyfriend. They used to walk all over her, making her miserable, and they were all as horrible as each other. But she never wanted to hear a word against them."

"You moved around with her?"

"Mostly, I lived with my dad. He used to like it when I rolled his joints and laughed at his jokes." She smiles a little, but not in a fond way, more like she's trying to soften the effect of what she's telling me. "He took me with him when he went out robbing houses. I could wriggle in through the smallest windows, then let him in the door."

"Father of the year."

I make a mental note to be sure and let her father know what I think of him if I ever get to meet him. It pisses me off that he didn't take better care of his daughter, but at least this conversation is wilting my boner.

"Every time Dad went to prison, I had to move in with Mom." The twist of her mouth tells me how much she'd hated that.

"Until you got arrested as well," I say.

She nods. "And hello juvie."

"Considering your early life, you seem well-adjusted."

This time, her smile is real. "That's because I met my real family in juvie. Including the lawyer who got me out of there."

"You're close to your lawyer? I can't imagine being friendly with any of mine."

"Aunt Alejandra is the best. I love her so much." Her expression is so soft and warm, it makes my chest ache. I'm certain that nobody, not even Gaby, has ever looked like that when talking about me.

"Your lawyer is your aunt?" I'm careful not to let my voice reflect anything but mild curiosity. Certainly not envy.

"We're not actually related, but that's what we all call her. She got us out of juvie early. Kayla and Jamie had homes to go to, so it was easier for the courts to release them. But seeing as Dad was in prison and Mom had disappeared, I would have had to stay where I was or go into the foster system. Aunt Alejandra became my temporary guardian so they'd let me go, and I got to move in with her."

"That was good of her."

"I was lucky. I call her my aunt, but she's like a mother. Better than a mother. Now I have people I can count on." She lifts her eyebrows. "What about you? Who do you count on?"

"Gaby," I say.

"That's all?" Her eyebrows drop, creasing together as though she feels sorry for me.

"I have enough money to solve my own problems. I don't need anyone else." I make my tone firm. Although I have a handful of good friends, and dozens of acquaintances, I'd never think of asking them for anything. Far better to be self-sufficient.

"Everyone needs family." Her tone is gentle.

"You need family. I have employees."

"But you're mean to your employees!"

"I'm not mean."

"Rude, then."

"I'm not actually rude. My requests are never unreasonable. I pay them well and give generous benefits."

"You make everyone call you Mr. Anders. And you're not friendly. Just ask the hotel manager."

A memory of how much I once cried over my old nanny flashes though my mind, and I shift uncomfortably on the pillows. "I'm not friendly because I don't want to blur any lines. My employees aren't my friends. It's better for everyone if I don't treat them that way."

Her face softens, even as her perceptive gaze seem to grow sharper. "Why do you think that? Did someone hurt you?"

"Of course not." I push thoughts of Helena firmly from my head. "How could an employee hurt me? They're paid to do a job, and I expect nothing more or less. Keeping things formal works for everyone."

I could tell her about Helena, how I'd come to think of her as a mother. But it was foolish of me, and now I'm smarter than that... except when it comes to Scarlet. Somehow, she makes me want to break every one of my rules.

There's a knock on the door and then a male voice calls, "Concierge, Mr. Anders, with your pajamas."

Scarlet starts to get up, but I tell her to stay where she is and answer the door myself. She wrinkles her nose at me when I come back into the bedroom carrying some plain charcoal pajamas.

"Are those brand new?"

I furrow my brow. "What other option is there? They don't sell used pajamas, do they?"

"Ever heard of thrift shops, Bob?"

"No," I say honestly, going into the bathroom to change.

While I'm in there, I take the time to jerk off, picturing Scarlet as I fist my greedy cock.

I imagine unbuttoning her red pajama top and pulling down her silky pants, leaving them around her thighs. Then I'd turn her away from me, bending her over the sink so we're watching ourselves in the mirror. I'd bury myself deep inside her wet pussy, with one of my hands entwined in those wild curls of hers, and the other reaching around to play with her nipple.

Her green eyes would blaze at me in the mirror, her full lips forming the 'o' shape they make when she's surprised.

Almost as soon as the image is in my mind, I come fast and hard, gritting my teeth so I don't make a sound.

When I eventually emerge from the bathroom, Scarlet's sitting up in bed, writing in a notebook with pillows tucked behind her. She raises her eyebrows as she looks me over from head to toe.

"Those are sensible pajamas."

I glance down. The loose pants are dark gray, with a snug, matching t-shirt. "Melissa's a sensible woman. She knows not to send up clothes that require the use of sunglasses."

Scarlet adjusts the position of her notebook on her knees, and I admire the way her silky pajamas drape over her breasts. She's not wearing a bra, and the fabric catches on her nipples. Whenever she moves, I hear the rustle of silk. So I don't take too long in getting into my side of the bed. Even after jerking off, I'm in danger of getting hard again. I might be new to wearing pajamas, but I can already tell they're not ideal for hiding boners.

"I'm making a list of murder suspects." She bites the end of her pen. "You should show me the death threats you got."

Oh yes. Our suspects.

Instead of thinking so much about Scarlet, I should be focusing on the assassin who's out to kill me.

"We don't need to worry about those death threats," I say.

"They're not serious threats. My investigator already ruled them out."

"Are you sure?"

"Certain. He traced them to patients affected by Selexitron. They saw on the news that I inherited my father's share of Anders Pharmaceuticals, and they're desperate for someone to acknowledge the damage the drug has done. The death threats were a cry for help. Governor Salmanca's new charitable foundation will prioritize their needs."

She shoots me a smile warm enough to make me want to smile back. "That means we can cross them off the suspect list?"

I nod. "The board members have the clearest motives for stabbing me."

"But there are plenty of other reasons to want to kill you. SO many reasons." Her smile turns into a wicked, lopsided grin.

I respond with a disapproving frown, one of my most serious ones. This particular one has made grown men cry. But apparently, Scarlet is the one person in the world who's immune.

"Besides the board members, everyone mentioned in your father's papers has a motive, right?" She taps her pen against her cheek.

"It's a big box of dirty secrets. If you're making a list of all those people, you're going to need a bigger notebook." I lie down on my side of the bed.

"What if we just add the people with the worst secrets?"

"Bigger notebook," I repeat.

"So it's hopeless trying to narrow down a suspect?

Everyone wants to kill you?" She lets out a frustrated huff. "We need to find a way to trim down the list."

Lying on my back, I put my hands behind my head, saying nothing. The only way to find the assassin is to tempt them into trying to kill me again.

Scarlet puts the notebook on her nightstand, moving aside her magic rocks, deck of platitude cards, and stinky candle to make room for it. Then she takes the pillows out from behind her so she can stretch out. She switches off the lamp that's beside her and rolls onto her side, facing me. Her hair fans out so appealingly over the pillow, I want to bury my hands in it.

It's a lot more difficult than I expected to have her beside me in bed and not to reach for her. So I stay on my back and turn my face up to the ceiling. Maybe not looking at her will help.

"Well," she says after a moment. "Goodnight."

"Goodnight." Switching off my own light, I lie in the darkness and listen to her breathe.

It's too dark to see her, but she's very close and I can picture her clearly. I can imagine how her silky red pajamas would feel under my hands, how she'd gasp as I popped the buttons of her top and slipped my fingers under the waistband of her pants. I can imagine kissing the soft skin of her throat and sliding those ridiculous silk pajamas all the way off her.

Knowing her, she'd have something smart to say about it. Some teasing comment to make me laugh. And I'd act stern even though I'd like it.

Then I'd spread her legs and sink my fingers into her while I teased her nipples with my tongue. Soon, all she'd be able to do would be to moan my name. I'd torment her clit until she begged me to let her come. When I finally buried myself balls-deep inside her, it would be immensely damn satisfying to feel her clench around my cock with her shuddering climax.

I'd make her come so loud and so hard, she'd be hoarse for weeks.

My fantasy is so vivid, I have to bite back a groan of pure torment. Sliding my hand silently into my pajama pants, I fist my hard cock. I can't jerk off again, can't even risk stroking myself with Scarlet lying next to me. I can only squeeze its unrelenting iron.

I'm burning up. All I want is to touch her.

But I can't let myself touch her.

Fuck.

What made me think sharing a bed was in any way a good idea?

This is torture, plain and simple.

I've never in my life been so conflicted, and I sure as hell don't like it.

CHAPTER 19

Scarlet

When I wake the next morning, Zar isn't in bed with me. There's nothing next to me but a wide expanse of cold sheets. Probably a good thing, seeing as I was afraid I'd snuggle into him in my sleep and wake up realizing I was trying to big-spoon him.

Rolling over, I see Zar sitting at the small desk in the corner. He's wearing jeans and a t-shirt, and he's leafing through some documents. On the floor beside him is a big box that's full of more papers. The box isn't one I've seen before.

My heart speeds up. He must be looking through the treasure-trove of his father's secrets. Aunt Alejandra's photographs could be in that box.

Zar is wearing his frown of concentration. It's the same focused, intense expression I saw when I broke into his house. He wears it so well, I just want to lie still and stare at him.

Then he glances up at me, catching me staring.

"Morning," I say with a yawn, pretending I only just woke up. "Sleep well?"

He grunts something noncommittal. "You?"

"Very well," I lie. Truth is, with him next to me, it took me forever to get to sleep. I was edgy and restless... and extremely horny. When I finally got to sleep, I had sex dreams, but not satisfying ones. They were frustrating. I was stark naked, chasing Balthazar through a series of long, damp tunnels. And I couldn't catch him, no matter how hard I tried.

I pull myself out of bed and stretch. He watches me with his brow even more furrowed and his eyes glittering, demonstrating that his serious look of concentration is just as sexy when it's focused on me.

"What you doing?" I ask.

His heated gaze stays on me for a moment, taking me in. Then it drags back to his papers.

"Looking for secrets bad enough that they're worth killing for." His tone has an edge to it. As though by standing in front of him in my pajamas, I'm doing something wrong.

"Find any?" I ask.

He taps a stack of papers at the end of the desk. "A lot. And Dad's investigator was thorough. Each report has a lot of detail."

"If I help, we can get through it quicker."

"Get dressed," he orders sternly. "Don't stand around like that."

My mouth goes dry thanks to the sexy number six frown he angles at me. And I immediately want to argue. An expression that demands obedience is my own personal catnip, and I'd be the kind of cat who smiles at you as she knocks everything off your shelf.

"Tell me the truth, Zar, do you have a grudge against dragons?" Letting out a mock gasp, I widen my eyes. "Was it a dragon that carried away your good humor?"

He grunts, not taking the bait. "I want to have more meetings today."

"Who else do you want to talk to?" Moving closer to the table, I crane my neck to look at the papers he's scattered.

"Uncle Earnest, for starters." He taps the stack of serious secrets. "He's made a string of bad investments, and his son has an opioid addiction."

"You really think that's worth killing for?"

"Earnest was also making regular payments to my father. A lot of people were, but Earnest has debts, and his son is in an expensive rehab facility."

"Does Earnest seem capable of murder?" I hitch up my pajama top so I can scratch an itch near my waist.

He watches my hand move on my bare skin, a muscle clenching in his jaw. "Anyone would be capable of murder if their victim was still in her pajamas instead of wearing clothes, when he'd already asked her twice to get dressed."

"Sheesh." Giving an exaggerated roll of my eyes, I let my top drop back into place. "Let the dragons live in peace, Bob. I thought I'd call Jamie and Kayla, then hit the gym for a workout before I take a shower."

"Then I'll shower now so you have privacy." He stands up and stalks into the bathroom, his gait stiff.

I blink at his rapid exit, surprised at how sudden it was. I hadn't expected him to give in so easily. Pulling myself together, I throw on my workout clothes in record time while

I have the bedroom to myself, and grab a rolled-up towel from the closet to take to the gym. I hear the shower go on in the bathroom as I'm dialing Jamie's number.

"Hey," I say quietly. "It's me."

"How's your weekend with the devil?" she asks.

I look at the large box full of papers. Zar left it on the floor. By leaving his father's box of secrets in plain view, he's clearly indicating a level of trust in me.

Now I'm about to break that trust.

"He's not the devil," I say. "He actually seems like a good guy."

"If he's so great, why did he keep Aunt Alejandra's photos?" demands Jamie.

"I don't know," I whisper. "But there must be a good reason."

I wish I could ask him about it, but if I do, I'll have to come clean about who I am and why I'm really here. And Zar doesn't seem like someone who'd take betrayal well.

"Why are you whispering?" Jamie asks.

"Balthazar is in the shower."

"You've snuck into his room while he's taking a shower?"

"I didn't need to. We're sharing a room."

"You're *what*?" Her voice rises so high, I wince.

"Long story. I'll tell you about it later." I cross to the box. "I'll see if I can find the photos."

"I need to know why you're sharing a room. Did he force you? Has he made you his prisoner? Should we launch a rescue mission?"

Ignoring her, I crouch and rifle quickly through the box. Zar has pulled out dozens of bank statements with balances that look like phone numbers, but the box is still overflowing with meeting summaries, handwritten receipts, reports from private investigators, inventory reports, and all kinds of other information.

At the bottom of the box is a large envelope that's stuffed so full, it's at least an inch thick. And when I pull it out to open it, I know I've hit pay dirt.

"Holy crap," I whisper. "There are dozens of pictures in here. Maybe *hundreds*."

"Any of Aunt Alejandra?" Jamie asks.

"Not so far." Shuddering, I flick through them. "There's a theme. Zar's father is fully dressed with naked women groveling at his feet. They're degrading."

"And Balthazar wanted to publish them? He *is* the devil. And he must have a way of brainwashing women to like him. First Melissa, now you."

"No photos of Aunt Alejandra yet." I'm trying to look through the ones at the bottom, but they're so old, they're clumping together. "Zar hasn't even looked at these photos." I peel one from another.

"How can you tell?"

"They're sticky with age. You know how old pictures can get? But now I'm pulling them apart, they're staying that way. They can't have been touched for months. Maybe years." I'm so relieved to know Zar can't have looked through them, I feel light. He's the opposite of his father, and I'm about to say as much when I find a photo of a woman who looks familiar. "Wait," I say. "Who's this?"

"Who? What did you find?"

I frown at the woman in the photo, then realize where I've seen her before. She's the short, pretty, red-haired woman who was with Zar in the photo I found in his bedroom. He was a child in that picture, while she looked to be in her early twenties, and they were smiling at each other.

This photo is very different from the one in Zar's bedroom. In this photo, she's naked, on her knees, her thighs spread and her hands tied. Blythe Anders is standing behind her, yanking her head back by her hair. The picture would be unpleasant enough without the smug look on his face. But one glance at his expression is enough to churn my stomach. He must have been a real narcissist to get off on taking photos like this. If I didn't dislike him enough before, now my hate burns with the power of the sun.

I hear the shower turn off.

That means I might only have a minute or two before Zar comes out of the bathroom.

"Call you back later," I hiss into the phone. Without waiting for Jamie to answer, I disconnect the call and shove my phone into my pocket so both hands are free.

Dropping the redhead's photo onto the desk, I frantically search through the rest of the pictures. There are so many photos, it's not a fun task. Zar's father must have been a sex-addicted, power-tripping, misogynistic asshole. If he weren't already dead, I'd want to kill him.

I'm about to give up when I finally I see what I'm looking for. Aunt Alejandra looks so startlingly young and beautiful that it takes me a moment to realize it's her. There are three photos of her, each worse than the next.

"Holy crap," I mutter.

Pulling out the photos, I shove the rest of the pictures back into the envelope and push it back into the bottom of the box. I grab the redhead's photo as well, and stuff the four photos I've stolen inside the rolled-up towel I'm going to take to the gym.

I've only just stashed the towel next to my nightstand when the bathroom door opens.

Zar comes out of the bathroom shirtless, wearing only a pair of jeans slung low enough on his hips to show off the delicious 'v' lines of muscle that arrow into his pants. He's fastened a clean dressing over his wound.

My heart is already racing too fast, and the sight of his bare torso almost causes a medical emergency. Though I've seen him bare-chested before, I can't seem to get used to how gorgeous he is when he's half-naked.

His waist is narrow, and his stomach muscles ripple like water over flat, shallow stones. The smattering of dark hair on his chest only accentuates the size of his pecs. A small trail of fine hair arrows down from his belly button, pointing to the bulge in his pants.

He's so gorgeous, he makes my head spin. He also makes my insides clench and highly pleasurable tingles start between my thighs.

He says something, but a buzzing has started in my ears. I drag my gaze away from his body in an attempt to focus on his lips, but my eyes keep dropping to admire the play of light over his abs. He has nice nipples. Dark pink and puckered. I've never seen a more inviting pair.

"Scarlet?" His voice abruptly cuts through the buzzing sound.

"Yes!" Blinking rapidly, I jerk my head away.

I need to snap out of it. As gorgeous as Zar might be, he's also the man I've just stolen from.

"Is something wrong?" he asks.

"Wrong? No. Nothing at all. What could be wrong?" Picking up one of my crystals from my nightstand, I concentrate on its cool weight in my hand. Amethyst for inner peace. I could definitely use some.

When I hear the sound of a drawer sliding open, I dare to take a peek. Zar tugs on a t-shirt. Thank goodness. Maybe now I can pull myself together.

He grabs a pair of socks, and I put down the crystal and choose a motivational card from my deck, hoping it might give me the inspiration I need to be able to stop thinking about how beautiful he is when he's shirtless.

"Is that your quote of the day?" asks Zar from behind me. He clearly remembers me telling him about it.

I hesitate, then turn to face him. "If I say yes, will you make fun of it?"

"Probably. Read it aloud." He tosses the rolled-up socks from one hand to the other, waiting. His eyes are glinting, and the sides of his mouth twitch up in anticipation.

Honestly, I'm looking forward to hearing his grumpy assessment. I love it when he's sarcastic, especially when he uses his bone-dry tone. Lord help me, but I find Billionaire Bob crazy sexy.

I clear my throat and read, "Life is ten percent what you make it and ninety percent how you take it."

Zar lets out a grunt of derision, his lips tugging higher. "That quote is a hundred percent pointless."

"Not as pointless as refusing to acknowledge the quote's wisdom. So I choose to take your opinion with the amount of disdain it deserves." I lift my nose in the air. "So much disdain. More than ninety percent of pure contempt."

"I give it one star." He moves closer.

"Oh yeah? Well, I give you no stars. Not a single star for you."

"Is that right?" He stops right in front of me, and he smells so good. Soap and shaving cream and expensive cologne. "What happened to that other corny quote about kindness?"

"That wasn't today's quote, so I don't need to be kind today. Kindness is off the menu."

Giving a little laugh, he sits on the bed to pull his socks and shoes on.

I step back, able to breathe again now there's more distance between us. "You don't like motivational quotes. What do you like?"

"If I were writing motivational quotes—which I wouldn't —but if I did, they'd be a lot better than the ones in your deck."

"Fine. Tell me one of yours."

"Okay." He finishes with his shoes and sits upright, thinking. His hair is damp and messy, like he just rubbed it briskly with the towel and called it good. His face is freshly shaven, his square jaw smooth. Truth is, he's just gorgeous with clothes on as without them.

"Here are some words to live by," he says. "Trust nobody, expect nothing, and you'll never be disappointed."

I swallow. I just betrayed his trust and stole from him. If he knew, he'd be horribly disappointed.

I feel like pond scum, but I force a laugh, trying to act normal. "Move over, Oprah! There's a new guru in town."

He tilts his head. "Well, am I wrong?"

I glance at the rolled-up towel that's hiding the photos.

The evidence of my betrayal is right there beside my nightstand.

"There are people I trust," I say. "Not many, but they earned it."

"Your inner circle. An exclusive club." Maybe he means to sound like he's teasing me, but there's a trace of something like wistfulness in his tone.

"Who's in your inner circle?"

He doesn't hesitate. "Gaby. My stepsister."

"And that's it?" I soften my tone. He doesn't realize how sad that sounds, but now I feel even worse. I know what it was like to have parents who didn't care and nobody I could count on. Everything changed for me when I found my real family.

"How many do I need?" he demands. "Enough to join hands and sing Kumbaya?"

"Enough to feel safe."

He gives me a smug smile, as though he just won the point. "Isn't that what I have you for?"

CHAPTER 20

Scarlet

"I'm going to the gym," I tell Zar, picking up my phone and the towel that has the stolen photos stashed inside it. "Back soon."

"Wait. Before you go, I have something for you." He riffles through the stack of papers on his desk that contain serious secrets, and extracts a page. Then he holds it out to me. "Here."

I put my phone and the towel down carefully on the bed, making sure the photos won't slip out before I take the paper that Zar offers. It's a report from a private investigator, dated several years ago, addressed to Zar's father. I skim it quickly, my heart rate kicking up when I see the name of the detention center I lived at when I was a teenager, and then Governor Salamanca's name.

When I get to the end, I read the entire report again slowly, taking in every word.

Once I'm done, I look at Zar. He's standing close, watching me with a half-smile.

I feel light-headed. Overwhelmed.

Everything Aunt Alejandra suspected is true. The proof is all laid out in slightly faded black type. There are payment dates and amounts. Even bank account numbers. The governor was earning a small fortune from stuffing as many vulnerable kids as possible into detention centers. Not just the center I was sent to, but others all over the state.

"Why are you giving me this?" My voice is hoarse.

"Because you were hurt by Salamanca. If you leak the report to the press, it'll destroy his career. If you give it to the FBI, they should be able to build a case to prosecute him. Or you could do both."

I stare back down at the report. "We've tried to find evidence for years."

"Now you have it."

There's a lump in my throat. What's worse than pond scum? Sludge? Sewerage? Whatever it is, that's me. I'm betraying the man who's just handed me something I've wanted for so long.

"Thank you," I whisper. "Really, Zar, this means so much to me. You have no idea." I throw my arms around him on impulse, pulling him in for a hug.

It's the wrong thing to do, absolutely nothing like hugging a friend. My body presses against the irresistible muscles I was dreaming about all night. My face collides with his shoulder and somehow ends up in the curve of his neck. Then I'm breathing in his delicious man smell with my arms around his waist and my lips a hairsbreadth from the soft-looking skin of his neck.

Danger.

All systems red.

Letting him go, I jump away. My face is suddenly burning. "I'm sorry, I shouldn't have hugged you without asking, but thank you. So much."

He clears his throat. "Weren't you going to the gym?" He sounds gruff. " Don't take too long. I have plans to blackmail, accuse, and offend the rest of the board today."

"Yes! Okay!" Pulling myself together, I grab my phone and the towel with the photos inside. "I'll be back soon."

"And this afternoon, I'm going to do some work in a private cabana next to the swimming pool," he says as I'm heading to the door.

I stop and turn, clutching the towel to my chest. "Why would you work in a cabana?"

"If I'm publicly accessible in a place everyone will see us, it might draw the murderer out."

I blink at him, shocked. "You want someone to try to stab you again?"

"If it'll help to identify them."

"You want to set yourself up as bait?" I shake my head. "No way. It's too dangerous."

"It's not your decision to make. Just don't be too long." His tone contains a stern note of finality, and he sits at his desk, dropping his gaze to his papers as though to dismiss me.

I leave and get into the elevator in a daze. But instead of going to the gym, I head to the hotel's huge, grand lobby. Hurrying to a far corner of the lobby where nobody will be able to overhear what I'm saying, I call Aunt Alejandra.

"Scarlet," she says, her voice as warm as always. "How are you?"

I can hear traffic noise, and she's puffing a little as though she's walking. She must be on her way to the Court of Appeals building to start work.

"Do you have a minute?" I ask.

"I always have time for you, mija," she says. "I'm due in court soon, but I can talk while I walk."

"I have evidence about what Governor Salamanca did," I blurt. "He's guilty. All our suspicions were right."

She makes a sound of shocked delight. "You have proof?"

"Undeniable proof. Everything we need to send him to prison for the rest of his life."

"That's wonderful news! Can you show me?"

"I'm in San Dante for the week, but I'll take pictures of the report and send them to you." I stop to draw in a deep breath. "And there's something else." I brace myself for her reaction. "I got your photos from Balthazar Anders, and I'm about to destroy them."

"What?" Her voice rises. "But how did you get them?"

"I'm doing some security work for Balthazar."

"And he gave them to you?"

I swallow. "Not exactly."

She's silent for a moment. Then she says, "You promised you wouldn't do anything reckless." Her tone makes me wince.

"I know, but I have the photos now, and I'm going to destroy them. You'll never have to worry about them again."

"Scarlet—"

I don't want her to tell me she's disappointed in me, or demand I give the photos back to Balthazar, so I cut over her, rushing to explain. "I'm sorry, tía, but it would have been awful if the photos were made public. After everything you've done for me, I couldn't stand the thought. I had to take the photos back because I love you so much."

"I love you too, mija." Her voice softens. "But I don't want you doing anything illegal. You're not that person anymore."

The rumble of cars going past cuts off, and I imagine she must have reached the building and gone inside.

"You know I wouldn't do anything to hurt anyone," I say. "But Balthazar shouldn't have had the pictures in the first place, and he should have given them to you when you asked."

"Stealing is never the right thing to do."

"I agree. Usually."

"Scarlet—"

"Ninety-nine percent of the time, I'm a law-abiding, responsible citizen. I don't do anything illegal anymore. I don't even forget to use my turn signal. But if someone threatens you, I can't just stand by and let you get hurt. And if you're about to suggest I give the photos back, I won't do it. I'm going to destroy them no matter what!"

She lets out a heavy sigh, sounding conflicted. "Legally, the photos belong to Mr. Anders."

"Morally, they belong to you."

"The law is important to me, Scarlet. It's been my entire career."

"It's important to me too. But in this case, I have to do what I think is right. I'm sorry, but you can't talk me out of this."

"Then there's not much I can do." Her tone softens even more. "Other than to admit I'll be relieved to have the photos gone. Thank you for wanting to help me, mija, even if you've used the wrong method."

"You're welcome."

Her voice gets stern again. "Please don't do anything else that you shouldn't. No more reckless behavior, okay?"

"Okay." I hesitate, but there's no easy way to find out what I want to know, so I plow straight into it. "Tía, may I ask you a question?"

"Of course."

"I was wondering what exactly Balthazar Anders said in his email when you asked him for the photos back? Would you mind forwarding it to me?"

"Why are you asking?"

"Well, I'm working for him, and he doesn't seem like such a bad guy. Which is confusing because threatening to release your photos is such an awful thing to do. So I was wondering how he phrased it, and I thought maybe if I could read the email..."

"I'll send it to you if you promise to obey the law from now on."

"Of course. I promise not to do anything illegal for the rest of my life, except if someone I love needs me to do it."

"Scarlet!" She gives a half-laugh, half-sigh.

"And I'll delete the email after I read it," I add.

She promises to send it to me when she gets time. After we say goodbye, I head to the gym. There's a woman's restroom connected to it, and I shut myself into one of the stalls. Then I rip up the photos of Aunt Alejandra and flush them down the toilet. It's a relief to watch them disappear.

I'm tempted to do the same with the photo of the redhaired woman, because it's truly awful, a lot worse than my aunts'. But I want to know who she is, so I don't. Instead I stash that photo more securely inside my rolled-up towel. I can work out without using the towel, and hide the photo in my suitcase when I get back to the room, at least until I figure out why Zar has a picture of the woman on his bookcase in his bedroom.

When I get inside the gym, there are a few people there working out, and I recognize some of Zar's family members. Thankfully, Uncle Orson isn't there, but Orson's young, tiny wife is on an exercise bike. She's wearing ear buds and flicking through a glossy magazine that's balanced on the handlebars while she pedals. Orson must have told her what Balthazar said about the director payouts, because when she looks up and sees me, she gives me such a vicious, furious glare, I flinch. She might be pint-sized, but there's a whole lot of hate in her eyes.

Ignoring her, I stride to the other end of the gym. On my way, I pass Loretta, who's in front of the mirrors, doing squats. A handsome trainer is with her, handing her some weights and making sure she's doing it right. Unlike Orson's wife, she smiles, so I give her a wave.

"Looking good," I say to be friendly. "Great form."

"Thanks." She wrinkles her nose at the big man beside her. "This is Sergio. He's my dog nanny, but multi-talented. Pookie's sleeping so we're slipping in a workout."

I lift my eyebrows. She mentioned her dog nanny was highly skilled. And in his tight shorts, I can see why she was so complimentary.

"You want to borrow him?" Loretta asks. "I could use a break."

"No, thanks. I don't need him." I keep walking to the

weights rack to load myself up, determined to work out so hard, even Jamie would be impressed. And not just because I need to stay strong to protect Zar, but also because a tough workout might help with my sexual frustration.

Though I have to admit, I'm not too hopeful in that regard.

If we go swimming at the cabana this afternoon, there's sure to be swimsuits and bare flesh. Not to mention danger, which everyone knows is a potent aphrodisiac.

There probably aren't enough weights in the world to dampen my attraction to Zar, but considering I just stole and destroyed something that was technically his property, I'm going to do my very best.

CHAPTER 21

Balthazar

When Scarlet and I finally get to the restaurant for a late breakfast, we have an even angrier meeting with Aunt Maude than I had with Uncle Orson.

Aunt Maude is a severe woman, with pinched lips and a blunt hairstyle that's so firmly fixed in place, the breeze can't lift a single strand. She's over sixty but her skin is aggressively tight, as though she told her plastic surgeon to pull it up extra hard. Her white, frilly blouse has such a high neck that it cradles her chin.

Thanks to the reports done by my father's investigator, I know how much her two children hate her. Both are board members, but neither are here. And if even half of what the investigator wrote was true, they're unlikely to turn up.

When I tell her about my plans, and that I have proof of the physical and mental abuse she's heaped on her offspring, she lunges up with surprising speed and tries to slap me.

Fortunately, Scarlet leaps out of her seat with even more surprising speed, catching her hand before it hits my face.

Aunt Maude swears at me so violently, spittle flies from her lipsticked mouth, then she strides away with her heeled shoes banging like gunshots on the restaurant's tiled floor.

Afterward, Scarlet looks unhappy, chewing her lip and not being her usual talkative self, even when I try to lighten her mood. As we get in the elevator to go back up to our suite, she turns to me and says, "Please ask your security team to come to the hotel."

"Why?"

"Because I almost didn't catch your aunt's hand when she took a swing at you." Her body is rigid, and she stares straight ahead at the elevator doors. "She got too close. If I'd been any slower, you'd have a shiner right now."

"What are you talking about? I've never seen anyone move as fast as you. That was a Mr. Miyagi stunt."

"You've seen *The Karate Kid*?" She doesn't smile, which seems all wrong. Her lips are designed for smiling. She should look delighted that I know who Mr. Miyagi is.

"You snatched Aunt Maude's hand out of mid-air," I point out.

"There should be more protection agents here. What if she'd grabbed a knife?"

"One of the butter knives from the table? They'd barely leave a scratch."

"Your security manager's name is Alan, right? Let me get him out here. He can pretend to be a normal guest, and he'll help to keep you safe."

"You're doing just fine on your own."

She pushes back her hair, fisting her hand in her curls. "Only it's clear that I'm not. Part of the job is recognizing vulnerabilities, and I'm the weak link. What if you get stabbed again? Or shot?"

"If I agree, will it make you feel better?"

"A lot better."

"Then go ahead and call Alan."

Some of the tension eases from her body. She drops her hand and gives me a questioning look. "Really?"

"I don't think I need anyone else, but you're the expert. Fill the hotel with as many security guards as you want. Just make sure they keep their distance."

She lets out a loud breath, her shoulders sagging. "Thank you."

I shrug. "Aunt Maude is a bitch."

"Holy crap, she's SUCH a bitch!"

"One of my least favorite family members."

The elevator doors open. "She's Bitchy McBitchface," says Scarlet, stepping out. "From Bitchville, in Bitch City, capital of Bitchonia."

"She travelled here on the Bitch Express," I contribute, surprising myself. Maybe I shouldn't encourage her silliness, but I'm glad to see her smile back where it belongs.

Scarlet looks delighted I've joined in. "Her seat was in the bitch-class carriage." She laughs as we go into our suite, and it's a bright, bubbling sound. It's contagious. When she's laughing, I feel lighter.

She turns to me once we're inside, her smile still lighting her face. "What's next, boss?"

"I'll do a little work, then we'll head down to the cabana."

She looks alarmed. "You can't be bait before I have backup!"

"Then call Melissa and ask Alan to come here."

She tugs out her phone, and I head to the desk in our room. As I sit down and start looking through my papers, I can hear the murmur of her voice from the living room, though I can't make out what she's saying. It's a nice sound. There's something musical about the way she speaks. It's pleasant to work to.

I lose myself in my data for a while, and by the time Scarlet and I have a late lunch, Alan has arrived and I'm ready to set my plan in motion.

There's a row of private cabanas beside the swimming pool's longest side, and ours is the one on the end that's farthest from the restaurant and other public areas. The cabana is a tall, grand hut with a high vaulted ceiling. It's enclosed on three sides, with the front open to the pool area. Inside it are some armchairs and a coffee table designed to hold drinks, though I'm going to use it for the large stack of papers I take with me to read through. A large fan in the ceiling circles lazily to keep the inside cool.

Because of the angle of the cabana's opening, nobody can see into it. Which makes it both publicly accessible, and private. The perfect spot to encourage a would-be assassin to take another shot.

Alan and Scarlet have agreed he should stick close to the pool area, blending in with the other hotel guests like an undercover spy. He's far enough away not to be suspicious, but close enough to watch for anyone approaching our cabana.

"This is so nice!" exclaims Scarlet as she puts her large

shoulder-bag down, looking around the cabana. She has her curly hair tied back in a ponytail, and she's wearing a mid-thigh-length dress which hangs loosely from her shoulders in a straight line and shows off her shapely legs.

I sit on one of the armchairs and spread my papers out on the coffee table. I've already started going through them, sorting them into piles according to my level of interest in them.

"What's all that?" she asks, sinking into the chair next to me.

"Mostly updates from companies I've already invested in. And proposals from new companies that are looking for funding."

She wrinkles her forehead. "Are you seriously going to keep working when it's a beautiful, hot day, and we're sitting right next to a swimming pool?"

"Some of these companies are doing exciting things." I grab a proposal from the stack of companies I'm least likely to invest in, and hand it to her. "Look. This one's woo-woo. You'll probably like it."

She frowns at the proposal. "What do they do?"

"It's an online motivation hub. Their app gives you access to coaches, videos, music, cheesy motivational quotes, the works. All in one place."

"Ooo, I love that!"

"Shocker."

"Are you going to invest in them?"

I shake my head. "Not my thing. There are some companies here with artificial intelligence projects and that's the current big thing."

She's still scanning through the woo-woo proposal. "This

actually looks cool. And helping people adopt a positive mindset is important."

"So are advances in AI. It's growing fast, getting exponentially better."

"But as AI improves, the world starts changing more rapidly, right? Which means more people will go looking for ways to feel like they're on steady ground, mentally speaking. People like stability. And rapid change is only going to make them like it more."

I tilt my head to the side, considering her point. "That's true, I suppose."

"Everyone wants to invest in AI, but it's people who really matter. And when everything seems chaotic and unpredictable, people are willing to do whatever it takes to feel better." She gives me a serious look, handing the proposal back. "My entire childhood was chaos, so I know what I'm talking about."

"I'll think about it." I move the proposal to the pile of investments I'm interested in.

She stands up. "I'll get a better view of anyone approaching if I'm out there on the lounger." She points to one of two loungers positioned in the sun, mid-way between the cabana and the swimming pool.

I grunt. "You'd better be wearing sunscreen."

"I am. But will you do my back?" She takes some sunscreen out of her shoulder bag and hands it to me, then grabs her dress at the hem and pulls it up, over her head, and off.

Several things happen instantaneously. My jaw hits the floor. My pants shrink to a fraction of their size. All the moisture vanishes from my throat. And a sound vibrates in my ears that could be the singing of angels.

Scarlet is wearing a red bikini.

Her body is curvaceous, with the defined muscles I've spent the last few days admiring, only now they're on full display. And combined with the delicious heaviness of her bottom and breasts, it's no wonder angels have burst into song. In her high-cut bikini bottoms, her legs look longer than I could have imagined. And her skin is noticeably darker on her arms and legs, and lighter where her breasts spill out of the twin triangles of the bikini top.

She's breathtaking.

And my cock agrees, because now I have a boner that feels larger than some states. It's a good thing Scarlet immediately turns her back to me, lifting her ponytail high, or she could hardly fail to see it. And it takes me a moment to realize she's waiting for me to apply sunscreen to her back.

Getting to my feet, I squeeze sunscreen into my palm, then rub it into her silky skin. Touching her brings its own pleasure, and even though my hand stays around her shoulder blades, it does little to reduce the problem of my hard-on.

Although I take my time, I can only rub sunscreen on for a limited amount of time before it becomes awkward. So I concentrate on calming my body's reaction while I complete a very thorough application. Then I clear my throat.

"What's your tattoo?" My voice comes out raspy.

She glances down to the small, flying bird on her hip. It's just the outline of a bird, with an unusual design inside it.

"It started as a lock and key, a homemade tattoo I got in juvie." She gives a soft smile as though it's something she likes to remember and reaches down to trace the heart's rough edge with her finger. "We all gave ourselves the same tattoo in the same place, all the girls in our over-stuffed dorm. Mine's a little wonky." She moves her finger to the more professional looking tattoo around it. "After we got out, Kayla, Jamie, and I all got a bird tattooed around it to symbolize being free." She gives a little laugh. "We went to a proper parlor for that."

Staring at the appealing jut of her hip is threatening to destroy the tenuous control I have over my arousal, so I sit back down. "You're all done." I hand back the sunscreen.

She goes out to the sun lounger and lies on her stomach. Though she looks relaxed, she turns her head every few minutes, scanning for any approaching assassins. But the pool area is deserted apart from us. This is only one of the resort's swimming pools, and it's designated for adults only. Presumably the family pools are busier.

I read through some proposals, but I'm distracted by the sunbathing beauty outside and the exquisitely tempting curves of her ass. Eventually, I can't stand it any longer.

Standing up, I strip off my t-shirt. Before I came down to the pool, I removed the dressing covering my knife wound. The skin has knitted back together, and the stitches are inside the wound and will apparently dissolve on their own. It's been healing quickly.

I walk out of the cabana to where Scarlet is lying, and she sits up, looking questioningly at me.

Her gaze travels over my bare torso, so I flex my muscles accordingly. Her cheeks flush pink, and I have a sudden urge to laugh, mostly at myself. But I like that she's a little flustered. Especially seeing as the sight of her in a bikini was impressive enough to turn my brain into mush.

"I'm going for a swim," I say.

"Are you allowed to get your wound wet?"

"Stop fussing. It'll be fine."

She draws herself up to standing. "Not only am I'm not fussing now, I've never fussed in my life." With an indignant huff in her voice, she's even more magnificent. "But if the wound gets infected, I want the record to reflect that I protested, and you went ahead anyway."

"I won't deduct any Yelp stars if I get an infection and die."

Truth be told, I'm touched by her concern. I'm not used to anyone worrying about me. If I got sick at boarding school, I was told to stop complaining.

"You ask me to shoot assassins, but you're happy to risk your life in the pool. That's on you."

"Did you bring a weapon with you?" I ask curiously.

"Of course. It's in my bag." She nods at the large shoulder bag she left leaning at the entrance to the cabana.

"Are you coming for a swim?"

She glances at the water. It's inviting in the heat, with the sun reflecting off its rippled surface. Then she shakes her head. "I shouldn't."

"Why not?"

"I'm on duty."

"Maybe I can't remember how to swim. You should get in the pool with me in case I start to drown."

Her gaze slides back to the water. I can see how tempted she is.

"What will Alan think?" she asks.

"Who cares?"

She looks across the pool to where Alan is sitting. He's at the far end, in front of the restaurant, at a table with an umbrella. He's wearing shorts and a t-shirt and drinking a fruit juice.

"What kind of bodyguards let their clients swim alone?" I ask. "Two-star bodyguards, that's who. Alan would be shocked if you didn't go in with me."

She screws her nose up. "Promise not to get shot while we're in the pool?"

"Too many rules," I complain. "Don't get shot, don't die from an infection. Anything else?"

She grins at me, then takes two giant steps and dive bombs into the pool, hugging her knees to her chest. When she hits the water, big cold drops splatter all over me.

I dive in after her, cutting through the water with clean precision. I tug on one of her legs while she's underwater, then surface next to her.

She laughs and whoops like a teenager, splashing me in retaliation. Her face is alight with delight. Something tugs in my chest. What would it be like to be so carefree and light-hearted? Watching her unrestrained pleasure, I can almost feel that way myself.

All at once, I have an almost uncontrollable urge to pull her against me so I can lick the water from her lips. I want to capture her slippery limbs and run my hands through her wet hair, and kiss both of her closed eyelids, just to feel her long eyelashes flutter beneath my mouth.

Before I can do anything, Scarlet ducks underwater and swims along the bottom of the pool, not surfacing until she gets to the other end.

I admire her graceful movements while she's not looking, then force myself to lie back and float, looking up at the sky. The cold water feels great, but all I can think about is how her limbs would feel tangling with mine. When Scarlet moves to the side of the pool to rest, I do a few lengths, swimming fast, trying to shake the compulsion out of my head.

When I stop at the edge of the pool, Scarlet moves next to me. Her gaze is on a man coming around the edge of the pool, striding purposefully toward us. He's wearing a suit, so he's not intending to swim, and I don't recognize him.

"That man has a bulge in his pocket." Her tone is low and urgent. "Could be a weapon. Don't move. Don't get out of the pool. If I yell, duck underwater." As she's firing off orders, she's pulling herself out of the water. She motions with her hands to someone, and I turn to see Alan still sitting at the far end of the pool, farther away from us than the rapidly approaching man in the suit.

Alan jumps up and trots toward us. But he's too far away to get here in time.

Moving impressively fast, Scarlet dives into the cabana. Yanking a gun from her bag, she crouches behind the curtain.

The man in the suit comes straight to the side of the pool in front of me. He has no idea Scarlet has her gun trained on him from behind, or that Alan is hurrying into position. His hand goes to his pocket, and I see Scarlet tense. My heart beats faster. If she fires, I'll grab the man's ankle and drag him into the water with me. It's not what she'd want me to do, but it would mean he couldn't turn and fire back at her.

As the man tugs the object out of his pocket, I put my hands next to his foot, ready to snatch his ankle.

But the object in his hand isn't a gun. It's a digital device, a little larger than a phone.

"Would you like a drink, sir?" The man switches on the device. It's clearly some kind of electronic ordering system, and now that I look more closely, he has a name badge pinned to his lapel. Apparently, my waiter's name is Terry.

"We have a fine range of cocktails," Terry adds. "Today's special is a tropical mimosa."

It's probably a good thing Terry will never know how close he came to being shot as I yanked him into the swimming pool.

Behind him, Scarlet lowers her gun. She signals to Alan, telling him to go back to his table. My muscles have relaxed so much, the water is holding me up. I want to let out a laugh but manage to swallow the impulse.

"Sir?" repeats Terry.

"Come to think of it, I could murder one of your killer cocktails," I say, straight-faced. "Give me a Death In The Afternoon."

Terry frowns down at his device, then back at me. "I'm sorry, sir, it looks like we don't do that one."

Scarlet's cheeks are turning pink. She stuffs her gun back into her bag.

"Then I'll take a Revolver."

Another frown at his device, and a long pause while Terry searches the available options. "I can ask the bartender, but that's not on our menu either, sir. Um. What's in it?"

"Never mind. Make it a Bloody Mary." I raise my

eyebrows at Scarlet. "Want one? Or would you prefer a Blood Orange Martini?"

Scarlet levels a highly impressive glare my way. If looks could kill, the assassin's job would be done for him.

And I have a such an overwhelming desire to kiss the stern, sexy line of her mouth, I'm no longer sure how long I'm going to be able to hold myself back.

CHAPTER 22

Scarlet

I spend another night having weird dreams about my high levels of sexual frustration, and wake up glad that I didn't put the moves on Zar in my sleep.

He's already up, as usual, and I suggest he showers first. While he's in the bathroom, I sit up in bed with my phone and check my email.

Aunt Alejandra has forwarded me the message he sent her.

Feeling inexplicably nervous, I open it.

The email is brief and impersonal. It didn't come from Zar's email address, but from a lawyer.

Be advised that all items received from the Anders' estate are solely the property of Mr. Anders. Any information, data, notes or images may be disclosed to any person or authority at the sole discretion of Mr. Anders, including but not limited to being released for public scrutiny. No requests for confidentiality or compensation will be entertained. Mr. Anders may choose to

respond further to your request in due course, however no further
correspondence will be entered into unless initiated by him.

I read it three times with relief slowly washing over me. It had to have been written by the lawyer, not Balthazar himself. He inherited stacks of private papers from his father with information about a wide range of people. Maybe he was getting all kinds of requests from people afraid their secrets might be in there. After all, it looks like the kind of email he might send to any of them. Vaguely threatening, but mostly ass-covering.

My verdict? Balthazar isn't a monster, and he doesn't have an evil twin.

He's stern, cautious, reserved, and protective. Flawed, like we all are. But also incredibly kind and generous. His heart is pure.

No matter what the email says, he wouldn't have released Aunt Alejandra's photos to the public. That's not who he is. I'm relieved the photos are gone, but I'm also glad I can let go of the idea he did something awful.

"Everything okay?" Zar asks.

Jerking my face up, I swipe to close my email. "Fine. I didn't notice you'd come out of the bathroom."

And man, how could I not have noticed? Not only has a knee-weakening scent of cologne drifted out with him, but he always looks especially gorgeous with his hair freshly washed and towel dried, so it's messy rather than perfect.

At least he's fully dressed, shirt and all. There's no way I wouldn't have noticed him if he wasn't.

"You were engrossed." He crosses to his side of the bed.

"I was reading an email."

A wave of guilt washes over me and I feel my face

heating. Luckily, he's sitting down to put his shoes on rather than looking at me.

I'm here on false pretenses. I've already resolved to confess the truth to Melissa and apologize for what I did to her. But Zar's less likely to forgive my betrayal. From his brief mentions of his childhood, I can tell he's been hurt. And like me, he has trust issues.

I'd find my actions hard to forgive, so will I be asking the impossible from him?

My heart aches at the thought.

Truth is, I feel close to Zar. There's a connection between us. Something special. And I hate the thought of hurting him. The idea that he might never want to see or talk to me again is hard to stomach, and I hope it doesn't come to that. But once Zar is safely back in LA, and the assassin has been caught, I'll have no choice but to come clean with him.

And I need to accept I might lose him.

"Are you getting up?" he asks.

"Hmm." I try not to sound despondent.

His forehead crinkles with a number two frown. "You're sure everything's okay?"

"Yes." I drag myself up, shaking my head to clear it. "Sorry. I'll be ready for breakfast in ten."

We eat breakfast in the restaurant and after enjoying the buffet, Zar sees Earnest, his uncle with the bad investments and addicted son. We move to his table to talk to him. Then we speak to his other aunt. These meetings go pretty much the same as when he spoke to his Uncle Orson and Aunt Maude. His family is awful.

Watching his aunt jump up from the table and storm out of the restaurant, I meet Zar's eyes. An entire wordless conversation passes between us as we silently share our disgust at how horrible she is.

Mind you, my blood relatives aren't any better than Zar's, seeing as Dad's still got several years to serve on his latest sentence, and Mom vanished without a word while I was in juvie. If it were a competition, we'd probably have to share the worst birth-family award.

The mystery is how Zar became such a thoughtful, moral person when he was surrounded by selfish jerks when he was growing up. Maybe his stepsister had something to do with it, seeing as she's the one family member he likes. If so, she must be an amazing person.

"So what's your plan for the rest of the day?" I ask, leaning back in my chair. "Do you want to hang out in plain sight again, tempting the murderer to attack?"

He pushes his aunt's half-empty coffee cup further away from him. "That would be okay with you?"

"I don't love the idea that you're putting yourself in danger. But if I can stick close to you, and Alan backs me up, I'll go along with it."

His eyes stay on me, as though he's studying me. I don't mind his gaze. Truthfully, I like having his attention. He's a gorgeous man doing important things, and it's flattering when he puts his focus on me.

Besides, I like studying him right back.

He has such a long thin nose, narrow eyes, and sharp cheekbones, he looks severe when he frowns. But the crease between his eyes is mostly smoothed out now. And there's such vibrant awareness in his eyes that if I didn't already know how smart he is, I'd be able to tell just by looking. His jaw is the only part of his face that's not narrow, but blunt.

Assertive. The bottom of his face is a barroom brawler. The top half, a judge. And incredibly, the two halves don't just fit together, they make a beautiful whole.

I love his face. I'd never get tired of looking at it.

"You enjoy danger," he says eventually, when he's apparently ready to render a verdict.

"Not if you're the one who's in danger."

"But at heart, you're a thrill seeker."

I shrug. "The possibility of catching a murderer red-handed does add a touch of excitement to our day, don't you think? I mean, as long as you don't get killed."

He lifts a brow. "Or wounded?"

"Not even a lightly stubbed toe," I promise.

"I'm not afraid."

"I figured. When you insisted on being bait for a murderer, it pretty much gave that away."

He tilts his head. "You do home security audits, but that seems too dull for you. It must bore you."

I glance down at the remains of Zar's aunt's breakfast. Though the buffet is groaning with a selection of delicious options, she restricted herself to fruit and coffee. Talk about dull. Her meal choice was the poster child.

"Are you forming rash ideas about me just because I ate a pancake piled high with a dozen different toppings for breakfast?" I ask.

"I'm getting to know you." His gaze is level.

"It can get a little boring, but at least I'm working with my best friends."

"Some people like routine. I can't see you being suited to it."

I wrinkle my nose. "Jamie, Kayla, and I each do what

we're best at. I happen to know about security, so that's what I do."

"Have you ever been sky diving or paragliding?" he asks. I shake my head.

"What about water sports? Scuba diving? Water ski-ing? White water rafting?"

"Those things all cost money, Bob. And you know the difference between money and confetti, don't you?"

"Mmm." His gaze lifts as though he's thinking. "I've decided to take a break from being murder bait today. The only question is, what shall we do instead?"

"You don't need to work?" I ask.

"I don't *need* to do anything."

"Nice to be you," I say, not even being sarcastic. It must be wonderful not to have to worry about paying the bills.

"Come on." He gets up and moves behind my chair to pull it out for me when I stand.

"Where are we going?"

"To not be bored."

He doesn't answer any more questions, just covers the ground to the hotel's reception desk with his long strides. At the counter, one of the receptionists asks if she can help him.

"Jet boating?" he asks, giving me a questioning look.

The idea is exciting. I mean, come on. Anything fast has to be fun, right?

Before I can form words, he must see the response in my face. His lips hook up and he repeats, "A jet boat," to the receptionist in a decisive tone.

"Certainly, sir." She looks unruffled, as though she's used to getting these kinds of requests.

She makes a call, and about an hour later, I find myself

on board the sleekest, most beautiful boat I've ever seen. At Zar's insistence, the driver stays ashore, leaving the two of us to take the boat out alone.

Zar drives the boat out to deeper water where he gives me a lesson on how to operate it, and I have a turn at the wheel. Then I relinquish control back to him and grip the front rail as we race at high speed across the rolling ocean waves. The boat flies from the top of one wave to the next, bouncing as it goes. The wind whips my hair away from my face and snatches my laughter. Zar grins back at me, windswept and gorgeous. I lean in to speak into his ear over the roar of the engine, inhaling the scent of sunscreen and salt.

"This is so much fun!" I exclaim.

"The best." His eyes sparkle as he steers the boat over the water. "Beyond expectations."

"You've done this before though, haven't you?"

"Yes, but this is better." His smile is unrestrained, his face relaxed. Even the crease between his eyes has smoothed away.

"How is it better?" I ask.

His eyes trap mine, and all at once his expression opens. He's not hiding behind sternness, or wealth, or expectations, or any kind of reserve. His gaze is so warm, it makes my heart beat faster. He looks at me with appreciation, as though he thinks I'm beautiful. And there's a kind of wondering in his eyes. It's as though he can't quite believe I'm here with him. As though he's so glad for my presence, he's marveling over it.

He lifts one hand from the wheel to bring it up to my

face. His knuckle grazes gently over my cheek. "It's better now, because the last time, I wasn't with you."

His words go through me like a buzz of electricity, warming me from my head to the bottom of my toes. I want nothing more than to kiss him.

Then we hit a wave, and the boat bounces.

Zar drops his hand and looks at the water in front of us, concentrating on steering. I still want to kiss him, but I don't want us to capsize or anything. So I push it out of my mind and just enjoy the thrill of the ride, the exhilaration of feeling on the very edge of control as we soar across the waves.

Later, when we're low on fuel and heading into shore, Zar says, "I'm hungry. Let's go straight to the restaurant once we're docked."

"I have a better idea." I point along the boardwalk. "There's a taco truck!"

He shoots me one of his cute, pretending-to-be-stern frowns. "Are you suggesting we eat food prepared inside a truck?"

I gasp, exaggerating my horror. "You've never had street tacos?"

"Strangely enough, I've never eaten from a car, motorbike, or lorry either. I prefer when my meals don't contain engine grease or road dirt."

"This is a serious! What if something terrible happens and you die young? If you've never eaten from a taco truck, how you could say you'd even lived at all?"

"The lobster thermidor at the restaurant is supposed to be excellent. We haven't tried it yet."

"Oh no, Bob." I wag a finger at him. "You're not getting

out of this. Lunch is on me."

As soon we're off the boat, I grab Zar's hand and tug him along the boardwalk to the truck. "Sit here." I push him onto the bench seat at one of the picnic tables near the truck. "I'll get the food."

"So bossy," he grumbles. "At least let me get it."

"This time it's my treat. You're going to love it. Forget about the lobster thermidor!"

I go to the truck and come back with cardboard plates loaded with delicious tacos, smaller containers with extra toppings, and drinks tucked under each arm. With a flourish, I unload it all onto the picnic table.

"I got carne asada, shrimp, and fish tacos, with extra spicy salsa, cilantro, and guacamole." I point to the drinks. "And beer for washing it all down."

Zar eyes the food doubtfully. "And you're sure this is safe? Before you answer, remember that we're sharing a bathroom, and my gallantry only extends so far. In certain situations, it's every man for himself."

"You know why I got limes for our beer?" I poke my wedge a little further into the neck of the bottle. "It stops the flies from getting in."

His frown deepens, and I barely manage to suppress a grin at his expression.

I wave a hand. "Don't worry. Alcohol is a disinfectant. It kills germs."

Zar drags his cardboard plate closer, studying it through narrowed eyes.

"Wait! It's not ready yet. First you have to pile on the salsa." I grab one of the small containers to dump hot salsa over a taco. "Then the guacamole. And finally the cilantro.

Okay, now it's ready."

"There's no cutlery. We're going to use our hands like cavemen?"

I give a cavewoman-like grunt, nodding enthusiastically. Picking up a taco, I take a huge bite. The burst of flavor is so amazing, I let out a muffled moan.

He raises his eyebrows, staring at my mouth with dark eyes while I chew. To encourage him, I make more 'yummy' noises, rolling my eyes with apparent ecstasy.

He clears his throat. "I want you to know, I don't trust easily." His tone is serious.

I swallow my mouthful of food. "Okay. I don't either."

"So what you're about to witness isn't done lightly." He picks up one of the tacos gingerly, his nostrils flared.

"Get ready for taco heaven! You're never going to want to leave."

He sniffs the taco. Then he takes a small bite. I watch closely as he chews, waiting for his reaction. I don't know why I'm so eager for him to like it, but I'm holding my breath.

To my delight, a slow smile spreads over his face. He nods, still chewing. "I'm still alive," he says, swallowing. "That's better than I expected."

"It's so good though, right? And you didn't even have close to enough spicy salsa on top!"

With my encouragement, he piles more toppings on, then takes another, bigger bite. "Mmm. I can barely taste the engine grease at all."

"And look, no flies in our beer! What did I tell you?"

His eyes crinkle with amusement, their warmth so clear to me now.

It's been an incredible day. Easily one of the best days of my life, eclipsed only by the day I got out of juvie. Zar seemed to guess what I'd enjoy almost before I did, making sure I got plenty of time behind the wheel of the jet boat. And when it was his turn, he took just enough risks to make it exhilarating.

An important realization forms in my brain and floods every cell in my body.

I want Zar, and I don't care about the consequences.

I'm desperate for his hands on my body and his mouth on mine. I want to kiss the place between his eyes where furrows are etched. To stroke the tip of my nose down his long, serious, angular one. To lick his oh-so-tempting lips and nuzzle the squareness of his jaw.

Even knowing he might not forgive me after I confess my sins, I want to have at least one night of wild passion with him, forgetting everything but the incredible chemistry that sizzles between us.

I don't just want him. I *need* him.

Is that so wrong?

CHAPTER 23

Balthazar

It's still early, barely past eight o'clock, but Scarlet put on those damned red pajamas again, so I had to either walk around with a boner or go to bed.

That's why we're lying in bed together, on our sides, facing each other, the covers pulled up over our shoulders. My lamp is on, casting a warm glow over her lovely face. I'm not sure if she's stopped smiling since the boat ride, and her smile seems to automatically inspire my own.

Though I jerked off in the shower again, my boner just won't quit. It's the Muhammed Ali of boners, refusing to get knocked out. If there was a nuclear war, this boner would be one of the only things to survive it. Just the cockroaches and my boner. Indestructible.

"Thank you for today," Scarlet says.

"Enough excitement for you?"

"My life does feel a little dull occasionally," she admits. "But not today."

"Understandable. Our brain gets wired early in life. The experiences we have as children shape us as adults."

"Is your life exciting?"

"I work with some exciting tech companies."

She wrinkles her nose. "Stop. You're making my heart race too hard."

Her smart mouth is begging to be kissed. I have such a strong urge to reach across the bed to her, I screw both hands into fists under the covers to stop myself. I need to remember Gaby's warning and the promise I made. Scarlet is my employee, and I've forced her to share a bed with me. That fact alone should be enough to hold me back.

"I've done a few things you'd consider more exciting." I keep my tone level with an effort. "A few years ago, Gaby and I went trekking in the jungle. We carried our own backpacks and slept in hammocks."

"You didn't have anyone to carry your bags?" She gives an exaggerated gasp. "No valet to unpack for you? No chocolate on your pillow? Not even a pancake station at the breakfast buffet?"

"I battled killer spiders and didn't shower for a week. You wouldn't have recognized me."

Her eyes go a little distant and a small smile plays over her lips as though she's picturing it. "You and Gabby trekked to Machu Picchu?"

"How did you know?" I ask, surprised.

"Oh." She blinks, her gaze returning to me. "I'm a little bit psychic. And you seem like a Machu Picchu kind of guy."

"Have you been there?" I can imagine how much she'd love the ancient city.

"To Peru? It's on my vision board."

"You should go. It's a spiritual place, even for me."

"When was your Machu Picchu trip?"

"Eight years ago." It's surprising to realize how long ago it was. Where has the time gone? Work has consumed so much of me that the years have been slipping away.

"And no adventures since then?"

I give my head a small shake against the pillow. "I've been busy. Gaby used to be the one to suggest we take trips, but she's in Australia working on the Great Barrier Reef. She's part of a research team, working on ways to protect it from coral bleaching."

"Must be a rewarding job. I'd love to see that reef one day."

I make a silent decision to take her there after the weekend is over, when she's not working for me anymore. We could share an adventure she'll never forget. After all, I can do anything I want, go to any place on Earth, experience any excitement. I can't think why I've been working so hard instead of grasping all that life has to offer. Why haven't I been doing more?

"Where else would you go?" I ask. "If money wasn't a consideration."

Her smile widens. I love how big it is. How it makes her eyes crinkle and her cheeks crease.

"I'd go everywhere! I'd like to see and do everything. From abseiling in Alaska to zip-lining in Zimbabwe, I want to try all of it." She gives a wistful sigh. "Except I run a company and have responsibilities. I couldn't take off, even if I won the lottery."

"If you won the lottery, you'd stay in LA and keep going to work?"

"No!" The word bursts out quickly. Then she presses her lips together, considering the question more carefully. "Actually, I don't know. I'd want to go but wouldn't want to let down my friends. Good thing I don't have a lottery ticket, because I don't know how that would work, exactly."

She's so loyal.

Her friends are lucky. It must be an incredible feeling to know someone cares about you that much.

And it's torture, being on the other side of the bed from her. All I can think about are the things I want to do to her and can't.

"Can I ask you a question?" she says. "I've told you about my family and friends, but I don't know much about yours."

"There's not much to know. My parents were busy people, so I was mainly raised by a series of nannies."

"Did you have a red-haired nanny?"

I frown. "Why would you ask that?"

"I told you, I'm psychic. And a picture just flashed into my mind of you as a boy with a red-haired woman."

"Helena had red hair." There's no such thing as psychic ability, so how did she know?

But come to think of it, there are only a few basic hair colors. She probably just picked one and got lucky.

"Was she nice?" Scarlet asks.

My chest tightens at the question.

Helena was more than nice. I'd made the mistake of loving her.

In my defense, I'd been young. But I should have learned what would happen from the string of nannies who'd come before her.

"She was my favorite nanny." I make my tone light. "And

she hung around the longest. We used to have a lot of fun, at least from my perspective. She took me hiking, and camping, and rock climbing. I liked to pretend she was my real mother."

"Do you still see her?"

"Not since the day she left."

"How old were you?"

"I was about to turn eleven. One morning, I went into Helena's room, and my father was having sex with her. A few days later, Helena was gone. She left quickly, without a word, and I never saw her again."

Scarlet draws in a sharp, audible breath. "Oh my God. That must have been awful!"

"It's probably a good thing that I was too young to fully understand what was happening."

A feeling of disquiet is gnawing at me. By talking so openly about my past, I'm opening myself up to Scarlet. Growing close to her. Giving her the power to hurt me.

Surely I've learned my lesson many times over. Only I can't seem to help myself.

"I'm so sorry." Scarlet's bow is furrowed. "You must have been devastated."

I give a little shrug. "When my mother saw how upset I was, she lectured me about how Helena was just an employee who was paid to pretend to care, and if I grew attached to people who only cared about my money, I'd always be disappointed."

Realizing I'm squeezing the sheet in my fist, I ease my hand open.

My mother wouldn't understand why I'd bother to keep a photo of Helena on my bookcase. But the photo reminds me of one of the best days I'd had at that age. Helena had taken me hiking in the mountains, and we'd seen some deer. For some reason, the delight on Helena's face had been even better than my own sense of wonder.

Scarlet winces. "Your mother sounds cold."

"She was. But she was also telling the truth."

"Where's your mom now?"

"She died in an accident not long after that."

"I'm sorry," she says again. She looks genuinely upset for me, and I have a strange urge to comfort her.

"After Gaby moved in, life got a whole lot better," I say.

"But you got sent away to boarding school sometime after that, right?" I raise my eyebrows at her question, and she adds, "I read an article about you, but it didn't mention anything about your mother."

"My childhood isn't something I like to talk about."

She gives a little nod as though she understands. "Then we can stop talking about it. I don't want to drag up bad memories."

"What else do you want to know?"

She hesitates. "Um." She bites her lip as though she's thinking, though I'm fairly sure she already has a question on her mind. "What about your ex-girlfriend," she says after a moment. "Natalia Ricci, the fashion designer. What happened with her?"

"Natalia ended our relationship."

Her eyebrows shoot up as though she's surprised.

"What?" I ask.

"Nothing. It's just that I can't imagine any woman ending a relationship with you."

I can't help but smile at the implied compliment. "Natalia

had a career opportunity in Paris that she couldn't turn down."

"It must have ended on good terms for you to buy one of her dresses for me."

"You looked sensational in that dress." I like remembering how it clung to her body, accentuating both her curves and her muscles.

"Are you kidding? It was a stunning dress. A lizard would have looked sensational in it."

I start to protest, but she reaches out to touch my lips with one finger, silencing me.

"Stop. Don't compliment me, or I'll get carried away." She says it in a flirtatious way, and my cock gets even harder.

When she withdraws her finger, I'm sorry to see it go. If she'd left it there, I would have nipped it with my teeth. Or sucked on it. Probably both.

"Were you in love with Natalia?" she asks.

"No." The word comes out quickly and firmly. She registers it with a look of understanding.

"We're so much alike." Her words are soft. "Two people with trust issues. And the only person you can depend on is your stepsister."

"One person is enough. It's all I need."

"What if I were to barge my way into your inner circle?" She moves one leg under the covers.

Her toes touch my shin.

Even through my pajamas, I can feel the heat of her skin. Her eyes have gone hazy, and her gaze rests on my lips.

My cock starts to throb.

"If you touch me, I'm going to kiss you." My voice is rough.

She moves her other leg under the covers. The toes of her other foot land on my other shin. Pinching me with her toes, she quirks an eyebrow. "I'm double touching you." Her hand extends so her fingers find my chest. "Triple touching."

"I warned you." I move over her, and she drops onto her back, looking up at me with her lips slightly parted.

I drop my face to hers slowly, breathing her in. I love having her below me. The anticipation of our kiss is an exquisite torture. Her breath is fast and shallow. There's a whisper of silk from her dragon pajamas. She smells like oranges.

Our noses touch. I pause for a moment, holding my body above her so our only contact is that soft press of our noses. This close, even in the dim lamp light, I can see all the flecks in her lovely eyes and admire the graduation of colors. I can taste her breath. Feel the warmth of her. Recognize the hint of vulnerability in her expression.

Her hands snake around my waist. She tugs my body down against hers.

I take her lips with mine, flicking my tongue between them as I let my weight drop onto her. Her legs part for me, her thighs on either side of mine. She lifts her knees, hugging me into her. Letting me rub against her, sensible dark pajamas against sexy red silk. Hardness against softness.

I kiss her deeply, groaning against her mouth, wanting all of her. Needing to be inside her. To consume her.

Her hands are on my back, sliding from waist to shoulders. Pulling me into her. She makes a sound of need. The sexiest sound I've ever heard.

She's everything.

Everything.

A loud rapping comes from the door, startling me into pushing back from her.

Scarlet protests, but I sit up on the bed. Moving away from her is like emerging from a daze. Running my hand over my face, I drag in a breath. Despite my resolution, I'd been about to make love to her.

Whoever's at the door knocks again.

"Who the hell is it?" I snap loudly.

"Room service, sir." It's a man voice.

"Wrong room!" My annoyance surges.

The man calls back, "I have a gift for you, complements of the manager, sir."

I want to tell him to go away, but Scarlet's eyes have widened. "Free stuff?"

Shit.

I get off the bed. My erection pushes out my pajamas. My entire body misses the feel of her against me.

Scarlet grabs my arm as she scrambles out of bed too. "No, let me get it. It could be an assassin."

"Then you're not getting it. You're not opening the door if whoever's there could be armed."

Her brow creases. "But that's *literally* my job."

"I don't care. You're not getting yourself shot." I raise my voice to call to whoever's outside. "What have you got for us?"

"French champagne and strawberries, sir."

I still want to tell him to go away, but Scarlet exclaims, "Free champagne!"

What Scarlet wants, Scarlet gets.

Still growling my displeasure, I fling open the door to let

the waiter in. When he sees my frown, he almost drops the
champagne. And he doesn't hang around, just dumps the
tray he's carrying on the table and flees. As soon as he's done,
I pick up the hotel phone.

"What are you doing?" Scarlet asks.

"Calling the manager to make sure there aren't any more
gifts."

"Tell her thank you!"

After I get the manager on the phone, I make a point of
saying *please* before telling her not to send anything else,
then I say *thank you* while looking pointedly at Scarlet. She's
pouring the champagne and smiles back at me.

"You're most welcome," the manager gushes. "I've been
terribly worried about our mistake. Thank you for calling,
Mr. Anders. Really. Thank you."

I hang up before she can thank me a third time for
thanking her. Am I really that horrible to people that
showing the slightest courtesy can earn that much gratitude?

Maybe Scarlet's right. Perhaps I took my mother's lecture
a little too much to heart. It's entirely possible I've made such
a point of distancing myself from the staff I interact with, I've
actually become rude without realizing it.

When I turn to her, Scarlet has a glass of champagne in
one hand and a strawberry in the other. She looks pleased.

I, however, am not.

The interruption has kicked my brain back into
operation.

I keep thinking about the photos my father took and how
he used to prey on the women who worked for him. I can't
help comparing the things he used to do with the facts of my
current situation. Scarlet is my employee, so I'm in a position

of power over her. Bad enough that I've forced her to share a bed with me. I can't take back what I've already done, but taking any further advantage of her would be wrong.

"Grab your champagne. Let's take it back to bed." Scarlet gives me a hopeful smile. She's chewing on a bite of strawberry, the rest of it held to her luscious lips. She's utterly gorgeous and unbearably tempting, and all I want to do is agree.

I shake my head. "I need a shower."

Her smile vanishes. "But you already took one."

"I'm taking another one."

Heading into the bathroom, I shut the door.

Only I should have known a small thing like a closed door wouldn't stop her, because she barges right in behind me.

CHAPTER 24

Scarlet

Putting the champagne down, I dump my half-eaten strawberry onto the table and follow Zar into the bathroom. Too bad if he was about to use the toilet. I'm not letting him shut me out.

"What's wrong?" I demand.

It's a big bathroom, but small by normal room standards, so we're standing close. But he stands stiffly, his fists clenched, wearing his most severe frown. Maybe once I would have found that frown intimidating. Now it just worries me.

"I can't have sex with an employee." His tone is hard and final. "It's the kind of thing my father would have done. He seduced young women who worked for him and took pictures of them without consent."

At his mention of the photos, guilt flushes through me. "He did?"

"I'm taking a shower. Get out of the bathroom."

Oh, no. Guilty or not, he's not getting rid of me that easily.

"I'm taking a bath," I say defiantly, crossing to the tub and turning the taps on full.

Water gushes noisily into the tub.

"You're not taking a bath." He uses a sharp, domineering tone that would probably make his other employees crap their pants.

"Watch me." I unbutton my pajama top, tugging it back to reveal my chest.

His gaze drops to my bare breasts.

He goes completely still, as though he's suddenly stopped breathing. There's raw hunger in his expression. He looks like a man who's barely holding himself back, and the feeling of power that gives me is like a rush of adrenaline. It's like flying over the biggest waves on the jet boat, the sensation of being momentarily—gloriously—out of control.

"Stop." He grinds the word out, his tone rough. "Once you're no longer an employee—"

"Okay." I cut him off. "Then I quit."

He looks thunderous. "You're not quitting."

Putting my hands on my hips to hold my top open, I arch my back and thrust my breasts out. "I am quitting. I just did. Effective immediately. Now I don't work for you."

"You can't quit. I forbid it." His serious, growly voice sends shivers down my spine.

And my shivers intensify when I adopt a playful tone that's sure to make him even more growly. "Oh, but I already quit, so it's too late for you to forbid anything. I don't work for you and neither do my breasts. See?"

He definitely does see, because his eyes darken and his jaw clenches.

"Scarlet—"

"Zar." I pretend to glower at him, though I'm so turned on I can barely see straight. "You're no longer my boss."

He groans. "You're killing me."

"Wouldn't that be funny? You hire me to keep you alive, but I make you so angry, I kill you."

"Hilarious." His tone is bone dry.

It sounds weird, but I love the deadpan way he talks when he's being sarcastic. It makes me want to keep provoking him.

"One last chance," he says. "Button your top."

"You're not my boss anymore, remember? I already quit." I pull my pajama top right off and drop it onto the floor.

With a muttered curse, he steps forward and walks me back to the wall. He pushes me against the tile and brings his face close.

"No more chances," he growls. His eyes devour my lips and his t-shirt presses against my erect nipples in the most delicious way.

"Stop talking," I whisper. "Just kiss me already."

His lips come down hard on mine. His mouth bosses mine open, and his tongue sweeps in, taking charge. The sensation of cold, hard tile against my back makes the whole thing even hotter.

One of his hands moves into my hair, the other goes to my ribs and presses up against the underside of my breast. His kisses are furious, biting. His cock presses into me, thick and long. Its hardness ratchets my arousal.

I lift a leg, hooking it around him, grinding shamelessly against his hip.

He slides his fingers over my nipple, groaning when he finds it hard. I gasp into his mouth as he plucks at my nipple, and he grabs my lower lip between his teeth, biting gently. Then he grabs my ass, pulling it higher, helping me angle myself for maximum sensation. I'm practically wearing a hole in his pajama pants. It'd be better if he was naked, but his hand feels incredible grabbing my ass. I love his fingers digging into me, and the way it heightens my sensitivity.

"Fuck, Scarlet," he grinds out, his mouth against my neck. "You don't know what you're doing to me."

He's wrong about that. I have an excellent idea, seeing as his cock is pressing against my stomach like highly insistent steel. And I'm pretty sure he knows what he's doing to me without me having to spell it out, seeing as I'm wearing nothing but silky pajama bottoms and making needy little movements against him. But in case he hasn't managed to figure it out, I slide my hands up inside his t-shirt, grabbing at his flesh and eagerly scraping my fingernails over the ridges of his muscles.

He makes a sound of pain, and I suddenly remember his knife wound.

"Did I hurt you? I'm sorry!" I try to pull back, which isn't easy with my back against the wall.

His lips quirk. "This is what hurts." He puts my hand on his cock, squeezing my fingers around it for just a second. Then he drops my hand and turns to the tub to turn off the water. I must have tuned out the sound of the water, as I'd forgotten it was still running. We could have been knee deep, and I wouldn't have noticed.

"Take your pants off and get into the tub," he orders.

"Are you getting in with me?"

"Not while you're my employee."

"Then I—"

"You're going to touch yourself while I watch."

"Oh." Well, that doesn't sound so bad. "Do I get to watch you?"

Instead of answering, he pulls off his t-shirt. *Yum.*

I do as he asks and get into the tub, sliding my body into the hot water with a sound of pure pleasure. A sound that makes his gaze even hungrier.

Unzipping his pants, he tugs his cock free. It's just as long and thick as it felt when I was grinding against it. So long and thick it makes my insides clench. He wraps his fist around it, then slides his hand up and down, stroking its entire length.

Holy crap, that's hot.

I lie back in the tub, my knees lifted and apart. His gaze is so intense, it feels like he's caressing me with his eyes. My skin tingles wherever he looks.

"Slide your hands down your body," he says, his voice low and demanding. "Do it slowly."

I do better than that. First I give him some nipple action, tweaking and stroking them and moaning a little while I do it. Because I'm an overachiever and having his dark gaze on me feels so good.

"Open your legs wider, sweetheart." He strokes himself faster. "Show me how you make yourself come."

I move my hand between my thighs to play with myself. I'm so horny, I groan with relief when my fingers find the place I need them most. I've never done this with an audience before, and I don't think I could do it for anybody else. But even though being vulnerable isn't easy for Zar, he's opened himself up to me emotionally, so opening myself physically to him feels natural. It feels right. I'm not self-conscious or nervous. I'm too turned on for that.

I'm good at pleasuring myself, and in the warm bath, the sensation is incredible. Caressing my breast with one hand, I work myself with the other. Zar licks his lips, breathing fast. He's as turned on as I am, jerking his hand roughly up and down his cock.

My orgasm comes quickly in electric jolts that are strong enough to shock through my entire body, making the water splash over me. The relief of it is immense. I've been holding my arousal back for so long, it explodes out of me.

Zar comes a moment later, grunting his release with his eyes fixed to mine. I lie quivering with aftershocks, wanting nothing more than his touch. He grabs a towel to wipe himself off, then reaches for me, either sensing my need or sharing it. He takes my hand to pull me into his arms.

There's a faint click that sounds like the front door of our suite being unlocked.

Zar freezes.

I hear the door open. Then it snicks shut.

Zar and I both stare at the door of the bathroom. It must have swung closed when we came in here. From outside the door, there's a sound like a soft footfall.

"Someone just walked into our room," I whisper.

Zar nods, not moving. We listen to a scraping noise, like someone's moving furniture. Then he puts a totally unnecessary finger over his lips, as though I need to be urged into silence. But I'm all too aware there's an assassin targeting him. The bandage covering his knife wound stands out on his skin.

If the assassin figures out we're in here, we'll be sitting ducks. He could shoot through the door. Pick us off at his leisure.

I stand up as quietly as I can, water running off my naked body into the tub. "Get into the tub for cover," I command in a whisper.

My gun is locked in the safe, and there's nothing obvious I can use as a weapon. Running my gaze around the small room, I search for anything that could inflict damage on an intruder. All I see are bottles of shampoo and bubble bath. Soap. Toothpaste. A razor. All of it slim pickings.

In desperation, I grab the hair dryer. I'll pretend it's a gun to give me a split-second advantage over the intruder. And if all else fails, it'll give me something to throw. It's the heaviest item in the room.

"You're not going out there if you're not armed," whispers Zar. "You could get shot." Despite my command, he's not getting into the tub.

"I need to protect you." I move toward the door. "Lie down in the bathtub, Zar. I mean it."

"You're not putting yourself in the line of fire. I'm not letting you go out there, dripping wet and stark naked."

"This is my job," I hiss back. "Not the wet and naked part, the dealing with intruders part. I'm your bodyguard, remember?"

"You quit."

"I retract my resignation."

"Then you're fired."

He's wasting time. If the intruder isn't here to shoot him,

they intend to steal his father's papers. Either scenario is unacceptable, and I don't have time to get dressed or to argue with Zar. If the person in our suite hasn't realized we're in the bathroom, the possibility of surprising them is the only advantage I have.

Pushing past Zar, I reach for the bathroom door handle.

"I'm bigger and stronger than you are." He grabs me around my waist, pulling me against him. "I have a better chance of overpowering someone at close range."

"Let me go, or I'll put you on the floor, knife wound or not."

"I'll only let you go if you don't run out unarmed. I'm not going to watch you get killed!"

I grab his balls and squeeze. He grunts and bends at the waist. As soon as his grip on me slackens, I yank myself free and lunge at the door, flinging it open. Hairdryer held up like a gun, I let out a battle cry as I throw myself into the room, propelling myself toward the intruder.

"Freeze, asshole!" I yell. "Put your hands up or I'll shoot!"

The intruder staggers backward with a scream of shock. I barely have time to register that it's a woman before she throws something at me.

Instinctively, I dive sideways. I barely feel the burn of the carpet along the bare flesh of my side as I hit the ground, my hairdryer still outstretched in front of me. I pull the trigger.

Admittedly, if I were actually holding a gun instead of an unplugged hairdryer, pulling the trigger would be a lot more effective.

Launching the hairdryer at the assassin, I lunge to my feet, moving straight into a fighting stance.

The woman flinches sideways so the hairdryer goes right

past her. Even though it doesn't hit her, she screams even louder. Then she throws another missile.

That's when I register her maid's uniform.

She's middle aged and sturdy. Her graying hair is pulled back into a tidy bun. She's standing next to the head of the bed, and the sheets are neatly folded back. There's a chocolate on one of the pillows. My gaze flicks to the missile she threw. It's another chocolate, now lying harmlessly on the carpet.

"Oh my God!" My stomach turns over, and I stretch both hands toward her. "I'm so sorry! I didn't know it was you. I thought it was someone else!"

The maid grabs the remaining piece of chocolate and hurls it at me.

"Turn down service!" she shrieks. "Turn down service!"

From behind me, Zar starts to laugh.

CHAPTER 25

Balthazar

I close our hotel door behind the maid. She was only placated after Scarlet offered her many effusive apologies, and I pressed a large amount of cash into her hands. Now she's finally gone, so I walk back into our living room.

Scarlet is standing at the entrance to the bedroom. "That wasn't funny." She crosses her arms across her towel-covered chest and shoots a glare at me.

"Of course not." I can't stop another chuckle from escaping, though I'm trying to be sympathetic. She shouldn't be embarrassed. Her fearlessness impressed me all over again. If there really had been an assassin, she probably would have gotten the better of him somehow.

We're both wearing towels, hurriedly wrapped around ourselves. Scarlet's cheeks are flushed and her hair wild. Some of the lower strands are still wet from the bath, clinging to her shoulders, but the rest is an explosion of loose, messy curls. I love how they cascade in such wild abandon. They're just like her: impossible to predict or contain. I want to sink my hands into them. To pull her head back and claim her lips.

With one tug, her towel would fall right off.

She widens her eyes, assuming an expression of sympathy. "You didn't hurt yourself from laughing so hard while I was rolling around naked, did you?"

"If I hadn't laughed, the maid would have kept throwing things."

Her nose scrunches. "I suppose it was kind of funny. And I like your laugh. It's all deep and rumbly. You need to laugh more often."

"What would I have to laugh about if you weren't around?" Moving to her, I put my hands on her upper arms, relishing the softness of her skin. Her warmth.

My need to touch her is out of my control. She's the sun, and I'm starting to realize how starved of light and heat I've been for so very long. How can I keep away?

"The door is locked, right?" She looks up at me with her eyes darkening, as though she's as acutely aware of us being alone again as I am. "And the *Do Not Disturb* sign is up?"

I nod.

Problem is, in a moral sense, I'm in exactly the same situation as before. Nothing's changed.

The moment the board meeting is over, Scarlet's employment can end. Then she can decide whether she wants to have a relationship with a man who's no longer her employer. There'll be no consent issues to worry about. I won't be like my father.

But right now, her towel is inches away. One tug, and it

would fall away from her incredible breasts. One tug, and her irresistible body could be mine.

Letting go of her shoulders with a superhuman effort, I force myself to turn away and grab my pajamas off the bed.

"What are you doing, Zar?" Her tone sharpens.

"I'm going to put something on."

"Oh no, you're not." She moves closer, so she's standing inches from me. "You don't get to pull away from me now."

"You're my employee."

Her eyes flash green fire and her fists go to her hips. "Are you kidding? We're way past that. I mean, come on! You can't claim we haven't crossed any lines just because we haven't actually had sex yet."

The word '*yet*' makes my cock instantly swell, and the rush of blood leaving my brain threatens to scramble my will.

"We did cross a line. It was my fault. I'm the one in the position of authority, and I should never have allowed it to happen."

"We went waaay across that line." She pulls her shoulders back, making my gaze drop to her breasts, barely hidden by the towel. "So why not keep going? Make it a one-way street. No U-turns allowed."

Just. One. Tug.

My throat is dry. When my hands start lifting to her towel, I ball my fists. How could I have let us get into this situation? "I can't do it," I mutter, furious at myself. I should have insisted on two rooms. How stupid was I to imagine I'd be able to control myself around her?

Her back sags and she takes a backward step. Some kind of realization passes across her face, and she frowns. "This isn't what you want." Her tone flattens. She sucks in a breath between her teeth. "Sorry, Zar. I thought…" She shakes her head, walking to where her own pajamas are waiting. "It doesn't matter. I shouldn't have pressured you. Never mind."

Her shoulders slump as she picks up her pajamas.

She thinks I'm rejecting her.

Her feelings are hurt because she has no idea how much I want her. She thinks she was coming on too strong.

I can't stand the thought I've hurt her.

I can't let her stay so dejected. There's nothing I wouldn't do to put her smile back on her face.

With her pajamas in her arms, she turns back to face me.

"Now all this has happened, there's something I should really tell you." Her lips draw down. "I have something I need to confess."

Her expression sends pain lancing through my heart. I drop my pajamas onto the bed.

"Scarlet, I want you. The problem is mine, not yours. You've done nothing wrong. *Nothing*." Grabbing her pajamas out of her hands, I dump them on top of mine.

She swallows, her face still drawn. "But I have. I've done something very wrong. You need to know what I've—"

I draw her into my arms.

Better to cross every single line than cause her another moment of pain.

Bending my head, I kiss her fiercely. All I want is to show her with my lips and my body how much I want her. How badly I *need* her.

For a moment she's stiff and unresponsive. Her lack of response is a shock, and I'm about to draw back. But then her body softens and her hands snake around my neck. She presses into me, her curves lush against me.

"Zar," she murmurs against my lips. "I want this. I want *you*. So much."

One tug.

That's all it takes to send her towel to the floor.

My towel follows. Then her skin is on mine, her breasts in my hands, my mouth on her jaw, her throat, her neck.

I maneuver her onto the bed and lie over her, between her legs. She looks up at me with such fire and warmth in her eyes, it swells my heart.

She wraps her legs around my hips, dragging me lower, pressing my cock between her legs. I lower my lips to hers again, kissing her deeply while my cock throbs insistently and she grinds against it.

It's so good. *So good.*

Lowering my mouth to her breasts, I worship them the way they deserve. Her hard nipples tighten even more under my tongue, as though they're straining up to me, wanting more of my mouth. My hand slips between us, between her legs. I part her with my fingers and sink into her slick, wet heat.

She groans, her hands in my hair, grabbing fistfuls.

Her soft heat feels so good, I have to move down her body. I kiss and lick underneath her breasts and down her stomach. Moving down even further, I slip my tongue between her folds. Gasping her pleasure, she spreads her legs wider. I slide two fingers into her while I lap her.

She cries out as she comes into my mouth, her thighs clenching around my ears while she pulses around my fingers.

When her cries die down, I plant a soft kiss on her clit, then another on the soft down of hair on her mound. Then I get up and move to my side of the bed.

"What are you doing?" She's breathless and gasping.

"Getting a condom."

"Hurry. I miss your touch."

My heart swells again. "Me too, sweetheart."

The valet left my box of condoms in my nightstand, and I extract one and roll it on. When I'm done, I look up to see her sitting up on the bed, watching. Her eager expression and the heat in her eyes makes my cock jerk.

"Lie down," she says.

I quirk an eyebrow at her. "Feeling bossy?"

She grins. "Let's see how well you can take orders."

I don't obey fast enough for her liking, because she grabs my shoulders and tugs. I let her pull me down onto the bed and straddle my hips. From below, the curves of her body are even more gorgeous. Her breasts hang over me, begging for my touch. The swell of her belly is so sexy, I want to caress her everywhere at once.

She sits on the base of my cock, her slippery sex pressing hard against me. My cock presses back. She rubs herself up and down my shaft, making me groan with pleasure.

Truth is, I've wanted this to happen since the moment we arrived. She's been driving me crazy. Beyond crazy. I haven't been able to think about anything else.

Now I'm finally getting what I've been longing for.

She grasps me, angling me at her entrance.

A memory flashes into my head of our first night in this bed, how she walked out of the bathroom in her red silk pajamas, and my cock went hard. It's been constantly hard for her ever since.

"Wait." Before she can sink onto me, I grab her waist, stopping the movement.

She stills, looking down at me. "What's wrong?" Her worried eyes search mine.

I reach out to grab the pajama top that's lying discarded on the bed. "Put this on."

She blinks, her brow creasing with puzzlement. "You want me to put my top on?"

"I've had to watch you wear those sexy fucking dragon pajamas all this time." My tone is rough with need. "Just put the top on, but don't do it up. I want you in it while I'm inside you."

Her eyes widen, then a slow smile spreads over her lips. It's her mischievous smile, higher on one side than the other. My favorite smile.

"Now who's the bossy one?" she asks teasingly, but she pulls it on, then sits back down on me. The shirt hangs open, her breasts thrusting out of it, her nipples like bullets. She looks fucking incredible.

"Lift up, sweetheart." When she raises herself up, I position my cock at her entrance. Then I put my hands on her waist to pull her down.

She sinks onto my cock with a moan, sliding me all the way into her, so I fill her. The sensation is incredible. Then she moves back and forth, rocking on my cock, grinding down on me. Her wild curls toss like waves on a stormy sea. I roll both her nipples between thumb and forefinger, then surge up to bite and kiss them. She pants and groans, a perfect soundtrack to our pleasure.

When I can't stand it any longer, I flip her over onto her back and push her legs up so I can drive myself more deeply into her. I use my thumb on her clit while I pound her with my cock, needing to hear her come again with loud, uninhibited cries of ecstasy.

I fuck her with all the frustration and longing that's been building from the very day I first met her, the day she sashayed into my office with her smart mouth, her oversized buttons, and her wide smile.

I love the way she comes for me. I love the hazy green of her eyes, the way her eyelashes flutter, the shape of her mouth, and the scrape of her fingernails on my back. I love how she tastes, how she smells, the weight of her tits in my hands. I love how she gasps my name and it's the best sound I've ever heard in my whole damn life.

I'm falling for her so damn hard.

When her cries of pleasure have finally turned into little mewling sighs, I make love to her gently, kissing her softly and whispering sweet, true things to her. I murmur how precious she is. How she's smart and funny. Warm and beautiful. Cherishing her, I gaze into her gorgeous eyes as I finally shudder my release.

It's not until later, after she's lying on me, wrapped in my arms, with her head on my chest and my mouth on her hair, that the full enormity of my feelings sink in.

I really have fallen for her. I'm head over heels for her. Oh. *Fuck.*

What the hell am I doing?

So much for the hard-learned truths of my childhood, all those painful lessons that should have drummed into me how dangerous it is to expose my heart.

CHAPTER 26

Balthazar

I get up just after dawn and sit at my computer for a while, trying to work. But mostly, I just gaze at Scarlet, marveling at how peaceful she looks when she sleeps. When she's awake, she's usually smiling, her eyes sparkling, hair wild, and laughter never far away. But at rest, her skin is smooth, and her long lashes kiss her cheeks. Her curls frame her face, cascading over the white pillowcase.

I've never seen anyone so beautiful.

All her woo-woo stuff is on the dresser. I enjoyed teasing her about it, but I'm not nearly as dismissive as I pretend to be. After all, it's a complicated world. Who knows what things are possible?

Maybe Cosmic Santa is real, and Scarlet is here because she's what I've been wishing for all my life. Gazing at her, it's not hard to believe she was sent here by some kind of divine intervention. After all, I didn't know she was everything I wanted until I got to know her.

She's bright and fun and smart, and I have no idea how I could have ever thought she was too much. She's just enough. Perfect. So fucking perfect, in fact, that it pisses me off. I never asked to meet anyone like her.

I wanted another Natalia Ricci. Good dates, good sex, then good-bye.

I didn't want to meet someone with the power to strip away every bit of armor I have. To crack open my ribs and expose my beating heart to pain and heartache.

Snatching my phone up, I head into the suite's living room, gently slide open the glass door to the balcony, and step outside so I don't wake Scarlet up. The sun is rising. I call Gaby quickly, before I can think better of it, punching the numbers on my phone so hard, it feels like I could stab right through it.

Gaby takes a while to answer the call. When she does, I've clearly woken her. The room is dark, and her hair is messy. She's propped on one elbow in bed.

"Bee?" she croaks. "You realize what time it is? Is everything okay?"

"The woman I told you I'd met," I say brusquely. "The one who works for me."

"Yes?"

"She's still my employee, but I couldn't wait any longer."

Understanding flashes over Gaby's face. She drags in a breath. "Oh," she says. "Okay. Give me a second."

She puts down the phone and I stare at her ceiling for a while. Her light comes on and I hear the sound of running water. When she picks up the phone again, she's sitting on the bed looking a lot more awake. She's wearing pink

pajamas, bright enough that Scarlet would probably like
them.

"Okay," she says, her tone brisk. "Tell me, how old is this
woman?"

"Twenty-nine."

"That's not too much younger than you. But have you
ever bullied or intimated her? Is there a chance she might
feel like you pressured her for sex?"

I fix her with a hard look, because that's the only answer
her question deserves.

She nods. At last, she gives me a little smile. "See? You're
nothing like your father. So trust yourself. You know what's
right."

"Yeah, I do. I'm not asking for permission." I run a
frustrated hand over my face.

"Then why are you calling me?"

I shake my head. "Beats me."

Her laugh is half amused, half puzzled. "Okay?"

"I suppose... I have feelings for her." I growl the words.

Admitting it out loud makes me angry. I never asked to
feel so needy, like my wellbeing is somehow tied up in what
Scarlet might choose to do. Having feelings for Scarlet puts
all the control into her hands.

"That's great!" Gaby exclaims, eyes wide.

Shows what she knows.

"What's so great about it?" I demand.

"Love is nice. It's a good thing."

"Is it, though?"

Her smile is soft and so full of understanding that it
compresses my chest. "Trust her, Bee. And trust yourself."

"Like it's that easy."

"It's not," she admits. "Not for people like us, who were brought up by selfish people who could only love themselves. But if you can let yourself trust her, it'll be worth it in the end."

"So many people have walked out on me. The more I expect from people the more they disappoint me." My throat is tight. Admitting the truth out loud is like coughing up razor blades.

"She might not disappoint you."

"Maybe."

"There's only one way to find out."

I grunt, ready for this uncomfortable conversation to be over. "Go back to sleep, Gaby. And thanks. I'm sorry I woke you."

"I love you," she says.

My throat closes even more. I don't usually say those words aloud to her. I figure Gaby already knows how I feel about her, and I don't need to. But this time, she's forced my hand.

"Love you too," I say gruffly. Then I cut off the call.

I feel better after speaking to her, even though I had to admit how I felt. And I'm not going to feel bad for making love to Scarlet. Screw Dad. I don't care what he used to do. I'm not him.

When I get back into the hotel room, Scarlet's still asleep, still more peaceful than I can ever imagine being. And as badly as I'm aching to claim her, I can't bear to wake her.

Maybe I'll let her sleep in. But as soon as she stirs, I'll get back into bed and find out if she wants me again as badly as I want her.

Sitting back down at the table, I take another look at my

laptop. Melissa sent through the spreadsheet I asked for. That'll be a good distraction.

Opening it up, I scroll through it.

"Shit!" I exclaim, forgetting to be silent.

At the sound, Scarlet stirs and opens her eyes. "Morning," she says sleepily, smiling at me.

Her smile makes all my anger at having developed such strong feelings for her vanish.

"Morning, beautiful," I say.

She stretches like a cat, and I forget everything but the urge to jump into bed with her. But before I can move, she asks, "What are you looking at?" and I remember what I found.

I motion to my laptop. "I asked Melissa to have a financial analyst go through all my father's bank accounts, pull out all the regular deposits, and figure out where they were coming from."

"Did something interesting pop up?"

"Check this out."

She gets out of bed and stands next to me, leaning close to the screen to read it. She's buttoned her silky pajama top. It's long enough that it hangs past her ass, but her gorgeous legs are bare and I have to fight with myself to let her read the screen without pulling her into my lap.

My father had a lot of regular deposits into his many personal bank accounts, but I wait patiently while she scans the summary.

Her sharp intake of breath tells me she's seen the same thing that I did.

"Leo?" she asks. "He was paying your father that much every single month?"

"That's what it says. And why would Leo be paying bribes to my father? There was nothing in my father's papers about him or Loretta."

She bends even closer to the screen, her forehead creased as though the answer might be there. "Your father didn't have any of Leo or Loretta's secrets?"

"His investigator gave him detailed reports about every board member, except for Leo and Loretta. I thought there was nothing worth reporting on, but maybe the reports have been removed."

She widens her eyes at me. "Even if Leo and Loretta were squeaky clean, the investigator would have put it in writing."

"I'll call the company." I call the number for the office where Dad's investigator works, but it doesn't even ring. Instead I get a recorded message saying the phone's been disconnected.

Scarlet's looking at something on her phone. "According to this news report, the office burned down six weeks ago." She's silent a moment while she reads, then her brows lift. "It says suspected arson." She lowers the phone, looking excited. "Are you thinking what I'm thinking? Leo and Loretta must have stolen the reports from your father, then killed him. And they burned down the investigator's office to destroy any copies."

I rub my jaw. "But Leo's short, and he's always seemed meek. My father was big and strong. He wouldn't have been easy to kill."

"And whoever stabbed you outside the ball can't have been Leo or Loretta. That guy was bigger and taller than both of them." She wrinkles her nose. "Maybe they called someone to turn up and take you out? Is there a rent-an-assassin service? Like Uber Eats, only you can get a hitman delivered? Uber Kills?"

"Sounds like a failed *Dragon's Den* pitch."

She sits on the edge of the bed. "I want to talk about it more, but I'm in urgent need of coffee."

"You and me both." Picking up the hotel phone, I tell them to deliver coffee and breakfast. Then I join Scarlet on the bed and we fool around. Seeing as she's not wearing pants, I can't resist the urge to make her come on my fingers. Though with room service on its way, I regretfully keep my boner in my pants.

The food arrives quickly, and we sit on our balcony to eat it. My near-constant state of arousal is a pleasant kind of torture now that I've decided to stop holding myself back.

Scarlet eats with enthusiasm, enjoying fresh bagels and coffee. She spreads generous toppings on the bagels, piling them up high. It's the same approach she has to life, and I love that about her.

"You think Leo and Loretta must be short of money?" she says as we're finishing breakfast. "They got sick of paying your father a lot of hush money every month, so they killed him."

I nod, swallowing the last bite of my bagel. "And there must have been something terrible in the investigator's reports. Something bad enough for them to be willing to commit arson to keep it quiet."

"If your father's investigator found out what it was, we can too." She makes a phone call, and when the person on the other end answers, she says, "Hi Kayla, it's me." From her tone, I guess must be speaking with one of her friends. After a pause, she says, "Yeah, we're at the resort." She pauses, listening. "It's really nice. Yes, I've been swimming. This resort has four swimming pools, can you believe it? And you'll never guess what I did yesterday!"

I drink my coffee, smiling a little as she tells Kayla about our day on the water, enjoying the excitement in her voice. She sounds happy, and I like that. I like it a lot.

Eventually, Scarlet says, "Hey, Kayla, would you do me a favor? Could you please look into a couple called Leopold and Loretta Anders, and find out everything you can about them."

"Put her on speaker," I say.

"Wait, Kayla, I'm putting you on speaker," says Scarlet into the phone. Then she holds it out between us so I can speak to the person on the other end.

"This is Balthazar Anders," I say clearly. "Can you hear me?"

"I can hear you." There's a wariness in Kayla's tone that makes me wonder what Scarlet might have told her about me.

"Leo Anders is a partner in at least three businesses. You should look into them." I give her all the information I know, then glance at Scarlet. "Please Kayla," I say, and add, "Thank you," for good measure.

Scarlet gives me a pleased little smile that makes my heart feel light.

"Got it," says Kayla. "Will do."

Scarlet hangs up, and I'm about to suggest we go back to bed, when she asks, "You want to take a look inside Leo and Loretta's hotel room? We might find something to explain all this."

"How would we get into their room?"

"They're probably having breakfast, seeing as they were at the restaurant buffet this time yesterday morning. I can sit with them and steal their room key."

I shake my head. "Too dangerous."

"It's too dangerous to sit with them in a public restaurant?"

"It is if they catch you taking their key."

"They won't catch me." She wrinkles her nose. "Professional, remember?"

"I don't like it."

"Well, I'm going to do it." She gets up and goes into the bedroom. A minute or two later, I hear the shower.

I finish my coffee, berating myself for having such strong feelings for her. If Scarlet were still just an employee, I wouldn't have a problem with what she's doing. But now, all I want is to keep her safe. Problem is, she's not the type of woman I can order around. If I tell her not to do something, she'll do it anyway.

Actually, if I tell her not to do something, she'll do it twice.

"You'll have to wait for me to shower and dress," I tell her when she emerges from the bathroom wearing red pants that stop at her calves, and a white blouse that makes her breasts looks sensational.

"Better if I go without you." She runs a brush over her curls.

"Not going to happen."

"But if you're not there, I'll have an excuse to have breakfast with them. I'll tell them I'm lonely without you and can't bear to eat alone."

"You'll have to make up another excuse. They could be

killers. I'm not letting you anywhere near them on your own."

Though she lets out a sigh designed to let me know she doesn't need me watching over her, there's something about Scarlet's expression that makes me suspect she's not completely unhappy that I'm worried about her. She may even be pleased, though she's unwilling to admit it.

She finishes getting ready while I shave, shower and dress. And it's not until we're in the elevator together that I get to kiss her again. She tastes like toothpaste, and I love how the red pants she's wearing cradle her ass.

"As soon as all this is done, I'm taking you back up to our room." I push a stray hair back from her face.

She smiles up at me. "For hot and dirty sex, right?"

"Hot and dirty sex is exactly what I have in mind."

"Then yes please." Her grin widens, and I'm kissing her again when I hear the elevator doors open and have to reluctantly let her go.

We head toward the restaurant together. Stopping in the sumptuous sitting area just outside the door to the restaurant, we peer in and spot Leo and Loretta at a table in the corner, deep in conversation as they eat breakfast.

"Wait here," Scarlet says. "You can watch, but keep out of sight, okay?"

"Be careful."

"Don't worry, Zar. I learned how to steal when I was in diapers. And if anything bad happens, I'm armed." She taps her little shoulder bag.

I hover behind a pillar where Leo and Loretta won't be able to see me and watch her walk over to their table. To avoid having to make conversation with anyone who's

headed into the restaurant, I put my phone to my ear and
pretend to be engrossed in a conversation.

Scarlet's back is to me, but I watch Leo and Loretta's faces
as she motions to the spare chair at their table, clearly asking
if she can join them. Neither looks particularly thrilled
about the idea, but Scarlet sits anyway. While she talks, she
gestures with her hands and occasionally leans closer to
touch their arms. After a while, both Leo and Loretta relax.
Their smiles look real. Whether they're murderers or not,
she's clearly succeeding in charming them, though I can't see
how she intends to steal a room key from them. Surely it's
impossible to slip a hand into someone's pocket while they're
sitting down?

The three of them talk until Leo and Loretta finish
eating. Eventually, they stand up. My cousin and his wife
head out of the restaurant, and I duck around the pillar as
they walk by.

Scarlet comes out after them and grabs my arm, pulling
me into the restaurant.

"I got it!" Her eyes are sparkling. "Suite 351. And they said
they're going shopping, so if we go now, we should have
enough time for a look through their suite before they get
back."

I smile back at her, enjoying her excitement. She's such a
thrill seeker, and who am I to spoil her fun?

"Then let's go," I say.

CHAPTER 27

Balthazar

Scarlet turns around in the middle of Leo and Loretta's hotel suite. "This is nice," she says. "Not as fancy as ours, but still nice."

We're in their living room, but other than a coat thrown over the back of the couch and a pair of shoes on the floor, it's empty of their personal effects.

"There's not much in here." I keep my voice low. "Let's check out the bedroom."

She grins like she's enjoying herself. "Thought you'd never ask."

My heart is beating faster than normal. Breaking into their hotel room makes me uncomfortable. If they catch us in here, Leo and Loretta will know we suspect them.

But at least neither of them have the slightest chance of being able to hurt Scarlet if they come back unexpectedly. She'd take them down easily. The thought is reassuring.

Their bedroom is less than half as big as ours. "You go through their nightstands," I say. "I'll take the closet."

I open the closet doors. It's a large walk-in one. Stepping into it, I find a light switch just inside the door, flick it on, and look around. There's a rack on one side, and on the other is a shelf around waist height. Loretta and Leo's luggage is sitting on the floor, and their clothes are hanging on the rack. I lift one of their suitcases onto the shelf and unzip it to check if anything's still inside it. In the bedroom, I can hear Scarlet opening drawers.

"Zar! Take a look at this."

It takes me a moment to turn, as I'm too busy staring at the objects inside the suitcase I've just opened. When I do, Scarlet is pointing at an enormous dildo.

"I found something too," I tell her.

She closes the drawer. Joining me in the closet, she gives a low whistle. "Impressive!"

I nod, staring at the bewildering array of sex toys. Not just floggers and whips, but ball gags, restraints, spreaders, handcuffs, and many more dildos and vibrators.

"I would have thought Leo and Loretta would be too uptight for all this." She snags something black with one pinky finger, lifting it out of the case until it dangles. It's a black rubber bodysuit. "Can you imagine Loretta wearing this? "It's crotchless. Oh look! It has holes for her nipples. That's fun."

"I'd far rather imagine you wearing it," I say honestly.

She drops the suit back into the bag and steps closer, angling her face up to me, her gaze on my lips. "Are you imagining it right now?" Her voice goes breathy.

Instead of answering, I pull her close and kiss her. She

responds enthusiastically, pushing her body against mine. I'm instantly hard. But not just because she's gorgeous and sexy, and I can't wait to be back inside her. It's also because of where we are and what we're doing. It's the thrill of finding Leo and Loretta's sex toys, and the chance we're going to get caught. And seeing as Scarlet goes straight for the button on my jeans, I'm pretty sure she's feeling the same urgent excitement as I am.

My button releases and she slides her hand inside my jeans, then under my boxer briefs. Her fingers curl around my hard-on, and I groan with pleasure.

Pushing up her blouse, I play with her nipple through her bra. Her breast is beautifully heavy in my hand, and I love the way she arches into me.

"That feels so good." She dumps her shoulder bag on the shelf next to the suitcase, then shoves my jeans down so she can free my cock.

I move my hand to her other breast, tugging down her bra to get access to her nipple. I bite her beautiful neck then kiss it. Her hand slides up and down my shaft, and my breath comes faster. All sensations seem heightened. It's like the intensity control has been wound all the way up.

"I want you," she whispers. "Let's do it here. Quickly, before they come back."

Though one part of my brain is telling me it's the best idea I've ever heard, some small semblance of reason and good sense makes me shake my head. "It's not a—"

"Right here, right now." She turns around, unfastening her pants as she turns, and shoves them down, dragging her panties down with them. Then she leans forward, bracing her hands against the shelf.

The sight of her luscious ass cheeks instantly wipes all reason from my mind. I grind out, "Spread your legs," in a voice so full of wanting, I barely recognize it as my own.

She toes her pants to the floor and does what I ask, spreading herself for me. I run my fingers between her legs and find her hot, slick, and ready. She spreads her legs further, her breath coming in small pants.

"Yes," she groans. "Now. Hurry."

I rub my cock between her legs, covering myself with her wetness. Her slick heat feels insanely good against my sensitive skin. Then I realize why.

"I don't have a condom with me," I tell her, cursing my lack of foresight.

"Don't need one." She sounds as wild as I feel. "Quick. I need you!"

There must be a good reason why we should talk more about whether to have unprotected sex, but right now I can't think about anything but my need for her.

My cock finds her tight entrance, nudging inside her. It's incredible. She's incredible.

Nothing has ever felt so good.

"Yes," she pants. "More."

I thrust right into her, burying myself deep, and she lets out a long groan of pleasure. She's so snug around my cock, she's perfect. I withdraw and thrust again, and she says, "Yes, yes," in a voice that tells me she's loving it as much as I am.

Running my hands further up the front of her blouse, I push up her bra to get better access to her breasts. Her nipples are bullets. As I roll them under my thumbs, she drops her head back, pushing harder onto my cock.

I slide one hand down to her clit to stroke her while I push inside her.

"Oh God," she gasps. "I'm close already."

From outside the closet comes a sharp clicking noise. Then the sound of a door opening.

It's the suite's front door.

Someone's walking into the hotel suite. They must be in the living room.

My heart leaps into my throat.

Reaching out from where I'm standing, I flick the closet light off and pull the door shut. It's opaque glass, not clear enough to be see-through. With the light off, nobody will be able to see us, even if they come into the bedroom. Assuming they don't open the closet, that is.

I'm still inside Scarlet, and I stay where I am. The shock of hearing someone arrive has made my heart race. But the pleasure of being inside Scarlet hasn't lessened. If anything, it's intensified. It feels fucking incredible.

There's a murmur of voices, but it sounds distant. They're definitely not coming into the bedroom. Hopefully Leo and Loretta just stopped in to grab something from their living room and they're about to leave again.

I withdraw just a little, then thrust deep inside Scarlet.

A soft moan escapes her lips, and I put my fingers against her mouth to remind her to be quiet. Opening her mouth, she licks my finger. Then she draws it into her mouth to suck it. I push it further between her lips for a moment, wanting as much of my body to be inside hers as she can take.

Sliding one hand to her hip, I gather up a handful of hair with the other, tugging it as I bury myself even harder into her.

Scarlet lets out a tiny moan. "That feels too good," she whispers. "I'm going to come."

I bend close to her ear. "Can you do it quietly?"

"Maybe."

Just to tease her, I can't resist tweaking her nipple between my thumb and forefinger. I've never been harder in my life, and I doubt I'll be able to hold back much longer, especially when Scarlet orgasms.

She hasn't asked me if I'll be able to stay silent.

Considering the situation, that's probably a good thing.

CHAPTER 28

Scarlet

With one hand teasing exquisite sensations in my nipple, Zar runs his other hand down the front of my body to the juncture between my thighs. I'm trying not to orgasm because I'm afraid I won't be able to keep from crying out. But I'm already on a knife's edge. He's filling me so deeply, and his hard thrusts combined with the skillful pressure of his fingers are making it impossible to hold back.

Bracing my arms against the wall, I squeeze my eyes shut. My pleasure is overwhelming me, and there's no way I'll be able to keep myself from coming. I can only be grateful whoever is here is still in the living room. The low murmur of voices still sounds distant. If Loretta and Leo are back, they're staying out there.

"You can let go, sweetheart," Zar murmurs in my ear. He moves his hand from my breast to my mouth, slipping one finger back between my lips. "Bite down on me. I've got you. I won't let anything bad happen."

My senses are heightened, and his warm breath on my neck and ear feel almost as good as the hand that's stroking between my legs and his erection thrusting deep inside me.

Waves of pleasure pick me up and carry me away.

I try to come as silently as I can, but I can't be sure how noisy I'm being. I'm too focused on how amazing it feels.

When the pleasure finally ebbs, leaving me gasping, I ease my teeth from Zar's finger and wonder how I managed not to bite it right off.

"Is your finger okay?" I whisper guiltily. "Did I hurt you?"

I pull my hips forward, and he grunts, holding me still.

"Don't move," he whispers. "I'm too close."

Ignoring his command, I bend lower to reach one hand right through my legs and behind me, so I can gently cup his balls. He doesn't get to have everything his own way.

"*Fuck.*" He hisses the word loud enough that for a moment I'm certain we'll be caught.

Zar pulls my hips hard against him, and I feel him pulse into me. He lets out a groan that seems loud enough for the people in the living room to hear, but I can't reach for his mouth to stop him.

He pulls out of me as I hear the sound of footsteps on tiles. Two sets of footsteps coming into the bedroom.

My stomach lurches.

Did Leo and Loretta hear Zar?

Fumbling for my shoulder bag in the dim light of the closet, I manage to find it and carefully ease out my gun.

"Take your clothes off," a man orders. It's loud and close, which means he must be in the bedroom. But I don't recognize the voice.

"That's not Leo," whispers Zar. "I don't know who it is."

There's silence for a moment, and I strain my ears trying to hear what's happening. Then a woman gives a low moan of pleasure.

"Get onto the bed," says the man. "That's it, doggy. Take your clothes off."

The bed springs squeak. The woman moans again.

I turn my face to Zar, widening my eyes.

"What are you going to do to me?" asks the woman. I recognize her voice. It's definitely Loretta.

The man chuckles. "Seeing as you're such an naughty dog, I'll need to teach you your manners."

I bite my lips together against the wild laugh that wants to bubble up. "Naughty dog?" I mouth.

Zar puts his lips against my ear. "Shhh."

"I'm a bad, bad doggy," Loretta coos. "And you're so big and forceful."

"I'll use my training stick on you! I'll make you obey me."

"But I love to be naughty. You'll have to use all your skills."

"I'm a dog handling professional. You'll do what I say!"

I clamp my hand over my mouth to keep my laugh in.

The mystery man has to be Sergio, Loretta's highly skilled dog nanny. The big, strong-looking man who was handing her weights at the gym. He's definitely multi-talented.

"Don't make a sound," murmurs Zar against my ear.

"I need to clean up," I whisper back.

"In a moment." He holds me close as the unmistakable sounds of lovemaking fill the bedroom.

Once the lovers are well and truly engrossed, Zar slips a piece of clothing from a hanger and hands it to me. It's a silky top that must belong to Loretta.

Oh well. It's all I've got to use as a cleaning cloth. And seeing as she's clearly having an affair with her dog nanny, and she may be a murderer, I can't even feel that bad about it.

We pull our clothes back on as quietly as possible. Fortunately, the noises from the bedroom don't stop. In fact, Loretta and Sergio's cries of pleasure get louder and faster.

Once we're dressed, Zar puts his arms back around me, and I press my face against his chest while we listen to them climax. Then I hear some muffled raps that sound like someone knocking on the hotel suite's front door. I jerk my face up to meet Zar's gaze. He rewards me with his classic number two frown of puzzlement.

"I'll answer it," says Loretta. The mattress creaks as she gets out of bed. She must be barefoot because her footsteps are silent, but I hear the telltale snick of the door unlocking and the creak of it swinging open.

"Hello, darling." Loretta's voice is muffled, but she doesn't sound worried.

"Hello, my love," Leo answers. Weirdly, he doesn't seem shocked at catching Loretta with her lover.

Zar is tense against me. "Did Leo just arrive?"

I nod, listening hard.

Leo's footsteps pass through the living room and stop inside the bedroom. "You started without me?"

"Not my fault if you're late to the party," says Sergio.

"But you said you'd wait for me," complains Leo.

"Don't worry, Leo-pie, I'll get hard again for you."

My lips part. Zar's eyes are wide with surprise, and I know just how he feels. Loretta and Leo share a lover?

"Plot twist," I whisper.

"We're both bad doggies." Loretta sounds eager. "We need training."

"Wait," says Leo. "Do you know where my room key is? I can't find it. That's why I had to knock."

"Did you leave it in the restaurant?" Loretta asks.

"No. I searched all around and checked with the staff."

"That bitch girlfriend of Balthazar's better not have taken it." Loretta's tone turns peevish.

I pout as though my feelings are hurt. "I thought she liked me," I mouth at Zar.

"You shouldn't have come to our room." Leo is presumably talking to Sergio. "We don't want anyone else finding out about what we're doing."

"Then take your pants off, Leo-pie. I'll train you until you're a good boy, then I'll deal with Balthazar."

Loretta says, "If you'd stabbed him properly when you had the chance, we could have avoided all this."

"No WAY!" I mouth silently.

Zar's jaw tightens. His lips press into a hard line. His eyes hold a dangerous glint, and I have a new frown to add to my list. Number seven, *murderous* frown. It's my least favorite of his frowns, sending a shiver of foreboding up my spine. Number seven frown is a little too scary to be sexy, and I don't want him doing anything reckless and putting himself in danger.

"Let's just stay here until they leave," I whisper. "No sense rushing into a confrontation."

Frown number seven dominates Zar's face for a moment

longer, then he sucks in a breath and his expression eases. His jaw loosens and he gives a small nod.

I sag a little, relieved. Crisis averted. We can hide for a while until they've gone, then slip out and let the police know what we heard.

Zar's cellphone rings.

The sound is shrill, the volume turned all the way up.

"Turn it off," I hiss, though it's already too late. Dammit, why didn't I think to go over a few basic rules with him before we broke in? *Cat Burglary 101: Turn off your cellphone.*

"What's that?" snaps Sergio.

Zar flicks his phone off with a muttered curse. Grabbing my gun, I try to push him behind me so I can protect him. It's like shoving a brick wall. Unfortunately, I don't have time to remind him that *I'm* the bodyguard and he's the client before the closet door flies open.

Loretta, Leo, and Sergio stand in front of the door, gaping at us.

Leo is fully dressed in the same clothes he was wearing in the restaurant. Loretta has a bathrobe on, and her bare limbs suggest she's not wearing anything underneath. Sergio is stark naked. His impressive penis dangles limply under an explosion of curly pubes.

"What the fuck?" Sergio shouts.

"Put your hands up or I'll shoot!" I yell at the same time. Unfortunately, the power of Sergio's roar makes my shout inaudible.

Ignoring my gun, Leo lunges at Zar.

Zar tackles him to the floor, and they thrash around violently, making it impossible for me to shoot safely.

Cursing, I shove my gun in my pants. Sergio is ignoring me too, planting punches in Zar's ribs while Loretta eggs him on. They all clearly see Zar as their only threat. Right now, it's three on one.

Dropping into a fighting stance, I shout, "Hey, doggy style!" to get Sergio's attention. Then I perform a roundhouse kick—the same kind I did when I was pretending to save Melissa from a mugger. Only this time, I don't soften the kick or aim for his chest. This time, I plant my shoe into Sergio's large penis.

He howls and drops to his knees, both hands clutched to his dog-training equipment. I don't wait for him to recover but aim an axe kick at his face. Unfortunately, he flinches backward just in time, so the sole of my shoe barely grazes his cheek.

Zar gets to his feet, leaving Leo lying the ground, groaning. He starts toward Sergio, clearly intending to help me take him down. But Sergio's a huge man, and Zar's already hurt.

I point to Loretta, who's disappearing into the living room. "Get her, Zar! Stop her from leaving."

Zar hesitates for just a moment, then he does what I ask, rushing after Loretta.

When I flick my gaze back to Sergio, he's struggling to his feet. I take a chance and jump in closer to aim an uppercut punch to his chin. The punch connects and his head snaps back. Pain shoots across my knuckles.

He falls to the side, dazed, while I shake my sore hand, then tug my gun back out.

"Stay down, dog man," I order.

Cursing me, he does what I say.

I cover him and Leo with the gun while I grab some fluffy handcuffs out of the suitcase to throw at them. "Both of you put those on."

They obey, looking surly. To stop them from being able to get up, I grab spreaders for their ankles and put one on Leo, then one on Sergio.

And once that task is done, I solemnly vow never to use a spreader on a naked man again. It leaves way too little to the imagination.

Once I'm satisfied neither of them can escape their bonds, I look around for Zar. It's weird he hasn't reappeared with Loretta.

"Zar?" I head into the living room and come to an abrupt stop in the doorway.

He's lying on the floor on his side, a pool of blood spreading out in front of him, dark against the light tiles.

"Zar!" I rush to him, my heart jumping out of my chest.

Thank goodness, his eyes are open. He groans. "I didn't know she'd grabbed a knife."

The blood is welling from a wound in his arm. It's a good place to be stabbed in that there are no major organs to worry about. But there's a very real threat of bleeding to death.

And *shit*, there's an awful lot of blood.

If the knife went through his artery, Zar could bleed out in a matter of seconds. And the blood is pulsating out, which is the worst possible thing it could be doing.

I jump up and grab a tieback from around the drapes so I can use it as a tourniquet to stop the bleeding. While I call an ambulance, I press my free hand down on the wound.

He's not going to die. Not on my watch. No, no, no. I won't let that happen.

"Scarlet, I..." He groans with pain.

"Don't try to talk, Zar. The ambulance will be here any minute. You're going to be okay. Everything's going to be okay."

"But Scarlet, I need to tell you..."

"What, my sweet Zar? What is it?" I bend so my ear is closer to his mouth. Whatever he's trying to tell me, it must be vitally important.

He groans again, then croaks out something about stars. Is that what he's seeing? Frantic with worry, I try to remember if dying people see stars.

"Don't go toward the light," I order. "You stay away from any light, you hear me! You're going to be fine. It's a flesh wound, that's all."

"Scarlet..." He mumbles something else.

"What?" I bend closer. "What was that, sweetheart?"

"Your Yelp review," he manages to say on a long exhale. "Still five stars."

I stare at him as shock and fear pulse through me. He's bloody and pale, and I'm out of my mind with fear for him. It would have been better if I'd been stabbed.

All the feelings I've been hiding from myself, pushing away and suppressing, come bubbling to the surface.

I'm more afraid for him than I've ever been for anyone. And all at once I come face to face with the one thing I've been refusing to think about or acknowledge.

What I'm feeling for him is more than just affection. It's real. It's *big*. And I can't try to deny it because it's as strong and certain as my own heartbeat.

"You're going to be perfectly fine," I tell him, my tone forceful. "It's barely more than a scratch. But so help me, if you so much as take a single step toward any bright light, I'm never ever going to forgive you."

CHAPTER 29

Balthazar

"It wasn't too deep a wound, just bad luck that the blade nicked my artery," I tell Gaby. "I bled a lot, but I'm fine."

"Are you sure, Bee? You're really okay?"

I give her as reassuring a smile as I can muster from my hospital bed, holding my phone up in front of me. "I'm really and truly okay."

This is the third time Gaby's asked if I'm okay. She didn't know I was in hospital when she happened to call, so it came as a shock.

"And Leo and Loretta murdered your father?" she says. "I can't believe it. They were pretty much the only ones in the whole family I could actually stand."

"Their dog nanny was manipulating them. He was controlling their finances and spending their money. He's the one who killed Dad."

"He's the one who stabbed you the first time, right? But Loretta stabbed you this time?"

I wince. "Loretta took me by surprise. She grabbed a knife and I didn't know she had it."

"She could have killed you."

"The police found her and arrested her. Scarlet had the other two tied up and waiting for them."

"Scarlet sounds great! When do I get to meet her?"

"Hopefully soon. I want to introduce you."

"So things are going well between you two?"

I can't stop the smile that spreads over my face. "Very well."

"You really like her, don't you?" Gaby smiles back at me, and it's a relief to see her obvious worry about me ease away.

"I do." A pleasant warmth spreads through my chest like it does every time I think about Scarlet. "She'll be back any minute, then I've got a board meeting to attend. I'm going to become chairman of Anders Pharmaceuticals, axe the huge payments all the board members were getting, and start making drugs a whole lot cheaper for our patients. The board members are going to hate it so much, I might get stabbed again."

"I wish I was there." Her tone is wistful. "You're going to have so much fun making them all furious."

"I'm looking forward to it."

"Just make sure you're protected, in case they really do have knives."

"Scarlet will be with me."

Not long after I disconnect the call, Scarlet comes back into my hospital room. "I got your discharge sped up," she says. "The doctor agreed we can get out of here and go to the board meeting, as long as you promise to go easy and not exert yourself."

I push the sheets off and swing my legs off the bed, wincing a little as I sit up.

"You okay?" Scarlet hurries to me, looking worried.

"Never better." I tug her closer so I can kiss her. "I had an idea. After the board meeting is over and all the changes in place, we should go and visit Gaby."

"What?" She pulls back a little, her brow furrowed.

"Gaby's working on the Great Barrier Reef. We could go scuba diving there. See some sights. Have some fun. It's warm there this time of year, and I want you to meet her. I think her work would interest you."

She narrows her eyes. "What sort of drugs did they give you? I need to know if you're hallucinating, or if you're fully aware of what you're suggesting."

Resting my hands on her cheeks, I cradle her lovely face. Then I assume my most serious expression. "I'm completely sober, fully aware, and a hundred percent certain that I want us to travel to Australia, where we can dive, swim, and have a lot of sex."

And yes, I'm shamelessly tipping the scales in my favor by dangling Australia in front of her. She's a repressed thrill seeker, and I'm certain the trip will tempt her. I've already seen how much she loves the ocean. It's like presenting a diamond ring, only better, because she wouldn't be as tempted by a diamond as by an offer of adventure.

But her eyes are still slits, and she's studying me as though she's worried about head trauma. "How many fingers am I holding up?" she demands, lifting a hand.

"Two."

"Correct." She bites her lip. "Which is the same number of times you've been stabbed and ended up in hospital while in the care of me, your personal protection agent. So are you really sure I'm good for you?"

"I'm certain you're good for me." I give her a confident smile, grateful for how I feel when I'm with her. She makes my life seem so full of possibilities, I'm practically a walking, talking motivational quote.

When she's with me, I can even believe in her vision board manifestation stuff, because why not? If a woman like Scarlet can breeze into my life and make me feel so happy, the world must be a better, more benevolent place than I ever imagined.

"I'd have to ask Kayla and Jamie if they could handle things without me." She still looks unsure. "How long would we be gone?"

"That depends. After we've seen the sights in Australia, we could go zip-lining in Zimbabwe."

"Do they have zip-lines in Zimbabwe?"

I shrug. "If not, we could go parachuting in Paris. Ski-ing in Switzerland. Caving in Columbia. Wherever and whatever we want. The entire world and all the fun it has to offer."

She licks her lips, and I can tell she's picturing how much fun we could have by the distant look in her eyes. "But I can't abandon my business." Her tone wavers. She wants to give in.

"Then let's go to Australia for a week or two and see what happens," I suggest.

"Can you take time away from your work?"

"I can do what I like. And because the people who were trying to kill me are awaiting trial, nobody seems to want to stab me anymore. I'm already getting bored."

"What would it mean for us?" she asks. "Would we start dating for real?"

I blink. "Did that not go without saying?"

"I suppose it did, if you speak Balthazarian."

"Balthazarian?"

"That's your language. Want me to translate what you asked into normal-person language?"

Her sass is back, and that's a positive sign. My smile is hard to contain. "Go ahead."

"You admitted you're crazy about me and can't live without me. Then you pleaded with me to consider being your real girlfriend. There were several pleases in there. Hearing you beg like that was actually a little embarrassing."

"So?" I draw in my breath, half-wishing that was what I'd actually said. "Is your answer yes?"

She presses her lips together, her eyes wide. "Real dating," she says seriously. "Will we need to practice real kissing? If so, I couldn't be more enthusiastic."

Relief floods through me. But I try to reflect her seriousness back at her, simply nodding as though she hadn't just filled me with a warm feeling of joy. "Real kissing is a certainty. And what about Australia? Are you up for that, too?"

I can see how much she wants to say yes. Her eagerness is written in every line of her faces. But to my surprise, she bites her lip and the gleam dims from her eyes.

"Could we talk about it more after the board meeting?" she asks. "We need to leave now to get there in time, so let's get that over with first. Then we'll have a real conversation, okay Zar?"

"A real conversation?" A sliver of worry cuts through my joy. "What does that mean?"

She shakes her head. "Later." Her smile comes back, though it's not quite as wide as I'd like it to be. "Come on. First, there's evil to defeat. Let's go and have some fun."

CHAPTER 30

Balthazar

The board meeting is held in a conference room at the hotel. Although non-board members aren't supposed to attend board meetings, I insist on Scarlet being there and nobody dares to object.

There are eleven board members present. Leo and Loretta are in custody. Uncle Orson, Aunt Maude, and the other board members glower at me as I speak, but they vote to pass every motion I propose. When I axe their payouts, it's even more satisfying than I expected, especially when Scarlet grins at them all, not bothering to hide her delight.

But after the board meeting, I can tell something's worrying her. Scarlet's quiet and thoughtful instead of happy and excited.

"What is it?" I demand.

She's chewing on her lower lip. "I have something I need to tell you." Her expression is serious enough to dampen the satisfaction that remains from the board meeting. "Can we go back to our hotel room and talk?"

I nod, and we ride the elevator in silence. Though I want to demand she tells me what's wrong, I know better than to assume it's something I can solve. All I can do is hope it's something I can fix, whatever it takes. Money can take care of a lot. But the thing it's powerless against is when people inform me they're leaving. They have a job elsewhere, or an opportunity they can't turn down. They've decided to choose something different instead of sticking with me.

I hate having to wonder if that's what's happening. My fear of it hurts worse than getting stabbed. Scarlet stares straight ahead at the elevator doors, and her silence is like a blade sliding between my ribs.

I love her.

I'm in love with her.

The knowledge hammers against my ribs, filling me with even more dread.

I know she likes me. Hell, she may even love me a little, or at least feel something close to it. But that doesn't mean she won't hurt me. Too many people have walked out on me. I'm all too aware of how unexpectedly it can happen.

Once we're in our suite, Scarlet takes me into the small living room. "Please sit down." She motions to the couch and I sit uneasily at one end. But she doesn't take the other end. Instead she paces in front of me, wringing her hands in front of her. "I have to tell you something about how we met. And why."

I give her a confused frown. "We met at your interview."

She sucks in a breath and straightens her back. "I took the job on false pretenses. I lied to you. And now the board meeting is over, I need to come clean. I need to be honest with you."

A metal band is tightening around my chest. She's pale, squeezing one hand tightly in the other. She looks like the confession is hard for her. I'd almost feel sorry for her if I wasn't so afraid of what she's going to say.

"Your father had naked photos of my aunt." She holds my gaze.

"Are you talking about your lawyer?" I ask, confused.

"She's not my *lawyer*, she's my family. And she worked for your father, years ago, when she was young. He took photos of her." She swallows. "I promised her I'd get the photos back, and that's why I arranged to meet you. Because I wanted to find a way to take the photos and destroy them."

I sit up straight, realization dropping into my gut like poison. "What do you mean you *arranged* to meet me?"

She swallows again, then gives a tiny nod, as though she's silently talking herself into answering. "First, may I just tell you one thing? Aunt Alejandra saved my life. She's spent her entire life working in the law, doing great things. She should be a Supreme Court Justice. She'd be the best one there ever was! But she was terrified her photos would go public, and her entire career would be over."

Her tone is imploring, but my own heartbeat is so loud in my ears, it's all but drowning her out.

It's happening. Of course it is.

Scarlet chose her aunt over me.

Exactly how many times does this need to happen before I stop being the fool who hopes for something else?

I cross my arms over my chest. "Answer the question. How did you *arrange* to meet me?"

"Melissa didn't really get mugged," she admits, pacing between the couches. "Well, she thinks she did, but it was a set-up. I wanted to get a look at the security system in your house, and I feel awful about doing that to Melissa. I'm sorry for tricking you too, Zar. I thought you were evil, and I was so wrong."

"You wanted to look at my security system... so you could steal from me?" My tone is harsh enough to make her flinch, but she nods.

"And the day after we got here, I took the photos of Aunt Alejandra out of your box of papers and destroyed them."

Her words sink in slowly. The pounding in my ears is building to a roar. It's making my thoughts sluggish.

"You went through the box while I was in the shower and took what you wanted?"

"Just the photos." She's twisting her fingers together. "That's all I took."

"How can you expect me to believe you?" Without waiting for her to answer, I lunge off the couch and stride into the bedroom. Scarlet follows. Her mouth twists when I grab her suitcase and tear the zipper open, but she doesn't object. Not even when I dump the contents of her bag onto the bed, scattering her clothes and personal items all over the sheets. Her pained expression reminds me of how she didn't want anyone to touch her stuff, and how important her privacy is to her. But the fierce heat of anger is like fire in my veins. Her pain doesn't stop me.

She betrayed me.

She hurt me.

Now it's my turn.

"But there's something else I have to tell you about," she

says in a rush, staring down at her belongings. "I found another picture—"

I spot a photograph on the bed and snatch it up with a triumphant exclamation that cuts her off. It's a photo of a naked woman, one of the pictures my father took. I recognize his bedroom in the background, and the grainy quality of the picture, like all the other photos in his envelope of shame.

But it's not just any woman in the photo. She's all too familiar.

My gut clenches. When I swallow, all I can taste is bile.

The woman in the photo is Helena, the nanny I once thought I loved more than my own mother.

"I was just trying to tell you about that photo," Scarlet says, her face pale. "You saw it before I could get the words out."

"Why do you have a naked photo of Helena? How do you know her?"

When I told Scarlet about my nanny, she'd asked if Helena had red hair. Then she'd laughed off my surprise by saying she was psychic. She was clearly lying, trying to cover up her web of deceit. Has a single word out of her mouth been the truth?

"I found that photo when I was looking for Aunt Alejandra's pictures."

"How did you know who she was?"

She licks her lips, her hands clasped in front of her in the prayer position. "I saw her photo in your bedroom when I broke into your house. I was looking for Aunt Alejandra's photos, and I thought you'd be asleep."

"*You* broke into my house! I thought it was an assassin."
The extent of her betrayal leaves me breathless.

"I know. I'm so sorry, Zar. I planned to slip in and out
quietly, without anyone ever knowing. It all went wrong."
She lifts her clasped hands, her expression anguished. "I'm
really sorry."

Turning away from her, I stride to the far side of the
bedroom. My fists clench and unclench as I struggle with my
anger.

"This whole thing was about those photos," I grind out,
keeping my back to her. "You tricked your way into my life
for them."

Though I want to shout with rage and punch something,
the anger isn't so bad. What's so much worse is that a big
part of me wants to simply turn around and forgive her. And
that's the part that terrifies me.

How many people get to hurt me before I stop allowing it
to happen?

"The feelings I have for you are real." Scarlet sounds raw.
"I wasn't lying about anything but the photos."

I turn my head to the side, giving her my profile.

"You're fired." To my relief, the words come out cold and
precise.

"What?"

"I no longer have need of your services."

Swallowing all emotion, I turn to face her. Her eyes look
big and dark in her pale face. Her fingers are tangled
together, pressing against each other so hard that the skin is
white.

"Please, Zar, don't treat me like—"

"Like an employee?" There's a strange pleasure in

hardening my heart and making my tone icy. Like pressing my fingers into a wound to feel the pain. "An employee is exactly what you are. Actually, it's what you were. Now you're fired, which means you're not anything to me."

"Zar, please don't. I'm so sorry."

Though she takes a faltering step toward me, I turn away.

"Good bye, Scarlet. Your employment is terminated."

CHAPTER 31

Balthazar

I take the helicopter home, but the ride couldn't be more different from the one going to the resort with Scarlet. That time, I'd taken a seat in back so she'd have a better view, and I'd gazed at her profile the entire time, enjoying her excitement. Her obvious delight had made it fun.

Now I have the best seat next to the pilot again. But I may as well be in a blacked-out submarine for all the interest I have in the scenery.

I don't want to think about Scarlet. I'd do anything not to think about her. But even dragging financial reports out of my satchel and trying to work does little to clear my head.

The trip home seems to take forever, but at least when I finally arrive, I'm rewarded with an enthusiastic greeting from Ringo.

"It's you and me now, boy," I tell him gruffly, and he wags his tail even harder.

My dog has the very best of care while I'm away, but he

still misses me. He'd choose me over anyone else. I can be sure of that, and it makes me love him even more.

Shutting myself in my office with Ringo, I tell Melissa that I'm not to be disturbed until further notice, not even by her. I tell Alan the same thing. Then I turn off my phone. All I want is to lose myself in work and investigate potential investments by reading what the figures tell me. Numbers don't lie. They tell straightforward stories about profits and losses, untapped potential and overblown expectations. They don't manipulate or betray me.

My room is silent and sparsely furnished, and I have meals brought in by my housekeeper, so there's nothing to distract me from work. Nothing but my own unwanted thoughts about things that aren't possible. Things I don't want to think about.

The next day, my phone is still off and my instruction to Melissa still stands. But a little before lunchtime, I'm startled by a soft knock on my office door.

"What is it?" I snap.

The door opens and Melissa comes in, looking nervous. She and my other employees work out of a downtown office. She's only allowed to visit my home when she's invited to a meeting, or to bring me items that need to be hand delivered.

"Sorry for the interruption, Mr. Anders," she says. "I got called in by Alan. He wasn't sure what to do and didn't want to disturb you. I thought it would be better if I came in person."

I lean back in my chair, annoyed. "What's the problem?"

"Scarlet is here."

"What?"

"Scarlet is here, asking if she can see you. Alan's repeatedly told her you aren't seeing anyone, but she's refusing to leave. Short of physically carrying her off the property, there's not much he can do. And because your instructions about not being disturbed were so clear, he contacted me."

I stare at her a moment, my mind racing, wanting to rushing into places I won't allow it to go.

Scarlet's betrayal was a good thing. It came just in time. I was in serious danger of growing too fond of her, which wouldn't have been good for me. If she were still alive, my mother would have told me what a fool I was for getting attached to someone who only wanted something from me. And my father would have ordered me to stop being weak.

Swallowing the hard, unwanted lump in my throat, I make my tone curt. "Call the police," I order.

Melissa gives a startled blink. "The police? Scarlet says she wants to apologize."

"I don't want to hear it."

"I get that." Melissa's tone softens. "She tricked me too. She explained why she did it, but I'm not sure whether to forgive her either."

The last thing I want is Melissa's sympathy, or to have to see any pity in her eyes. She's an employee who's just as likely to betray me as Scarlet was. I'll never let myself forget that again.

"Have the police remove her," I command again. "And instruct my legal team to serve her with a trespass notice. If she comes within a hundred feet of my house, I want her charged."

"Really?" Melissa's eyes go wide. "Don't you think that's a little--"

"Follow my instructions," I snap. "Unless you want to look for new employment."

She flinches. Then she straightens her back and gives me a stiff nod. "Yes, Mr. Anders."

I thought Melissa's sympathetic look was bad, but now her expression has turned hard, and I can't stand the way she looks at me as though I've let her down. A rush of guilt surges through me as she turns for the door, and for a moment, I loathe myself.

But isn't it better this way?

"Shut the door behind you," I call after her, because I don't want to hear the police turn up to escort Scarlet from my property.

There's no chance of Scarlet coming back after that, so everything will return to the way it used to be. I won't ever see her again.

And if Melissa quits after the way I spoke to her, well, it would have happened eventually anyway. She'll leave without a backward glance. They always do.

CHAPTER 32

Balthazar

I bury myself in work for the next couple of weeks, letting it consume me from dawn until late at night. Instead of sleeping, I prowl listlessly through the dark rooms of my house with Ringo trotting along by my side. He's clearly puzzled by all my late-night roaming.

It feels like something vital is missing. As though I've lost something precious that I'll mourn for the rest of my days. But I know the pain I'm feeling is for the best, and as hard as it is, I'll get it over it eventually.

I should have stuck with the kind of relationship I'd had with Natalia. The end of that relationship was easy. And if I'd been sensible enough to keep some emotional distance from Scarlet, I wouldn't have to suffer now.

Lesson learned. *Again.*

Gaby calls every day, but I don't feel like talking to her. Problem is, she's persistent. She doesn't seem to get tired of having her call sent to voicemail. She just keeps on leaving messages, slowly wearing me down.

One day, two weeks after getting back to LA, I curse angrily at her image on the screen of my ringing phone, then stab the button to answer her call.

"There you are," she says, frowning. "Oh look, you're alive. And oh my goodness, you still have hands. I was sure they'd been severed and that's why you've been ignoring me."

Gaby is at home, in her apartment in Australia. She's in her favorite chair in front of the window that looks out to the ocean. Her tan looks even darker than before, and her hair is sun-bleached. Outside her window, it's dawn. The endless sky is a riot of color that's reflected on the equally endless ocean.

A pang of regret that I didn't get to show it to Scarlet makes me scowl before I manage to repress the thought.

"I've been busy." I lean back in my office chair, wishing I hadn't answered Gaby's call.

Beside me, Ringo raises his head, startled by my sharp tone. He looks at me reproachfully and lets out a sigh.

"Why do you look so unhappy?" demands Gaby. "Did something bad happen? How was the board meeting? Why couldn't you answer just one of my calls, Bee?"

"The board meeting went as planned. I made all the changes I wanted."

"And Scarlet? Is everything okay with you two?" She leans in, furrowing her brow. "You didn't break up, did you?"

"We were never really dating. Not in her eyes."

"Oh. No." She sits back in her chair, her expression falling. "Are you sure?"

"You've told me you think I hold myself apart from people. Only this time, I'm the one who was honest. And I was living in a fantasy world, thinking she'd be different to everyone else who's let me down."

Irritated, I push at the piles of papers on my desk, toppling one into another, and sending some floating to the floor. Then I glower at the mess I've made. I usually like to keep a tidy desk and work methodically. It's only the last two weeks that I've been so unfocused.

"I'm really sorry." Her tone is soft. "What happened, exactly?"

"Scarlet wanted some of my father's photos. Instead of asking me, she stole them."

"Why would she want the photos?"

"Someone she knew was in them."

"Oh."

"That's what she wanted from me the entire time, only I didn't know it. And I was open with her. I *told* her things."

Gaby puffs out a breath, her eyes scrunched with sympathy. "That's awful, Bee. So you think she never actually cared about you?"

"Does that matter?"

"Well." She frowns. "Yeah, it matters. Of course it matters."

Gaby isn't getting it. I give my head an impatient shake. "Even if she cares, she made her choice."

"So she *does* care?"

"Well, she says she does."

"She's apologized?" When I nod, she asks, "You're not willing to give her another chance, then? You don't have it in you to try again?"

"*Again*?!"

She tilts her head. "Would it be so awful?"

"If you got run down by a train, would you stay on the track?"

"Yes, actually I would, if it meant enough to me." She sounds thoughtful. "And next time you might be the one driving the train that accidentally runs Scarlet down. Then it's her turn to forgive you and get back on the track. That's how relationships work."

"Let me get this straight." I steeple my fingers, giving her my most severe frown. "You seriously think people stay in relationships because they're too stupid to get off a train track?"

"They're not stupid. They're willing to forgive because they know it'll be worth it in the end. Being run down makes them stronger, and it makes the destination better when they finally get there."

I want to scoff. But this is Gaby, the one person in the world who has my best interests at heart, so I restrict myself to letting out a disagreeable grunt.

"There's no destination," I say. "Not for me."

"There could be. Scarlet made you happy, that was obvious. It was nice to see you smile."

"It was fake happiness, built on a lie."

Her brow crinkles. "I know you've been hurt a lot, more than anyone ever should be. It's not fair that your mother died and your father kept you from getting close to anyone else. But if you stay away from trains, you'll never get to go anywhere."

"I don't want to go anywhere."

She screws her nose up, clearly about to argue. The

expression reminds me of how Scarlet used to look when she'd call me Billionaire Bob, and the memory sends a pain shooting through my chest.

"Something's come up and I've got to go," I say gruffly, interrupting Gaby. "Talk to you later."

I hang up as she starts to speak, cutting off whatever she's trying to say.

Then I get restlessly out of my chair. Ringo gets up too, and I bend to pet him. We prowl together out of the room and down the hall, doing yet another pointless circuit of my house.

Despite telling Gaby I didn't want to go anywhere, I'm unsettled. All that talk of trains has me wondering if I should get out of here. I wanted so badly to take Scarlet to Australia. Gaby and Scarlet would have instantly become friends, and I can imagine how great it could have been to spend time with them both.

Instead I'm alone, prowling around my silent house. It feels too big. There's nothing to distract my eyes or my mind, just stark plant arrangements and starker walls. Scarlet was right, it's too black-and-white. It needs some color. Some warmth. Some *life*.

Heading back to my office, I make a call to Melissa and ask her to get an interior designer in urgently. I want colors on the walls, bold artworks. Vases filled with flowers.

"Flowers?" she repeats, the word rising incredulously.

"Just do it," I snap.

"Yes, Mr. Anders." Her tone becomes formal and strained.

Fuck.

Lately I've been ruder than ever. Scarlet would be horrified.

Maybe Melissa would leave me without a backward glance if she got a better job, but that doesn't mean I should push her away. She's a good assistant and a nice person. I don't want her to quit.

"Wait," I say before she can hang up. "I'm sorry."

"Sorry, Mr. Anders?"

"For snapping at you. I've been doing it for the last two weeks."

"Oh." She sounds startled. "It's okay, Mr. Anders, but thanks for the apology."

"Balthazar."

"Excuse me?"

"Call me Balthazar. And if I neglect to thank you again, you have my permission to pull me up on it. You deserve curtesy."

She's silent for a beat. Then she says, "Okay, Balthazar. I will." Her tone is cautious, as though she's wary it might be some kind of trick. Exactly how much of a monster have I been?

"How long have you been working for me, Melissa?"

"Six years."

"Longer than any of my father's employees lasted." I mutter it more to myself than to her.

"I like working for you," she says, surprising me.

"Even when I'm rude and demanding?"

"You're not that bad. Only the past couple of weeks you've been..." she trails off as though afraid to say more.

"From now on, I'll be more considerate. And I'll make sure my financial officer organizes a pay rise."

"Thank you, Mr. Anders! I mean, thank you, Balthazar."

When I hang up, I feel a little better but I still can't concentrate on my reports.

Eventually, for lack of anything better to do, I wander into my living room, sit on the couch, and switch on the TV.

There's some big breaking news, and a mob of reporters are surrounding the courthouse. It takes me a few minutes to work out what's going on, but when I realize what's happening, I jolt right out of my seat.

Governor Salamanca has been arrested.

"She did it," I say out loud. "She took him down."

The governor is in handcuffs, looking furious. Watching justice being done is the best sight I could have hoped for. It suits my current mood perfectly. After everything the governor put Scarlet and her friends through in the juvenile detention center, he's finally getting what he deserves.

I watch the coverage for a while, satisfied to know I helped Scarlet to bring a corrupt, selfish official to justice. And I can't help but wonder if she's in front of her own television watching the same footage as I am.

An hour or so later, I get a message from Melissa letting me know she's going to stop by with a delivery. When she arrives, she knocks on my open living room door.

I switch off the TV but stay seated on the couch as I wave her inside. She's carrying some papers and a mysterious-looking box with a red ribbon tied around it.

"Hello." She hesitates. "Balthazar." She says my first name awkwardly, as though she's testing whether I'll still allow her to use it.

"Hi Melissa. Please come in." I make sure my tone is polite.

Her face brightens and she walks more confidently to the couch. "I need to show you something." She hands me the papers, keeping the box under her arm. "These are the accounts for the Selexitron charity you set up for Governor Salamanca."

"The governor's in custody. I've been watching the news coverage."

She nods. "I've just taken a call from your accountant about that. He's recommended renaming the charity, but says nothing else should be affected, seeing as the administrators are independent anyway."

"Okay, good." I frown down at the papers. "Then why do I need to review the accounts?"

"Look." She leans over to point to a deposit she's highlighted in yellow.

"So? What is it?"

"An unexpected anonymous donation to the charity. And it's for the exact amount that we paid Scarlet for the work she did."

I jerk my gaze up to her. "You think Scarlet donated all that money to the charity? Why would she do that?"

"I haven't asked her," says Melissa. "But I assume it's another way she's trying to make amends. She feels bad about tricking us."

"What do you mean, '*another way*'?"

Melissa hesitates, and I'm sure she's thinking about how Scarlet turned up trying to apologize, and my response was to involve both the police *and* my lawyer.

Probably not one of my finest moments.

"Scarlet got me into martial arts," she says after a moment. "She's given me some really thoughtful gifts and done so much groveling, I couldn't not forgive her. And thanks to her, I'm getting really good at Taekwondo." She gives a little laugh. "The other day, this guy in a bar was being a rude jerk, and I flipped him right over! Now my friends all want me to pay a visit to their exes and…" She stops, biting her lip as though realizing she was getting carried away. "Anyway," she says, holding out the box. "Please don't get mad and shoot the messenger, but this is for you."

I narrow my eyes at it. "Why would I get mad? What is it?" It's small and square, and the ribbon tied around it makes it look like a gift.

She winces. "Scarlet asked me to give it to you. I hope this doesn't affect the restraining order, and if you don't want to open it, I'll give it straight back to her. But I thought it should be your choice."

My chest contracts. But I give Melissa a cool nod and say, "Thank you for bringing it to me."

Then I take the box from her and open it.

Nestled inside it is a gold watch. A vintage Rolex.

"That's nice," says Melissa, peeking into the box. "It looks expensive."

Pulling the watch out, I flip it over. On the back, there's a name engraved. *Max Oberon.*

It's Uncle Orson's watch.

Suddenly my heart is beating in slow motion.

"It's more than expensive," I say. "It's priceless."

Scarlet didn't steal Orson's watch while we were at the resort, or I would have found it when I searched her luggage. She must have gone looking for him after she left.

When I'd suggested to Scarlet that she might want to

steal Uncle Orson's watch, she'd said the only reason she'd take it would be if Kayla or Jamie had a deadly illness and the watch held the only cure.

But she tracked him down and stole it anyway.

To give it to me.

My chest is tight, my heart still pumping extra slowly. It feels as though it needs to fight for every beat.

The watch is heavy, weighing down my hand. It's real. And Scarlet must have risked everything to get it for me. No matter how good she is at stealing watches, the danger of getting caught would have been high. She put her entire future at risk to take this watch.

No, it's not a watch, it's a symbol. She sent it as a message to tell me how she feels. And an object can't lie.

Nobody has ever done anything like this for me before. Maybe her train ran me down, but I tried to do the same to her in return, and she's clearly still on the track.

She put everything on the line to get this. She did it for *me*. And now there's only one question that remains.

What am I willing to risk for her?

CHAPTER 33

Scarlet

I'm in our small waiting room, perched on a chair, talking to a client.

Usually, we prefer to meet our clients at their place rather than having them come into our office. I mean, we've done our very best with the place, but our nice, thick rugs can't entirely hide the uneven floor, and when the elevator breaks down, there's nothing we can do but use the narrow stairwell. Still, this client has overlooked all that and is studying the plans I gave him with enthusiasm.

"You say I need a new alarm system, new window and door locks, and security cameras?" he asks.

"That's right."

"Comprehensive. I like it."

He's acting like the plan I gave him is something special, but I've done so many of them now, I could have drawn it up in my sleep.

"That's the full price?" He points to my calculations. "That's competitive!"

"Uh-huh." I'm trying to sound as enthusiastic as he is, but the last few weeks, I've questioning everything.

I've been wondering if my job is enough for me. Maybe this isn't just broken-hearted sadness, and part of the reason I can't seem to snap out of it is because I'm bored. Perhaps I should do more personal protection, like Jamie does. Maybe if I could save a few people from being murdered, I'd be able to stop wondering if I'm a terrible person who's unworthy of love.

I heave a sigh, but the client doesn't seem to notice. We discuss the plan a little longer, then shake on the deal before he leaves.

Once the door closes behind him, I drag my feet into our command center where Jamie and Kayla are both at their desks. Kayla is doing something technical and clever, no doubt. Jamie has her feet up on her desk, next to an enormous, half-eaten sandwich. She looks like she's taking a nap. Most likely she's fallen into a food coma and is about to start snoring.

I sit at my own desk with another heavy sigh, and Jamie cracks her eyes open.

"Did the client decide do go ahead with it?" she asks.

"They signed the contract." I realize I've just sighed again, and resolve to try and last at least ten minutes without heaving another one.

Kayla sticks her head out from behind her monitors. "You're still feeling awful?"

I nod.

"If Balthazar can't forgive you after you gave him a watch

that's worth more than this entire building, he has no heart."
Jamie drops her feet off the desk with a decisive clunk. "He
doesn't deserve you."

Kayla assumes a sympathetic expression. "What can we
do to help you?"

"Nothing. I just need to get over it."

"Work out with the punching bags." Jamie waves toward
our training room. "Sweat it out."

Kayla rolls her eyes. "That's your answer for everything,
Jamie."

"Well, it works for me. That, or going to the shooting
range. Or a rage room. Smashing things is good therapy."

"Sometimes you worry me," Kayla tells her.

"I'll hit the punching bag for a while." I get back to my
feet. Right now, I'm willing to try anything. Though I'm not
angry, just desperately sad and full of regret, and I'm not sure
any of Jamie's therapies will help with that.

Still life has to go on, doesn't it? So I go upstairs to the
apartment to change into shorts and a tee, then head into the
training room.

I have boxing gloves on, and I'm working up a sweat,
when I hear someone come into our client's waiting room
and ring the bell our visitors use to announce their presence.

Jamie's boots clomp over the floor as she goes to see who
it is, then I hear the door to the waiting room open and
Jamie let out an exclamation of surprise.

A male voice says, "Hello. You must be Jamie."

Thanks to my workout, my heart is already beating hard.
But now it stomps on the accelerator. I've been hearing Zar's
voice in my dreams every night, and I was horribly afraid I
might never hear it again in real life.

But there it is. Low, gruff, and perfect.

"I'm Balthazar Anders," he adds.

"I know." Jamie's tone is curt. "And I'd say it's about time you showed up, but calling the police on Scarlet was such a dick move, coming here now is too little too late."

Tugging off my boxing gloves, I stride toward the sound of his voice.

"And the restraining order," Jamie adds. "Let's not forget about that."

When I come around the corner of the desks, I can see through the door into the waiting room. Zar is standing with his hands by his sides, turned slightly toward me, while Jamie has her back to me.

I stop dead so I can soak in the sight of Zar, taking advantage of the fact he hasn't seen me yet. He's wearing his number three frown of mild irritation. It's one of his gentlest frowns, and I doubt he even consciously registers that it's on his face.

He's not wearing a suit or anything fancy, just jeans and a navy t-shirt that fit him so perfectly they could have been designed specifically for him. My gaze lingers over his wide shoulders, muscled build, and square, boxer's jaw. He's an intimidating man, and he wears his charisma unconsciously, like an invisible cloak made of power and money. It's easy to see why people don't stand up to him often.

Not that Jamie is intimidated. She's angry on my behalf, because I was so upset after Balthazar called the police on me.

He couldn't have made it any clearer that he wouldn't give me a second chance. And it was an act that said he now sees me as a criminal. Irredeemable. Unworthy.

My reply was to send him the watch.

I meant it as an acknowledgement. A way to say that, yes, I have my faults. I'm not perfect. But I would do anything —*anything*—for the people I love.

And I love Balthazar. Even if it hurts, there's no point in trying to deny it.

"Doesn't your restraining order mean you can't legally see Scarlet?" demands Jamie, her hands on her hips.

"My lawyer didn't put in any paperwork." Zar crosses his arms. "It was an empty threat. I was angry and lashing out." Neither his frown or his tone are an apology. But then, he doesn't need to apologize. I hurt him first, and he hurt me back. I don't like it, but I get it.

With my heart in my mouth, my hair damp with sweat, and perspiration trickling down the small of my back, I walk into the waiting room.

"Hi," I say, my voice a little hoarse.

Zar spins to face me. His face relaxes, his frown smoothing away. His eyes drink me in with the same kind of intensity with which I'd been studying him.

"Scarlet," he says. "Could we talk?"

I glance at Jamie and notice Kayla is also hovering behind me. Both are ready to defend me if I need it, or to throw Zar out if that's what I want. But as sweet as they are, and as much as I love them, Zar and I need to talk privately.

"Let's go upstairs," I suggest.

The building has a narrow stairwell that goes all the way to the top floor, but the apartment that Kayla, Jamie and I share is only two flights up. I lead him up the stairs with my heart racing.

Why is he here?

I can't dare to hope that he wants to give me a second chance. Zar has been let down by so many people, he's developed strong defenses. I loved being allowed to get to know him. But after I landed such a painful blow, what right do I have to hope that he'll ever let me in again?

I unlock our front door in silence and usher him inside, motioning him to sit on the couch in our tiny living room.

He does what I ask, while I take the armchair that's opposite his.

"It's just as colorful as I thought it would be," he says, scanning the apartment. "You've done a lot with the place."

Considering what he's used to, our apartment must look like a hovel in comparison, tiny and rundown. But I appreciate his compliment.

"Thanks." I fold my hands in my lap, and my eyes drop to his wrist.

He's wearing the watch I sent him.

Is that a good sign? I feel like it could be a good sign.

Seeing that I'm looking at the watch, he puts his hand on it. "Thank you for this."

He's being weirdly polite.

"I'm pretty sure your Uncle Orson believes in karma now," I say. Then I suck in a steadying breath, because I'm nervous and his expression is hard to read. "Like I told you, I don't do that kind of thing anymore. But he's such an awful man, I can't make myself feel bad about stealing it."

I wish Zar would frown so I could tell what he's thinking.

His various frowns have become some of my favorite things. Well, frowns one through six, at least. It's not just the way they lend weight and substance to a face that otherwise might be too classically handsome. It's also the way they show how he's feeling. I love how honest his frowns are. They say so much.

"After what Orson called you, he deserved to lose it." Zar's tone is even. "But that's not why I'm here. Scarlet, I need to ask you something."

"Okay." I brace myself.

"Why did you give the money you earned to the Selexitron foundation?"

I blink. I'm not sure what question I expected, but it wasn't that.

I've imagined what I wanted to say to him a million times, but now he's actually in front of me, all the speeches I made up in my head have fled.

"Because protecting you might have started out as a job," I say after a moment, "but it didn't end that way. It didn't feel right to get paid for it, and seeing as it was your money, I thought it should go to the charity you care most about."

He nods as though I've given him the answer he expected. He's looking at me with an intent expression. His gaze mainly roams my face, but occasionally dips all the way to my bare, sweaty legs.

Maybe I'm only being hopeful, but his eyes seem warm.

"Anyway," I say. "I wish I hadn't lied to you, and I'm really sorry. If I could take it back, I would." I'm trying to project calmness. Anything but the desperate longing that's in my heart.

"I'm sorry for calling the police and threatening you with a restraining order," he says, surprising me.

"I understand why you did." I raise my shoulders. "I hurt you. And I'm not even talking about how I let you get stabbed. Twice."

"Still, like Jamie said, it was a dick move. Childish. I shouldn't have done it."

"If you can forgive me, I can definitely forgive you."

"I invested in the woo-woo company you liked." He leans forward on the couch.

Is a tiny smile threatening to lift his lips?

That must be a good sign. It has to be, doesn't it?

"Did you?" I ask weakly.

Hoping could lead to more heartbreak, but I can't help it. Hope is what's coursing through my veins and operating my lungs. Could he be willing to give us a second chance?

His lips inch up a little more. His frowns might be some of my favorite things, but his smiles take first place, no question. They're rare and gorgeous, and fill my chest with pure oxygen.

"And you were right, my house needed more color," he says.

"It so did!"

So much hope swells inside me that I can barely catch my breath.

He leans even closer. "I've missed you."

"You have?"

"I've been grouchy and rude to everyone."

"Oh my God, Zar. I've been so sad without you. You have no idea."

Hope has its hands locked around my heart, urging it to beat in double-time.

"I might always find it hard to trust people," he says. "But here's the thing. You're the one person in the world I most want to trust."

"You can trust me. I promise, I won't let you down."

He nods, his gaze steady on mine. "I believe you."

Three simple words, yet they hit me with so much power, they make me dizzy.

"Thank you." I say the words in a whisper.

We both stand at the same time. Zar pulls me into his arms. I grab hold of him like a drowning woman clutches at the person who can save her. When he kisses me, I kiss him back with enthusiasm and boundless relief.

He feels so good, I want to fuse myself against him. I have a wild thought that maybe we could join together and become a single person so I never have to be without him again. The sadness of the weeks I spent without him fades away, joy surging in its place.

As though he feels my need and shares it, he slides his hands down my back, then lifts me against him, locking my legs around his waist.

"I missed you," he murmurs around his kisses. "So much."

I make a muffled sound of agreement, unwilling to lift my mouth from his. Then I manage to tug the back of his t-shirt free from his jeans so I can run my hands up his back. His skin is smooth. All the muscles that Jamie taught me the names of—lats, traps, and deltoids—are beautifully defined. His chin is smooth shaven, and he smells like expensive cologne. I push my hands through his hair, messing it up. I want to claim him as mine. To put my name on him in indelible ink so he'll always belong to me, completely and forever.

One thing I know for sure. I'm never—not *ever*—going to lose him again.

And judging from the delicious savagery of his kisses,

and the rock-hard rod throbbing against me, my guess is he might feel the same way.

He draws back to look at me. "You stole my heart." He says it forcefully, one of his beautiful frowns making his eyes spark.

"And I gave you my heart." I cup his face in my hands.

"Take care of mine." His voice gentles and his frown smooths away. "And I'll cherish yours." He seals his promise by putting his lips back where they belong, on mine.

"My bedroom is down the hall to the right," I suggest helpfully, between kisses.

He carries me down the hallway and lays me on my bed. Then he hovers over me, alternating between more kisses and nuzzling my neck. His eyes and mouth are both hungry for me, and I love it more than I can say.

"You taste like salt," he says into my skin.

"I've been working out. I need to take a shower."

"We'll take a shower afterward," he promises. "I like the taste of you like this. And I want to find out if you're salty everywhere."

"But won't it be better if I shower..." I stop talking as he pulls my shorts and panties off.

Then he lowers his face back into the curve of my neck. "My body has been missing yours." Kissing down my throat, he pushes my t-shirt up, then pulls it off me.

"Mine too."

My bra comes off as if by magic. It's like he only has to look at it and the catch throws itself open. He's still got way too many clothes on, but now I'm naked.

He circles my nipples with his tongue while I make an ineffectual attempt to remove some of his clothes, only managing to undo his jeans and tug uselessly at his shirt. The sensation of his hands and mouth on me is too good for me to focus on anything but how it feels.

"I missed your breasts." His warm breath gusts across one nipple, sending shivers of pleasure across my skin.

"They missed you too." The words come out with a little moaning sound that I don't realize I'm going to make until it happens.

He pulls his t-shirt off quickly, then plants a trail of kisses from my breasts to my belly.

"I missed your stomach." He kisses around my belly button.

"What about lower down? Did you miss any of that general area?" I remember all too well how skilled he was with his tongue. When he went down on me in the hotel room, he made me come SO HARD. The memory would be enough to make me wet and get me panting, if I weren't already soaking wet and breathless.

He lifts his face so his dark eyes tangle with mine. His grin is wolfish and gorgeous. "I almost missed that part of you the most."

"Almost?"

"Your gorgeous mouth comes first. Always." To my almost-disappointment, he moves back up my body to kiss me on the mouth. "I missed your smile," he murmurs against my lips. "Especially your lopsided one, the way it makes your eyes light up. And I missed your laugh. Your sarcasm. Your cleverness. Even the way you call me Bob."

"I missed your frowns, Bob. Every single one of them, except number seven."

"Number seven?"

He gives me a number two frown of gentle puzzlement, and I'm so happy to see it, I draw his face down to mine to kiss the furrow between his eyes. With my hands on his cheeks, I stare into his warm brown eyes. "I love all your frowns almost as much as your smile," I say seriously. "Tell me, is that so wrong?"

Instead of answering, he claims my lips again.

Then, kissing down my body, he moves back to my breasts, tonguing my nipples and making me moan. "I love your big, beautiful heart," he tells me.

He flips me over so I'm on top of him, straddling him, though he's still got his jeans on. Taking me by the hips, he pulls me up his body so I'm sitting across his chest.

"I love all of you," he says from underneath me. "And I need you in my mouth." I gaze down at him, lips parted, so horny I can barely see straight. He tugs me up higher, toward his head. "I've missed the taste of you. I want you in my mouth, gasping my name. I need to hear you call me Zar as you come, sweetheart. Will you do that for me?"

God, I'm so wet. So eager.

I move up further, then lower myself onto his willing tongue.

After that, I don't have much use for words, except when I find myself gasping his name over and over. Apparently, when it comes to obeying the *right* command, I'm nothing if not obedient. Who would have guessed?

When my mind-blowing orgasm subsides, he slides out from under me and strips off his jeans. He kneels on the bed and pulls me onto him, my back to his front. With his arms wrapped around me and his mouth on my neck, he pushes so deep inside me, I know that I'll always be his.

We fit together like we were made just for each other.

It would be impossible to believe anything else.

A lot later, after we've both floated back down to earth, we lie next to each other on the bed. Both of us are naked. His arm is over my body. My leg is over his. And I'm wrapped in a deep, satisfied serenity. Everything is perfect in my world.

It's a wonderful feeling.

"Thank you, universe, for giving me Zar," I mutter out loud. "I'm grateful."

He turns his head to me, smiling with his eyes as well as his lips.

"Did you just thank the universe for me?"

"Of course. Because I asked the universe for you, so it's only right to say thank you."

"Was asking for me like taking out a cosmic ad?" His tone is gently teasing. "Did your ad say, *Charming, brilliant, handsome billionaire wanted? Must have an enormous—*"

I poke his arm. "That's not what I asked for. I asked to be happy."

His smile widens. "You're happy?"

"Can't you tell?"

He shifts a little so he can kiss my neck. "That makes me happy."

I arch my neck into his mouth, enjoying his lips on my sensitive skin.

He says, "I'll have Melissa send Cosmic Santa a thank-you card." Then he strokes one finger over my chest, tracing the curve of my breast. "Scratch that," he corrects, his voice deepening. "I'll make it a gift basket."

"Just be grateful," I say. "Let's not take anything for granted."

"You have no idea how grateful I am." He's not teasing any more. "I love you," he murmurs softly, his lips nuzzling my ear. "You bought color into my life when I didn't even know how much I needed it. And I'm serious about Cosmic Santa. This is too perfect to just be luck. *Something* bought you into my life, and whatever it was, I'll always be thankful."

I let out a delighted laugh. "Who would have thought I could turn Balthazar Anders into a believer?"

He kisses my earlobe, the softness of his lips sending pleasurable shivers down my spine. "I believe in you," he whispers. "And I believe in *us*."

EPILOGUE

Balthazar

"I like her," says Gaby.

"You've told me that already. Three times, by last count." I hand her the pot I've just finished washing so Gaby can dry it. Washing dishes is a new experience for me, but Gaby doesn't have any domestic staff, so I'm pitching in and learning new skills. And seeing as I had to scrub the pot for at least ten minutes to get it clean, I'm gaining a new appreciation for my housekeeper.

"Well, I really like her," Gaby says. "Scarlet is good for you. You two look happy together." She gives the pot a quick, perfunctory wipe with a dishcloth before sliding it into the cupboard. It's becoming clear to me that she volunteered for the easier of the two chores.

I glance out to Gaby's small living room. Scarlet's on the couch with her phone propped up on the coffee table. She's talking excitedly to her friends, a wide smile lighting up her beautiful face. I can tell by her hand gestures that she's describing the day's scuba diving adventures on the Great Barrier Reef. The way she waggles her hands around to imitate the way the fish swam in front of us makes me want to laugh.

"She makes me happy." I drain the soapy water out of the sink. 'Happy' isn't a big enough word to describe the way Scarlet makes me feel, but if I start raving about joy and contentment and feelings of bliss, Gaby will start making jokes about the shape shifter who must be inhabiting my body. Instead I say, "I'm in love with her," in a gruff tone.

Gaby throws her arms around me to hug me, wet hands and all. "I'm glad."

I hug her back, then let her go. "Is that all the household chores you have for me, or should I also expect to be scrubbing the floors and fetching water from the well?"

She rolls her eyes. "After cleaning two pots, you must be exhausted! Pour yourself a drink and put your feet up, Cinderella."

"One drink, then Scarlet and I will head back to our hotel suite." I dry my hands, smiling to myself with anticipation. As incredible as our day has been, when we get back to our big bed, it'll get even better. It always does.

"Should I read anything into the fact you two are staying in the honeymoon suite?" Gaby asks, waggling her eyebrows.

"I requested it. Honeymoon suites are our natural environment. I'm always going to book them from now on."

"Who'd have guessed you'd be such a romantic?" She pats my arm. "Now go and sweep the floor in the living room while I fetch you some socks to darn."

She bustles off to her bedroom, and I fix myself a whiskey. Stepping into the living room, I show the bottle to

Scarlet, silently asking her if she'd like me to pour one for
her. She shakes her head and pats the couch next to her,
inviting me to sit. Outside, the sunset has painted the sky in
shades of dark red. The sea is beautiful at this time of the
evening, and Gaby's apartment is positioned to get an
optimal view.

"Are you talking to Balthazar?" asks Jamie, her voice
coming from Scarlet's phone. "Is he there?"

"He's here."

I stroll over to Scarlet and sit down, putting my drink on
the coffee table next to her phone. Then I nod at the screen.
"Hi Jamie," I say to the tall, Amazonian-like woman with
long black hair. "And Kayla," I add, seeing the much smaller
woman by her side.

"Are you treating our girl right?" Jamie glowers at me.
Scarlet said she grew up in a boxing gym, and I've seen
Youtube videos of her wrestling bouts. She's a formidable
fighter. Her glower isn't something to take lightly.

"I already told you he is!" Scarlet protests.

"He'd better be, if he knows what's good for him." Jamie
points two fingers at her narrowed eyes, then swivels her
hand so those fingers are pointing at me.

"Hi Balthazar," says Kayla, looking and sounding far
more friendly than her friend. "Do you like scuba diving as
much as Scarlet does?"

Before we left LA, Kayla and I bonded when I asked her
opinion on a tech company I was considering investing in.
She's shy and sweet, much easier to win over than Jamie. She
looks a little like Bella Storm, the famous singer, and I could
probably arrange for her to get some very lucrative work

body-doubling for Bella if she ever wants to get out from behind her computer monitors.

Scarlet puts her hand on my leg, and I put my hand over it, then curl her fingers in mine.

"I've just had one of the best days of my life," I say honestly. Scarlet's delight at all the marine life we saw during our first scuba dive was contagious. I spent the day impressed all over again by how fearless she is, and enjoying myself exponentially more than if I'd had to come here without her.

Lifting Scarlet's hand, I kiss her knuckles. She smiles back at me, her eyes warm. She's so beautiful she takes my breath away.

Jamie makes throw-up noises.

"Hey Scarlet," says Kayla. "You remember how I was looking for Dani?"

"Of course I do," Scarlet says.

"Well, I managed to track her down. I've spoken to her."

"No way!" Scarlet sits forward, and I let go of her hand so she can concentrate on what her friend's telling her.

"After she got let out of juvie, Dani had to get lost for a few years, because those guys were after her."

Scarlet's eyes go wide. "So all the stories she used to tell us were true? The men she'd double-crossed really did want to kill her? I always assumed she was exaggerating because it sounded so much like a movie."

"It was all true," says Kayla. "If anything, she underplayed the danger she was in."

"But apparently she's safe now," adds Jamie. "Those guys can't bother her anymore. And we were hoping you wouldn't mind if we ask her to join our team?"

Kayla nods. "She needs a job and we thought she could help with home security. But we don't want you to feel like she's taking over your role."

"Of course she should work with us! When I get back, I can show her the ropes." Scarlet's gaze flicks to me and she scrunches her nose before she turns back to the screen. "Actually, there's something I need to ask. Tell me if this isn't cool, but Zar and I were thinking about staying in Australia for a few extra days so we can do some traveling around. See a few more of the sights."

"Just a few more days, huh?" Jamie glares at me as though I'm a kidnapper.

"Maybe an extra week," Scarlet admits.

"That's fine." Kayla elbows Jamie. "We can handle things while you're away."

"Sure, don't worry about us," Jamie mutters with a frown. "But you'd better come back *eventually*."

"I will. Thank you." Scarlet gives them a smile. "I love you guys!"

After she gets off the phone, Scarlet stretches her legs over my lap, and I massage her calf muscles while we talk about the things we want to see while we're in Australia. It's one of the things I've come to love most, talking like this, with her. The world seems like it belongs to us, and her excitement to experience everything it has to offer makes me feel more alive and enthusiastic than I ever have.

After a while, she starts talking about her business, the things she loves about it, and the things she wants to change. Mostly, I just listen. But when she mentions they're worried about a patch of mold that keeps appearing on the ceiling of their training room no matter how often they clean it, I have to speak up.

"My staff work from my office downtown," I say. "I don't spend much time there, but it's a big building, and the second floor is empty. What if you moved into it?"

She lifts her eyebrows. "Move our business?"

I nod. "You could have the same kind of set up there, with a training room and everything. Only it'll be bigger and nicer. No mold."

"It sounds nice, but the rent's cheap in the building we're in, and our apartment is there too."

"But you're going to move in with me, aren't you?"

She blinks. "Am I?"

"Of course you are. We have to be together. And could you picture Jamie's face if I moved in with you?" I move my hands down to rub her feet, surprised I haven't thought to ask her sooner. It's not like me to overlook something so important. But Scarlet spent every night at my place before we left for Australia, so I assumed it would be a permanent thing.

She scrunches her nose. "So you want me to move into your mansion? Like, with its giant swimming pool, and housekeeper who does all your washing, and your home cinema room with reclining chairs and popcorn machine?" Though she's pretending to squint doubtfully, her eyes are sparkling. "I don't know, Zar. I'm not sure if I can bear to leave behind all the cockroaches and rodents in my apartment for a life of unimaginable luxury."

"That's a yes?" I ask, wanting to be certain.

She rests her head on the back of the couch, clearly

enjoying her foot massage. "Of course I want to. But what about Jamie and Kayla?"

I circle my thumbs around the balls of her feet, coaxing a sound of pleasure from her lips that makes me want to throw her over my shoulder and carry her away to our honeymoon suite so I can hear more. As soon as we've finished our conversation, it'll be time to leave.

"I'll convert part of the building into an apartment for Jamie and Kayla," I tell her.

"You'd do that?"

"Consider it done." I shrug to indicate how easy it'll be.

"But I'll have to talk to them about it first." She groans as I caress her arches. "Mmm, that's so good."

"And if you want more wealthy clients for your business, the guys I meet with for our Saturday night poker game all need security services."

"You can't make them hire us!"

"Nobody can make them do anything. I'll just tell them how good you are, that's all. It'll be up to them to take it further. Oh, and one of them is going to be in a charity boxing match, and he's looking for a trainer. I could suggest Jamie."

"She'd probably love that. I'll ask her." Scarlet squeezes my thigh. "Thank you for being so generous and thoughtful. I'm sorry Jamie's still being a little prickly."

"Jamie may not be my biggest fan yet, but if I can make you ecstatically happy for the rest of your life, she'll warm to me."

"For the rest of my life?" Scarlet raises her eyebrows, her face lighting up at the suggestion.

"I'm goal driven," I tell her. "It gives me something to work toward."

She gives a contented sigh as my fingers work into her soles. "Just spending time with you feels so good. Everything we're planning is amazing." Then her expression turns serious and she lifts her head to gaze into my eyes. "But you know that I don't need luxury, right? I don't need a fancy new office, or a mansion to live in, or billionaire clients, or any of the things you're trying to give me. If I were locked in an empty jail cell, I'd still be okay so long as you were with me. All I need is you, Zar."

"Partners in crime?" I tease.

She gives a soft laugh that warms me to my core. "Partners. Always."

❧

Thank you for reading The Billionaire and the Burglar! I really hope you enjoyed spending some time with Scarlet and her friends.

If you're wondering whether Jamie accepts the offer to train Balthazar's poker buddy for a charity boxing match, the answer will be revealed in *The Billionaire and the Booty Call.*

I'm supposed to be training a billionaire for a charity boxing match, but my new boss hasn't bothered to show up.

Bored, I decide to film one of my popular YouTube wrestling videos. I strip to my bikini, oil myself up, and send a message to the man who volunteered to be my wrestling partner.

Only... whoops! I send the message to the wrong number.

The wickedly hot stranger who appears at my door seems shocked when I grab him in a body lock and maneuver him into a bottom position. He thought my cryptic text was a mysterious booty call and wasn't expecting me to perform a takedown.

And I don't realize I've pinned the wrong man until my suit-wearing opponent comes up with a few impressive *moves of his own.*

Things get oh-so-much worse when my mistaken-identity wrestling partner turns out to be my new billionaire boss.

That's when our real sparring match begins...

ALSO BY TALIA HUNTER

THE LENNOX BROTHERS ROMANTIC COMEDY SERIES

No Funny Business
No Laughing Matter
No Fooling Around

THE LANTANA ISLAND SERIES

Boss With Benefits
The Engagement Game
The Devil She Knew

ABOUT THE AUTHOR

Talia Hunter likes to include her three favorite things in her novels: toe-curling romance, snort-laughs, and heart-warming friendships.

She recently moved to Australia, where she's constantly amazed and not at all freaked out by the weird and wonderful critters. When she's not writing, you can usually find her with a glass of wine, a good book, and a jumbo-sized can of bug spray.

She loves to laugh, and if you feel the same way you can keep up with her new releases and special deals by visiting her website.

www.taliahunter.com

www.ingramcontent.com/pod-product-compliance
Lightning Source LLC
Chambersburg PA
CBHW020259120726
47904CB00001B/264